I0581512

# Jesus Christ Joe

## Selby

CATLETT, VA

CABAL

CABAL

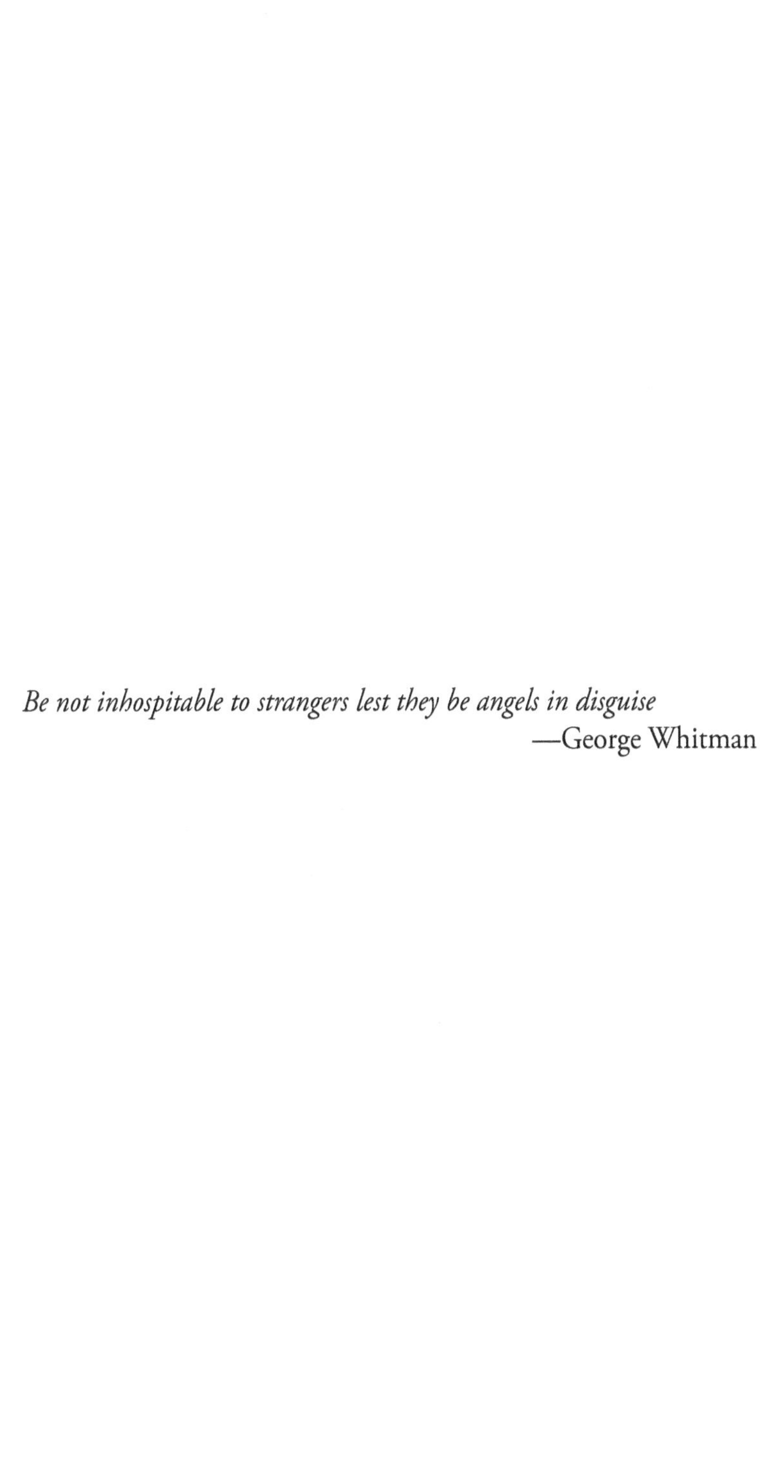

Be not inhospitable to strangers lest they be angels in disguise
—George Whitman

# The Beginning

Here the story begins, with our protagonist Joe, a young man, not quite eighteen sitting at the bedside of his dying grandfather, his only known remaining relative. It's late, the air is hot and stale, dust motes dancing in the pale lamplight. Despite the heat coupled with the smell of farts and decay, Joe doesn't open the window. Grandpa had been shivering cold earlier, no fat left on his bones to warm him, skeletal, his skin wrinkled and loose, draping his frame like oversized clothing. But now, with the help of morphine, Grandpa drifts listlessly between half sleep and vague lucidity, weakly clutching his blankets to his frail chest, his breathing laboured and raspy, his face grotesque. Joe waits. Hours earlier Grandpa told Joe that there was not long left, that when he was gone Joe should open the letter sitting beneath the lamp on his bedside table.

Joe waits.

# Heeding Advice

Grandpa's letter says,

*Joe. I have nothing much to leave you, no legacy. What little money we have is in the jar on the kitchen shelf behind the knife block, as you know. I've withdrawn every penny I can from the bank, and, having anticipated my demise, I've been frugal. Hide it as soon as you've finished reading this! Don't tell anyone about it.*

*I never had much money. I smoked and your Grandma drank. We had enough to get by but any wealth went on our vices, but no regrets, my life's been easy. There's over £3,000 there currently at your disposal. Now I'm gone, sell what you can; there's not much of value. Perhaps the car and the furniture?*

*This is the deal. Do not photosynthesize here, do not stagnate in this small-minded, deprived, decrepit town. Do not get caught up in the system. You are so young and can achieve so much. Fuck education or your lack of it, because you're already smart, boy! Perhaps you think it'll open doors that you wish to enter, but I don't think you need it. This culture promotes a formula for life satisfaction and prosperity, proclaiming that it can only be achieved through education, work, possessions, marriage, kids. And most people live by this blueprint. But do you think that's the only formula for happiness? Does that formula even equate happiness?*

*No, Joe, it does not! But, this is the expectation imparted on us by society. Conform… think debt, think divorce, a job you hate. I wouldn't waste your money or time. Do you want to owe for the best part of your life? Of course you don't. Some of the dumbest people I've met had the best education and some of the smartest I met did not. You can do anything, but I want you to keep away from that soul sucking system as best you can, avoid it at all costs. Steer clear of the Government and the Church, neither can be trusted.*

*This is what I think you should do: shed the material, start over! Be responsible for nothing but yourself! Pack a bag and head to The City. Set yourself up with the money that you have and LIVE YOUR LIFE! Get laid. Travel if you wish, get a passport and fly away. You can go anywhere, Joe. New York, Tokyo, Berlin! Doesn't that sound appealing? I think any young person who doesn't take advantage of such opportunities is denying themselves a fulfilled life. Get out of here!*

*Meet interesting people and make friends. You could really do with some friends. I loved your grandma very much. But we were young and things were so different. There wasn't the concept of experiences, opportunity or enjoyment back then; we left school, got jobs, got married, had children. This was mapped out for us from the day we were born. Living carefree and without responsibility never occurred to us. But, as I grew older I realised that there were people out there, living extraordinary lives and having incredible experiences, they've always been there! They chose their own paths, rejected the ideals of their forebears and did whatever the hell they wanted to! Boy, if I could articulate a wistful sigh in this letter right now, this is where it would be, such is the gravity of my feeling. I wish I'd known these things, wish I'd had the courage to follow a dream. I don't even know what my dream was anymore, but hell, I bet I had one, and if I were your age with £3,000 and the freedom this age bestows, I'd have some bloody fun! I missed out. Again, no regrets; I had my beautiful wife, a beautiful daughter and then, beautiful you, Joe. You all were the best things about my life, and I consider myself lucky, I do.*

*But you, with your youth, you can do whatever, without anyone dictating what that should be. Be creative, really think about what you want for yourself; go for it, full pelt. You're a great artist, don't stop doing it. Share it. Try new things. You're handsome too, though you might not realise it. Please, keep your head up and shoulders back, and stand tall like the man you are now. I don't know Joe, just do the things you enjoy, whatever that is.*

*Don't seek wealth, seek experiences. Try to enrich people's lives. Leave a mark. But remember to be considerate and stay gentle. You have a good soul Joe, no malice, no spite. Give freely, share. Help and be kind. Don't hurt people if you can avoid it.*

*Eventually, once you feel you've lived enough, experienced enough, maybe then find yourself some company, true love if you're lucky! Don't rush though, don't be in a hurry to fall in love. Because I believe companionship of that sort stifles creativity. That said, and I know it sounds contrived kid, but love is all there is, it's the key to happiness. Just don't hurry, don't expect it to drop in your lap. Find yourself before you find love.*

*If you'd rather not bother, find a menial girl and settle down in this pathetic town, work a menial job for menial pay, live a menial life with your menial car and kids, bills, responsibility and a pension plan then fine. You can join that colourless rat race, shackled to responsibility and monotony. Worrying about insurance, new school uniforms and boiler servicing is mundane, but if it's the life you choose I accept you're not up to the challenge.*

*I THINK YOU ARE DESTINED FOR GREATER THINGS! Believe in yourself. Be brave. Speak up! Don't compromise yourself. WHATEVER you do, Joe, I'm proud of you. Always. Despite everything, the hardships of your childhood and ending up in the care of an out-of-touch old man like me, you turned out decent and you changed my life for the better. You're clever and different, Joe. Different in a good way! You have youth and promise. Read the above. Mull it over. Break the rules. Do or die.*

*Love, Grandpa*

*P.S. Look under the bed.*

Well, shit, I didn't expect this. I look under the bed. Nothing but a dusty old rucksack, military maybe? It looks empty. I drag it out, open it; inside a folded piece of paper, which upon investigation holds another note from Grandpa.

*Joe, I got you this bag for your travels. From the charity shop in town. It's big and sturdy and should hold everything you need. Fill it and go!*

*Love, Grandpa.*

For fuck's sake, Grandpa, you're still warm and you're kicking me out already? That's what I think right now. I can't even comprehend embarking on whatever adventure he's encouraging. Like, give me a break? You literally just died.

Yeah, the letter's heartbreaking, and frankly, confusing. The Gospel of Grandpa, one Hell of a scripture. Poor Joe, only seventeen, feeling conflicted. All the instruction is too much to process. Joe has no idea how to live up to these expectations, he's only a kid, and he's frightened and alone. Get a passport? How? He'll Google it later. Joe tells himself the letter is simply the ramblings of an old dying man, verbalizing his regrets and lack of interesting life experiences. Figures it'll be safer to get a council flat and a job, get by. He'll still draw and stuff, maybe really work at trying to sell his art. He thinks he doesn't have the guts to go… but, this is just it! He does go! Go Joe!

Before we continue, allow me to introduce myself. I, dear reader, am Joe's tutelary, or guardian if you prefer. I am his cosmic companion, his familiar, his patron. I don't care; call me what you will. Perhaps you're thinking I'm an angel right? Fine, if that's easier for you, pigeon-hole me, makes no difference. I know how attached you guys are to the angel imagery, and that's alright. I get it, it's ingrained in you and it's nothing but complimentary. I even like it; you think we're pure and virtuous, and I'm not going to pass up or criticise attitudes like that, I'm flattered.

We've been interpreted many ways, in every culture since you developed sentient thought. The Norse called us Valkyries, the Pagans called us Faeries; the Egyptians, the Sumerians, the Aztecs, all deified us in some form or other. Some call us spirits, some call us daemons. Some call us aliens.

Whatever your conceptions, religious, spiritual or otherwise, whether you believe or not, I can tell you, you're probably wrong. I will tell you that we do not expect or require prayer, worship or even acknowledgement, nor can we respond to it. It has no power and is thus fruitless on your part. Same as you, we simply are, we exist, and occasionally under special circumstances, we accompany a mortal throughout their tiny, fragile yet complex lives. We grow fond of you. Our power is limited but we attempt to help if we can. Most of you don't have one of us.

Yes, you're all beautiful unique snowflakes and ultimately equal in worth. And I'm not using the word snowflake as an insult.

Actually, if I may deviate a moment, I think it's sad how that word has been commandeered once again to harbour such negative connotations. How the term is now used to mock those who dare to fight for their idealistic views. Why is it considered derogatory to be sensitive or to believe in one's individuality? Sensitivity leads to compassion. Self-belief leads to achievement. How can those characteristics be bad?

In a literal sense, snowflakes are one of nature's perfect designs. You think they're weak and fragile? They're not. Those ice crystals, sometimes an army of them amalgamated as one, survive the fall through space, through extremes. There are so many of them, and at first glance they all appear to be the same. Just like humans!

Upon inspection we see their variations, their foibles and uniqueness. We marvel at the diversity. Together they create blizzards and avalanches, they are powerful. Remarkable and beautiful. Just like you! So carry on being snowflakes. Speak up at injustice. Be empathic. Be emotional. Be offended. It's not so audacious to wish for a better world.

An incidental remark if I may; the word snowflake has been used previously to describe humanfolk. Once, those opposed to the abolition of slavery were described so, used as a preference for white skin over black. Fucking nonsense. And then later, to euphemise and understate the human ashes that fell on Nazi Germany. Disgusting. I didn't like it then, don't like it now. Stop hijacking the word. Snowflakes are beautiful. Pick a different word, fascists.

Moving on, understand we can't be there to oversee everyone's plight and lives. Can you imagine the logistics? It'd be so crowded! There aren't enough of us for starters, we don't breed willy-nilly like you lot. We don't breed at all. Most of you have no need for us, with your privileges and selfish, imagined tragedies, your properties and medicines and your support groups, your footwear and remote controls, kickstarters and patreons. Most of *you* will never know what it is to truly suffer. No criticism intended, just count yourselves lucky within your developed regions.

So, we're only deployed in exceptional cases, the circumstances of which may or may not become clear as Joe's story continues. We try, often in vain, to prevent your self-destruction. Without us you'd be screwed; humanity is constantly fucking itself over, marginalising, hating, killing. It's a wonder that we bother, but we do. Ultimately we believe in you and we like you. Most of you are good and that's what we focus on, else we'd have given up on you many thousands of years ago.

Also, please understand that time is not linear to us, but fluid. I have already seen Joe's beginning and end and all in between, I can accompany him at any point I wish, and, if I'm fortunate, make a difference. I can attempt to alter the course of history, which although it sounds like it's a privilege, is something we do for recreation. I don't mean to sound flippant, sorry if I do —I promise we do so with the best of intentions.

Just to reiterate, because I struggle to let this shit go, it is beyond me why religion still exists upon your planet. Because you have science! Incredible science, that as yet, has provided no evidence of anything otherworldly or meaningful. Your denial of something deemed as actual fact is both incredulous to me and admirable at the same time… must you challenge everything? Your faith based assumptions are quite amazing, I'm honestly fascinated at your need to cling to an unknown and dubious hope.

You're a strange lot. I get that you're scared to die. You yearn for some promise of immortality. Nice idea, and I understand the comfort the notion offers, but you have no proof of it. No evidence whatsoever! I'm sorry to say that for many of you, your beliefs are a pathetic venture, and to waste your brief, infinitesimal and valuable time upon Earth, absurdly abiding by the rules and requirements of fantastical ideals will not benefit you. All those fanciful doctrines were created by your long gone predecessors as a method to order, control, blame or oppress. Or, maybe just to create a sense of community and belonging. Even so, although they may once have promoted unity amongst you, they're nothing more than stories. Spending your precious reality in preparation for some fictional or spiritual realm is futile. Look where it's got you so far! Please don't waste your time. Just live, it's all you need to do. Just be. I'm not suggesting you should all take a nihilistic approach to life; we trust you to be good, rather just know that you do not know.

I apologise that I sound a bit preachy, I get excited, I don't mean to put you down. I just want you to know that you don't *need* Gods and Deities to be decent beings. You can cling to it if you must, but perhaps you could just question it. What good is blind faith? You are your own God.

My advice is that you trust in your science. Proof is everything. Don't just make stuff up. I know, science doesn't know everything right? But that's the point of it, to discover and prove. Only then you can be sure of your affirmations. You've still got a long way to go, but listen, I'll give you a heads up, maybe check out M-theory, string theory. Quantum tunneling. You people might be onto something there. Yeah it sounds like fiction and fantasy, still worth a thought. They're just theories, hypotheses, but I've seen worse. Maybe open your mind to the idea that other universes could exist, and maybe, just maybe, the advanced ones could influence others? Take Greek mythology; remember the stories, and then the movies? Those Gods, messing about with the mortals, dishing out justice and vengeance. Consorting, often surreptitiously, with the humans, to influence them, impregnate them (Zeus was a weirdo). Sometimes those Gods rewarded, were empathic. Where d'you think that idea might've come from? And all mythology to be fair, all religion? If you ever believed such outlandish ideas, then you should look to those scientific suppositions for your Almighty. Just maybe, God is a lie, to make your slavery more bearable. Trust me.

Or don't. I'm not saying it's spot on, but it's something to mull over, right? Now, there's some dichotomy for you, science or religion, rebellion or conformity. You choose.

I've said too much already, shit. And what about me? What proof do you have that I'm telling the truth? Maybe I too am mortal, spinning yarns to satisfy your fantasies? Do you have proof otherwise?

No, you don't. So just enjoy the ride.

# Edification

The nurse confirms Grandpa's passing. She makes the relevant calls, rubs my shoulder and offers meaningless words of comfort. I do not cry. I don't remember the last time I did. Not even when my mother died. I have no issue with people crying, I just can't do it. I don't know if that's healthy or not; I still have feelings, but they stay forever locked in my head. Is it wrong to admit that maybe I think it's weak to show that kind of vulnerability? Whatever, I'm cool with it.

I go downstairs, sit on the sofa and the nurse comes down. Her name's Leanne, she has eyebrows that have been tattooed on and she makes me a cup of tea. She washes the dishes in the sink. Within the hour the local funeral director turns up and he and his assistant take Grandpa away under a purple blanket; it's all very quiet and respectful, but it's strange too. He looks so small under there, childlike size, and I'm almost compelled to tear back the covering, check it's really him. I don't though, and they leave, doing a weird bow as they go. Leanne's tired, she doesn't want to leave me, technically a minor, but I assure her I'm OK. She has two teenage children and a taxi driver husband who she rarely sees, we've gotten to know each other well over the last few months. I tell her that Grandpa and I had been expecting this for long enough, I persuade her, I just want to sleep. Eventually she leaves. I do not sleep.

Grandpa grew up Catholic, and told me that when he was a young man he trained to be a priest. Not for long though, because some epiphany made him realise the futility of it, that religion was the biggest pile of horseshit he'd ever been subjected to. And he didn't want to die a virgin either, said what kind of spiteful God would deny man the right to a woman's warmth? It's our nature after all. His devout parents were dismayed when he quit his training and took on an apprenticeship as a signwriter. He met my grandmother soon after. They married, then tried for years for children to no avail, until, when they had given up all hope, my Grandmother finally fell pregnant in her late thirties. Their miracle child.

'We had a lot of fun trying, Joe!' I remember him laughing. Here I am as a consequence.

Grandma died before I was born. My mother died when I was ten. Ovarian cancer. Her decline was rapid and brutal, leaving no time to prepare for what would come after. She just got thinner and sicker until she collapsed one day at work, and upon returning from the hospital she had a terminal diagnosis. Advanced and incurable, there was nothing but palliative care left, same as Grandpa. I don't suppose I understood the gravity of the situation at the time, I didn't even know what an ovarian was (yes I know what an ovary is now), and like I said, I shed no tears. I realise that might sound weird; I was sad and loved her very much, but crying didn't seem like it would achieve anything. Who was I going to cry to?

Another thing about my mother; she was estranged from her father, Grandpa, so I never knew him until after she died. He'd been angry at her youthful pregnancy, she'd said, her falling so after just a few weeks together with my dad. She told me that her father had kicked her out of their house, but Grandpa denied this vehemently. He looked crestfallen when I told him. My mother was all he had left in the world, he said, she'd broken his heart leaving. I believed him more, because it felt like I knew him better than I knew her, if that makes sense? Of course, he'd been disappointed, worried at her embarking upon her relationship with this man, a virtual stranger whom he considered aggressive and controlling. And he was right; I remember him, my dad.

I never saw my father after we ran away, my mother's face all bruised and swollen again. I didn't even know his first name until I saw my birth certificate in the weeks after her death. For all I know he's dead too, or maybe in prison, but whatever, either the authorities couldn't trace him or didn't consider him fit to look after me. And so, I was placed in foster care, thankfully briefly, until my grandfather claimed responsibility for me. He didn't have to and I wouldn't have known any different if he hadn't. Grandpa hadn't seen me since I was a baby, we were complete strangers, so he owed me nothing as far as I was concerned. He hadn't known of my mother's death until weeks after, missed her funeral. I think it took him some time to get over it, and I don't know, maybe he felt guilty about not being there for her and treated my care as some kind of redemption? Whatever, it turned out that we became good friends, housemates. I remember when he came to meet me that first time at my foster home, his shock of wild white hair and that crazy yet amiable spark in his eye, his grin. There was a happiness about him, a sense of enlightenment; I think that's rare. I haven't seen it in any other person I've ever encountered. The day he came to take me home, he threw my hold-all in the boot of his car, opened the front passenger seat and waved me inside with a smile and a flourish of his hand. He shut the door behind me, walked around and sat himself at the wheel, turned to me and said with authentic enthusiasm, 'Well Joseph, let's do this! I think you'll be good for me, and I'll do my best to be good for you!'

I'd never been referred to as Joseph in all my life so that was weird, but I felt immediately at ease, and once the grief had softened our household became a happy one; quiet and undramatic. Content. I don't think I'd really known anyone cheery before then, my mother was always frightened and quiet, my father always angry and threatening. The cheerful people had merely flitted past, neighbours, folk at shop checkouts and school.

In time, social services left us to it, satisfied that Grandpa was doing an OK job of feeding me and keeping me alive.

That Christmas I learned there was no Father Christmas, because he told me, straight out. I'd already had my doubts to be fair, and he seemed almost horrified that I had been taught to believe such mythology. 'Well, I'm not going to lie to you boy! That won't do any good will it? *I* bought these presents Joe, because I love you. Have I upset you?'

'No.' Yes.

'Good, good… I just want to always be truthful with you. Listen, there's nothing wrong with imagination and wonder, they are both important and beautiful things. But with this, I'm not happy with letting someone else, a commercialised new messiah, take all the credit. And besides, you'd find out the truth sooner or later.'

I was wounded, despite my doubts and those naysaying kids at school, I had hoped, if Santa was real, that he was a decent guy. I never had him down as a marketing tool, and my eyes were suddenly opened to the adult world. Grandpa sighed, I know he felt bad, regretted this sudden admission. He tried to claw back, reason with me.

'I'm sorry, Joe, I wasn't thinking, I could have done this more tactfully. Sometimes I'm an arsehole without meaning to be. The concept is real Joe! Father Christmas, he was a real person, once, sort of. Well fuck, I don't know how to repair this, I'm sorry. Your mother believed too, and I've never forgotten the disappointment and tears, Joe, when she found out the truth. She felt betrayed! We felt like the worst parents in the world! Then, it seems she went and perpetuated the lie with you. I don't know what to make of that.'

Me either. My mother had lied to me. I sort of already knew, I told you I had my doubts. I might've been one of the last to know because I started secondary school that year. Still, it was a shock. It had been a tough year. I was glad he'd told me the truth.

He was always very animated, Grandpa, energetic and eternally cheerful, but he would curse and rave like a madman. I got used to that quickly. I asked him about it once, early on, why he swore so much.

'Because it's fucking powerful Joe! You chuck a curse word in a sentence and it can convey exactly what you feel! Call it lazy if you want, but sometimes no other words will do. Is it offensive? Why? Eh? It's an excellent way to emphasise your statements, and to be honest, it feels good too. Try it!'

I didn't, not then. He didn't pause anyway,

'Swearing can be both positive and negative in its use, don't underestimate it, learn how to exploit that. The word "fuck" is everything. A noun, a verb, an adjective, and adverb, an interjection.

It's one of the most versatile words in our language. Fuck it, offend people Joe, it's good for them!'

He was the smartest man I've ever met, super artistic too. The clever *and* happy combination is super rare, right? He loved to draw and was good at it, although he told me he didn't start until he was in his forties. It was not for any particular gain, he just enjoyed it, gave him something to do. He almost always had a cigarette gripped precariously between his lips, and he'd be sketching into little sketchbooks and notepads. People mostly, those he saw sitting on benches or sweeping their doorsteps, sometimes me. I didn't like those ones, my hair covering my face, slouched shoulders.

When he wasn't smoking, swearing and drawing, Grandpa would be reading. There were books everywhere; art, philosophy, politics, and he had a particular penchant for sci-fi. I never read any, but Grandpa had read them all. So many shelves crammed, books balanced above books balanced above shelves. I mean, there are still shelves, and books, but somehow the whole thing feels like the past already. It was Grandpa's reality, and he's not here now. Every room has at least one bookshelf. There's one in the bathroom, one in the kitchen, two on the landing, because he'd run out of space to put them anywhere else. He was the definition of a bibliophile, always buying books from charity shops, borrowing from the library; he amazed me with his thirst for knowledge. Am I supposed to return those library books? They're at least three months overdue. That's a hefty fine, I'll just ignore it.

Grandpa once told me he was an idealist. I didn't know what that meant, except my history teacher told me that Hitler was one too. Honestly, Grandpa was nothing like Hitler. I don't know a whole lot about Hitler, other than he was a shitty person, and I think my history teacher might be deluded to think such a thing. Whatever, I know about Grandpa; besides his unrivalled energy, his greatest characteristics were his kindness towards the world, his humanity and his propensity for humour and fun. He always saw the good in people, even when they were complete bastards.

There wasn't much money, just Grandpa's state pension and whatever benefits he received for looking after me, but we never went without. At least, I didn't.

Grandpa didn't think television was a good thing so we didn't have one. He thought it a waste of our valuable time, that it killed people's creativity, preyed on our insecurities and poisoned minds with material desire and political brainwashing. It made us dumb, a propaganda tool. He was probably right.

I didn't tell anyone at school that we didn't have a telly, I would've looked like a weirdo. It would be social suicide, not that I had any social involvement with anyone, so I don't know why I was trying to save face. I never said anything at home, but Grandpa must've felt bad for me because he would afford me the stuff he figured boys my age might want; material things that might earn me normal healthy friendships and inclusion. Although he was one of the least materialistic people ever, he understood that teenagers are superficial creatures and accepted that displays of conformity and faux-wealth were of some importance within school walls. It didn't work but I was still grateful. Nike Air, Converse high tops, the overpriced, branded jeans, hoodies with the right logo, the phone, they all made me seem like less of a freak, helped me blend in, even if the reality was I would never be like the rest of them. I can tell you now, the right clothes and accessories do not make you any more accepted amongst your contemporaries. And actually, the phone was a useless prop because I had no one to call; had no friends, everyone around here had grown up with one another and they didn't feel the need to welcome anyone new into their fold, especially a weirdo like me. I used the phone as my music player though, pretty much lived with headphones in my ears.

I like to think I am not a slave to the system, Grandpa made sure of it. But I understand that system, I play a part, I get it. I am equally complacent in its dominance as I am a fighter against it. Yeah, I realise the conflict in my feelings, but please, understand; on the one hand, I am (was) Grandpa's protege, and I trust his advice implicitly. But, even *he* allowed me to integrate myself within that accepted structure, understood the necessity, with the trainers and the phone and all that stuff. I know I should care, I know I'm a sheep, but at least I have some self-awareness right? I see the injustice, the restlessness, but what can I do? I don't know how I can 'avoid the soul-sucking system' like he asked. It pisses me off that I'm a pawn of the establishment, but I don't have the fight in me to change that. I want to be decent but I am not a perfect person, I am sorry. Anyway, forget it, I think I'm an idealist too.

That shit aside, we'd go into town every Saturday. Grandpa would give me some money and I'd go to the comic shop. In my opinion it's the only shop in town worth going to. Yeah, I'm definitely not a realist.

They don't mind you sitting in there flicking through the books, and I always bought something. Grandpa used to shrug and say, 'Well, any reading is reading Joe, and there's art too, can't be all bad.' And he was right, yeah? I like comics; the visuality of it, the art, and the escape. Complete removal from real life.

I've thought a lot about what it takes to be a superhero. Could I ever be one? I mean, I have a good origin story. A sad and vaguely tragic beginning, dead parents. A nemesis in the form of the entire world except for Grandpa. A weakness? Too many to mention. A superpower which I still haven't figured out. OK, maybe not. But superheroes are complex and relatable, and it's more enjoyable to read a book with pictures. I would copy the linework and pictures from those comics into sketchbooks. Still do. I've got a ton of sketchbooks.

**Joe is such a hero, he just doesn't know it yet. Just you wait.**

To my astonishment and delight, for my fourteenth birthday, Grandpa bought me a laptop computer and an internet connection. Mr. Parks from three doors down came and set it up for me, and suddenly I had access to the vast and unbridled world of media, music, and film.

Grandpa warned, 'It is for educational purposes only, Joe! Use it to cultivate your mind. Be careful, because the media lie. I hear the internet is full of misinformation and pornography, but it also has all the education and knowledge you could ever want! The biggest library in the world! So use it wisely, feed your mind with good ideas."

It was an eye-opener. Obviously I got hooked on clickbait and porn. And I got to watch movies and TV shows that kids at school talked about. But most of all I found therapy in music. It became my everything. The night the internet went live, I shut myself away in my room and binged on music videos (the porn came later).

There was this guy who worked at The Comic Store (It's actually called that, I'm not being vague). He was friendly and would comment on what I bought, usually with approval, or he'd recommend stuff. He was always wearing these band t-shirts, every time I went there. I guess I wanted to find some common ground with him because he seemed cool, so I figured I'd check out the music he was advocating. To start with it was Metallica. Which, well, wow. Changed everything. The Saturday after that it was

Slayer. Also wow. I'd never heard anything like this stuff before, so excuse my naivety or whatever, but it changed my life! I developed an obsession then, watching both their entire works via videos, streaming and live performances. I won't lie, I don't care how out of date I sound, I was immediately drawn to it, the catharsis of music, I felt I'd found my therapy. Those guys were so cool, so different to anything or anyone I knew in real life. The tempo, the darkness, the aggression, and intensity, the masculinity, all of it. It soothed me. I felt affiliated, almost a sense of belonging. I felt cool.

Grandpa quickly decided he didn't like my taste in music, which, he (and I) pondered was probably the way it was meant to be.

'Why all that doom and blackness, Joe? I don't get it. Doesn't it make you feel miserable? You should listen to The Shadows and The Beatles!' Or surprisingly, referencing Slayer, 'I have to say, the orchestration of this song is incredible Joe, so complex, so many layers, that riff, those drums! So powerful! Aggressive!' I probably rolled my eyes, whatever. Everyone likes South of Heaven, it's mainstream as fuck.

Anyway, a few weeks later I went to The Comic Store and the guy was wearing a Nirvana T- shirt. I'd listened to the entire back catalogue of Metallica, chronologically from Kill 'Em All to Hardwired. And Slayer, from Show No Mercy to Repentless (RIP Jeff Hanneman). I *still* hadn't found the guts to manage to strike up a conversation about our mutual taste in music, and now he'd gone and thrown me right off course with this. Went home, straight on YouTube. And that was it. I found him; my icon. Someone I could truly identify with. Lyrics that meant something to me, even if the guitar playing was a bit sketchy. Kurt Cobain, symbol of alienation and dissatisfaction. Lyrically, the music spoke to me on a visceral level, does that make sense? Kurt didn't give a shit about cool looking hair or Flying V guitars. He was less image, more emotion. Less Satan, more human. Slayer, those guys are just actors, but Nirvana, it's all real. Or was.

I was gutted when I realised Cobain was dead. Anyway, everything changed then because I didn't actually care what T-shirt guy thought anymore. I finally felt a genuine alignment, a bond with someone of significance. In fact, I was kind of pissed off that comic store guy couldn't just pick a side.

Aesthetically, Grandpa could see I was becoming somewhat influenced by the bands I was listening to. When I refused a haircut he didn't argue, just let me be. He didn't mind that I'd swapped visits to the comic shop for visits to the music store. The CDs, the band shirts, posters, he never questioned my choices. He was horrified by Nirvana as musicians though.

'Jesus Christ, Joe! That guy can't play guitar for shit, it's just noise! Can't understand a word he says, he just murmurs. What a miserable bastard! Slayer are better, by a mile.'

The way it's meant to be. I think Kurt played beautifully and spoke pure poetry, but Grandpa was not to be argued with, so I kept it to myself.

At school I sat alone at lunch, drawing. Nobody bothered with me. The bullies never targeted me either, by luck or by my sheer lack of significance, though cruel remarks were occasionally thrown my way. Freak was common, sometimes faggot. I get that I'm not particularly macho or whatever. I didn't care that I was different. It's not like being gay is a crime anymore, or detrimental. Anyway, I'm not gay, so what if I was? Those kids at school can fuck off, I've never needed them.

One parents' evening, my English teacher told Grandpa, as I sat beside him, that she thought I may be on the autistic spectrum, She said, not in a negative way, maybe Aspergers? *I just see that Joe struggles on a social level, but he's very bright too.* Grandpa got agitated and told her that he would not allow me to be labelled anything, thank you very much. I should be treated the same as every other kid at school. And that was that.

'Fuck school!' he said later that evening. He was a bit angry. I don't think I'm autistic, or else I'd be super good at maths. I'm just quiet and awkward. In a way it would be easier with a label, at least I'd have an excuse for being different.

We lived on a diet of sandwiches, toast, tinned spaghetti and beans. Frozen curries and biscuits. Bacon and eggs. Apples and oranges. Cereal. On Sundays we'd go to the cafe down the road for a roast dinner. Highlight of the week, food wise, and usually the only day I ate fresh vegetables. Grandpa had been too sick lately, so it's been mainly sandwiches. You can put pretty much put anything between bread and it's acceptably tasty.

As you know, Grandpa smoked like a chimney and swore like a sailor, basic similes I know, but true, and I'm nothing if not unoriginal. They were his only vices, and he dedicated himself to them with passion and enthusiasm. The house was permanently filled with a nicotine infused fog, every ceiling and furnishing tarnished with a greasy brown film, and every carpet an ash scattered blanket. His last cigarette was attempted less than four hours before he passed. Rolled and lit by me, Grandpa propped up on pillows, and despite missing half a lung and coughing up blood he laughed and said it was like sucking on angel titties. They were his final words.

As you're probably already aware, angels don't have nipples. I wish I did, they look fun. Still, I'm sure you can appreciate the analogy. Joe's grandpa was a good guy and was never meant to enter priesthood, else Joe wouldn't exist. And Joe's existence upon this planet right now is important. I'll let you get on.

He taught me to roll his cigarettes early on. It was time consuming and he was running out of it, would I be kind enough to help him out? By the time I was thirteen I'd steal some for myself, because I was curious about the appeal and because it seemed like something cool people did. You've seen that Kurt Cobain picture? With his guitar and leather jacket? I don't think it gets any cooler than that. And not just Kurt, what about the predecessors; James Dean, Hepburn, Clint Eastwood? Hendrix, Slash, Johnny Depp? Smoking used to be cool.

So, I'd spark one on the way to school, and one on the way home, taking the lane behind the houses so my neighbours wouldn't see me on the road and tell Grandpa. Yeah, I know it's disgusting and despite the graphic horror pictures on the packets, I still thought I was badass. At seventeen, my smoking fingers have already developed a yellowish hue and I've resigned myself to a lifetime of the addiction that killed my Grandpa and actually, I'm beginning to feel ashamed. It's still a *bit* cool though right?

Let me interject readers, *Spoiler Alert!* I can tell you now that lung cancer will not be the cause of Joe's death, no such luck will he make it that far. But now you have an understanding of Joe's relationship with his grandpa, and a little history on his upbringing, perhaps now you may realise my affection for the boy. Sweet kid, right?

We had this stupid boy/girl rule at school—you had to sit next to a member of the opposite sex in class. Apparently it encouraged a more civilised atmosphere within the classroom and improved behaviour. Casey Parks from three doors down always sat next to me in English and Art. She was studious but also popular, because I suppose she *was* hot in that basic bitch way. Long, glossy chestnut hair, eyeliner, that weird contouring shit going on where her cheekbones glow bright white under the artificial lights at school. I don't know why she sat with me. She would try to talk, maybe because we were neighbours she didn't think I was some kind of alien or something. I just felt awkward. She seemed to like me though, because a couple of years ago when I was on my way home from school, minding my own business on the lane behind our houses, she caught up with me.

'Give me twosies on that?'

'Twosies?' I asked. I'd never heard the term.

'Share your smoke?' She looked at me, perplexed but smiling.

'Oh right, OK.' I passed her the cigarette, and she'd clearly smoked before because she inhaled like a pro, no coughing.

'What's your deal, Joe? You're so quiet.' I just didn't have anything to share out loud. She continued, 'You know, you don't help yourself, you could be more friendly.' I didn't know how. I am friendly, just shy. 'Will you roll me another to take home?'

'I don't have anything on me, sorry, I rolled that this morning before I left.'

'OK, well, will you roll me one for tomorrow then?'

'OK.'

'Thanks. So, you wanna hang out for a bit?'

'OK.'

'You say anything other than OK?'

'Yeah.'

She laughed, 'Jesus Christ Joe, you're fucking weird.' I shrugged. She asked, 'Are you gay?'

'No!' I responded, too quickly. Do people think that? I'm attracted to girls, most of the time, all of the time. I mean, it's OK to notice if a boy is good looking or attractive or whatever, right? Doesn't mean I want to do sex stuff with them.

She grabbed my hand and led me to a small gap between two garages that lined the lanes behind our houses. I was nervous, not being accustomed to female company outside of class. Without warning, shielded from view by concrete and corrugated iron, she planted her mouth on mine, forcing her tongue through my lips. Freaking out, I tried to respond as best I could. She started to rub her hand against my crotch, through my school trousers. I gasped, grabbed her wrist. It was a bit much.

'Relax.' she said, looking me right in the eyes, and I loosened my grip, let her continue. I had no experience of anything sexual other than the porn I mentioned earlier. We'd had the odd sex-ed class at school, and I remember my form teacher saying that we should not think sex in real life was anything like pornography. Obviously right? I'd never seen any woman or man behave the way they do on PornHub, but right then, Casey was doing well at convincing me otherwise. Where the fuck did this come from? We hadn't even had a proper conversation. She'd unzipped me now, her hand seeking me out. I had no control, my dick had a life of its own, and nothing I could do would stop it. I felt the cool air hit right there, and she dropped to her knees, taking me in her mouth. Jesus fucking Christ! It felt good, it felt wrong, my legs were shaking, I was like, what the actual fuck? She was going for it, full XXX Videos treatment. I glanced down to see her blue eyes looking right back at me, lips slick and wet, taking as much as she could, bobbing back and forth. The eye contact was disconcerting. Reminded me of that POV porn, so I closed my eyes. Her hand got involved then, and I was gone. Without warning I came in her mouth, surprising myself with a porno gasp and moan. She spat, into the sweet wrappers and cans and debris gathered around us. Holy shit!

**Well, lucky Joe! That is all.**

I remember when I first heard the term blow job, some older kids at the bus stop. I knew it was sexual, from their conversation, but I thought it had something to with actually blowing. Just me? Whatever, call me naive. But it seems a weird word to use when you think about it. Shouldn't it be a suck job? I don't remember when I figured out what it really was, maybe after the porn. I googled it once, what I got was, what would happen if a girl blew air down your piss hole? Potentially an embolism, so shit, I hope that never happens. I think everyone needs to start calling it something else, just to be safe.

Casey had a reputation at school, I'd heard the talk when I got changed for PE. It was still unexpected though, that blow (suck) job. I'd presumed her promiscuity was reserved for the popular boys. The next day, except for her knowing perma-sexual smile, it was like nothing ever happened. She caught up with me in the lane, I was standing there feeling a foot taller than yesterday, and I gave her two cigarettes I'd rolled the night before. She barely stopped, just took them from me with a 'Thanks' and walked off through the back gate of her garden.

I did well in my exams, despite a lack of revision and interest in the curriculum. Sport bored me, I just don't have any competitive leanings. The science and math was interesting enough, but all that logical stuff was not where my heart was. Like Grandpa, I favoured the creative. I love to draw and read comics. Everyone at school had to meet with the careers advisor to discuss our subsequent plans. He told me my grades were good, asked what I'd like to do. I didn't know. I liked art, hadn't thought about the future. He told me my education would lay the foundations for the rest of my life, that I should map out a strategy, prepare ahead. I had a promising record, the world of future employment my oyster. Art would be unlikely to result in a proper career. I shrugged. He became uninterested, disappointed by my lack of ambition and enthusiasm. He suggested teaching.

Grandpa appreciated and nurtured my artistic inclination. Perhaps because of his own ardor for literature, art, and music, he always encouraged my drawing and writing, providing me an endless supply of materials with which to record my efforts. He never said I had to think about my future, just do the stuff I liked, the rest would fall into place. We had a piano, which Grandpa played a little, but I could never pick it up. It was my Grandmother's, who apparently was really good. He bought me a guitar that Christmas, just a cheap Japanese acoustic. I called it Frances and watched online tutorials and learned a few chords. I'm not really any good, a four chord wonder. I can play *Come As You Are* and *Polly*.

# Death Party

The days after Grandpa's death are strange, I fret over the letter and my future, alone and unprepared. I keep thinking of him, as he took his last gasping breath, in those thirty year old pyjamas that he'd worn for a week. There was no warning or ceremony; just nothingness. One minute he was sleeping, fitfully I suppose, the next he was gone. It didn't seem painful, no death rattle or anything, but it was obvious, that final exhalation. I'll remember the sound forever.

Mrs. Parks brings me food every day, plated hot dinners, sandwiches, fruit. I accept them graciously, because otherwise I might not bother eating. As I'm Grandpa's next of kin (and only kin) I am, despite being under eighteen, consulted upon regarding funeral arrangements. There's not a lot for me to contribute, even though we both knew he was dying we never discussed it much. I don't think he would give a shit. No religion, he said, he hated that stuff. He called funerals 'death parties'. But they ask me for music ideas and I remember what he'd said about this. Nina Simone, *Feeling Good.* Odd choice and he didn't explain. Social services advises and Mrs. Parks insists on accompanying me, mothering me.

I have no funeral clothes, so I wear my black jeans, school shirt and my black leather jacket. Mrs. Parks loans me her husband's black tie and gives me a lift because the council won't pay for a limousine. The funeral is poorly attended. Me, Mrs. Parks and Casey, a couple of neighbours and nurses who had tended to Grandpa in his final days. The crematorium staff pad out the congregation slightly. I listen to Nina Simone and it feels like a message. Otherwise, the event passes me by in a blur.

I've just finished school, second year of sixth form, but I haven't attended for weeks and I missed my final exams, so yeah, I failed. I only moved up to sixth form because my grades were good enough and I didn't know what to do otherwise.

Grandpa believed formal education was a waste of time, which I should find mildly comforting. Aside from learning to read, write, and do basic math he could not understand the value people placed on schooling beyond that. It was the law, and I had to go, but he made it clear.

'No autonomy, Joe! Schools teach like they're creating factory workers, they only educate you to work and follow rules. You know, they haven't changed their teaching methods for over a hundred years, hardly keeping up are they? Shitty system, a fucking joke Joe, they'll beat any creativity, energy, and joy for knowledge out of you.'

And so, unsurprisingly, he *really* disliked Universities.

'Higher education is elitist Joe, for the moneyed. You know what that shit costs? It's a trap. Earns you a lifetime of debt, shackled to the system! It's not in any way related to your capacity for intelligence or knowledge, in fact, in many ways it's the opposite! The constraints of such supposed education does nothing but wipe clean all your genuine free thoughts and opinions, replacing them with the pretentious and regurgitated ideas of whoever or whatever is deemed fashionable at the time! You're all forced to read the same books, at the same time and place which is, in my opinion, frankly inconvenient! It dictates when, what and how you should learn, it's bollocks! Why should you HAVE to learn anything that you have no interest in? It's so constrictive! And what for? Pieces of paper? No need for it, Joe! You know, it's like the military for the sheltered and privileged; I got no time for it. Machines! Designed to break you down and remould you into someone different. It's Government manipulation! We are, all of us, learning everyday. Ancora Imparo! You know who said that?' I didn't. 'It's accredited to Michelangelo, at the age of eighty seven. It means, "I am still learning" And we are! Always! You think I learned that at school? No I did not. Don't limit yourself to learning what other people tell you you must. There's so much out there to know, and you're better off discovering it yourself!'

Yeah, he was passionate about stuff. You see all those exclamation marks? That's how Grandpa spoke. All. The. Time. With conviction and assertion. My English teacher would have a fit. I'm personally aware that such formal education in today's world enables one to actually get a job. And you know, surgeons and stuff? Isn't it a good thing they have to train and qualify for such an important role? I didn't tell Grandpa that, because I could see his point. Didn't want to piss on his chips. Anyway, he reluctantly accepted my choice, saying it wasn't the worst decision I could make at that time; I should avoid the burden of responsibility for as long as possible.

'Don't worry about it, Joe, you've got plenty of time. No rush to make decisions, just wing it!'

I've gone off on a tangent again, but what I'm saying is; unemployed and penniless, Grandpa's funeral was that of a pauper, a basic public health service and cremation paid for by the local authority. Hardly a party.

There was no religious sentiment because we know how Grandpa felt about that. Afterwards, Grandpa's ashes were scraped into a cardboard scatter tube, ready for collection, but Joe would never collect them. They were later unceremoniously bestrewn by a member of the crematorium bereavement team in the garden of remembrance. Grandpa legally had no money to leave Joe, because we know that he had been withdrawing every penny he received and stashing that cash aside in the event of his death. He'd worried that if it was left in his account it would all be seized to pay for his funeral. He didn't really know a whole lot about intestacy law (who does?), but he did know he didn't want Joe to worry. As it goes, Grandpa had enough left in his account to cover Joe's phone bill, before said account was frozen.

After the funeral Mrs. Parks brings me home. I sit in the backseat behind Casey who keeps eyeing me in the mirror on the sun visor (liner on fleek). I avoid her gaze, look out the window instead. The radio is on, some guy talking about our society's collective dissatisfaction; how everyone needs to man-up and buckle down, work harder and not feel so entitled. Says we're losing our right to free speech. He sounds like a twat, I have no idea what he's on about and neither do I give a fuck. Mrs. P drops me outside Grandpa's house, and with sympathetic eyes,

'Dinner later?'

'No, thanks.'

I let myself in and flop down on the sofa. The house feels weird, empty, too quiet and I just sit in silence, eyes closed, my mind flying a million miles an hour. I'm tired. After ten minutes someone's knocking the door. I ignore it, almost dozing, but they're persistent. So, cranky and irritated I get up and answer it, intent on telling them to fuck off. It's Casey. I don't want for company, my only wish is to be left alone. But I don't tell her to fuck off.

'Can I come in?' She steps inside before I can answer, brushing against me in the doorway.

'I guess.' I mumble, and let the door fall shut and we stand there in the hall.

'Just wanted to know you're OK, Joe?'

'Well yeah I suppose, considering everything.' Her mother probably told her to come check on me. Casey reaches for my hand and leads me back to the sitting room.

'Come sit with me.' she says. I do, and within seconds she's unbuttoning me on her knees between my thighs, grasping at my crotch. Man, I don't need this. I'm nervous as fuck, but she sucks me soft into her mouth, and as I involuntarily harden as I give into the sensation. For fuck's sake.

Two minutes later, if that, I've shot my wad into her throat. She stands and walks to the kitchen, discourteously spits my seed into the sink, and pours herself a glass of water. Returning she asks,

'Better now?' All slutty smile, faded lipstick, sucking in her cheeks like she's posing for a selfie, channelling her Kardashian.

'Er yeah, thanks.' I say, because what else can I? It was a distraction. I'm looking at her eyebrows. They're kind of strange, unnatural. All angular and villainous. Same as most the girls at school, they all do that weird pencilling thing. The day has been really fucking overwhelming so far. Casey drops down next to me, leaning into my space, trying to look all hot and seductive, pushing her tits together with her arms, still in her funeral clothes. She brushes a strand of hair from my face and says,

'You're so nineties Joe, why don't you get a haircut?' I shrug. Whatever, I was born too late.

'I like my hair.' I say. She shrugs, looks around.

'Man, this place is like a time capsule… you wanna go upstairs?' I really don't. It's a mess up there for a start. I don't know if she wants me to fuck her or whatever, but I'm like,

'Nah, I gotta go somewhere, but thanks for coming over.' I'm not really thankful but it seems like the right thing to say. I've got nowhere to go. Too much death and sex for one day, I just want to be on my own and don't know what's expected of me anyway. I mean, my dick's getting sucked as Grandpa's body is being incinerated; it's just fucked up. She looks pissed off but gets the hint.

Standing she says, 'Whatever Joe!' All huffy, she turns, walks towards the front door. I remember something,

'Wait!' She stops, swings around, looking hopeful. 'Here,' I pull off her daddy's tie and hold it out to her, 'Tell your dad thanks.'

I take some money from the jar behind the knife block and go to the chip shop. Come home and sit on my bed watching YouTube. I'm distracted though. Grandpa has really messed with my head. I mean, we could've discussed this. I have no one to ask for advice now. Seriously, what am I supposed to do? I have nothing. I'll be kicked out, and then what? The money will get me nowhere, a couple of months at best. Thanks, Grandpa. I'm not angry with him, but I don't know what he wants me to do. All that seeking experience stuff, avoiding the system, meeting interesting people;

I'm still going to have to get a job to survive, toe the line. You can't buy groceries with experiences. This sucks. I've never felt so conflicted in all my life, and I never expected Grandpa would make me feel this way. Maybe I am angry? I don't know. I'm alone.

See what I mean? Poor Joe! What would you do? He's just a kid. You couldn't blame him if he just climbed into his bed and ignored all that was happening around him. At best, he'll get a council flat and a job in telesales. Struggle. Settle for a girl. Get her pregnant. Feign happiness in raising a whining kid in a world of poverty and disappointment. But no, he won't do that. He trusted his Grandpa, has faith in his advice. Come on Joe, I'm rooting for you. We're rooting for you! You can fucking do this!

I might do it. I might take the money and go, like he said. After I ate, I counted it out, £4479. That's a lot. I mean, I know it's not really, but it's the most money I've ever seen; God knows when he wrote that letter. What's the worst that could happen? What have I got to lose? Literally nothing.

No, it's stupid. I can't. I'm not up to this, no way. I've never even left this county. It's ridiculous, I'm not that kind of person. I'm a safe and easy type, not into drama and adventure. I'm tired, I want to sleep. I'm going to bed, I can't think straight.

I lie on my bed. I can't even imagine getting a job, I have no idea how. This house is so cold.

OK Grandpa, I'll do it! I'm pissed off and I think this is a stupid plan, but I'll do it.

I don't know why I keep talking to him in my head. I don't believe in Gods, an afterlife, any of that. I'm just comforting myself. I miss talking to him.

The rucksack he bought for me is still in his bedroom. I go in, notice the greasy imprint on his pillow, how the bedclothes were turned back from when they took him away. The curtains are shut and I shudder, it's a little creepy. I grab the bag and take it to my own room. It's definitely an army rucksack and I momentarily entertain the idea of joining the military. What a stupid fucking idea. Grandpa would be horrified, he was 100% a pacifist. The army is the last place I should go.

What should I take? I drop the bag and pick up my guitar, sit down, strum a little. Yeah, I suck. I should pack clothes. Maybe I'll need my birth certificate? As proof of ID? My National Insurance number. I have no other proof of who I am. I'll miss Frances, my guitar, but I don't have a case for her and she'll be cumbersome.

# Upping And Leaving

Next morning I give myself a pep talk in the bathroom mirror. I'm showered, shaved, packed. I examine my face. I don't look too bad. My hair's long on my shoulders. I'm not getting it cut.

I check out the house, each room. Seems weird to just abandon everything, Grandpa's entire history, his weird little mementos, his books. A lifetime of belongings. My belongings too. I haven't sold anything because who do I sell it to? The car hasn't been started for months. The tyres are flat and it's rusted, ancient, worth nothing. It's difficult to pack, to know what to leave behind. Am I crazy?

My books, CDs, my laptop are too bulky to take with me, but I take my phone and charger. Got my music on, and I guess I could connect to free WiFi around the place, if I really miss the internet (of course I will, the internet is my life). Clothes. The money. My favourite sketchbooks. Drawing is all I have now. Pencils and pens.

The council will come and empty this place out in a few weeks, once they realise I'm not here anymore. They'll send everything to landfill. The thought makes me anxious, but I remember Grandpa's letter; *Shed the material stuff, start over.* He wouldn't give a shit about it. I think about some council bailiff taking my laptop home for his kid, consider clearing my search history before I leave. Nah, there's nothing particularly incriminating, and my computer is years old, no one will want it. But I realise how fond I am of the things I own. Weirdly I look at the pillow on my bed. I like my bed and its pokey springs and I am tempted to climb in now and ignore everything. Instead, I walk out the room, my brain screaming at me, *No! Don't go! What about…?*

I check all the plugs are unplugged. There's a plate and a knife in the sink from my toast this morning. Fuck it. The lights are all off. I lock the back door. I just can't bring myself to walk out the front door. But I'm ready. My clothes are layered up. I have snacks, water, money. I can choose to go anywhere, do anything. It just seems impractical, shouldn't I plan something first?

Grandpa's letter is in my pocket. Do or die I think, what does that mean? I should Google it. I can't, I've unplugged the router. And so, in a moment of boldness, holding my keys in my hand, I hoist my rucksack on my back and I'm out the front door pulling it closed behind me. Standing on my doorstep, I swallow hard, take a long, deep breath, and head into town for the train station. Trains have WiFi, right? Fuck you school, fuck you, Casey, fuck you shitty small town life, I don't need you.

Fuck it, what do I have to lose?

# The Haiku Man

My train arrives at The City and I've never seen crowds like this. All the people look different here. I wouldn't see any of these around my hometown, not really. Overcome but undeterred, I follow signs that lead me to the underground.

No idea where I'm going, I buy a ticket and climb aboard the first tube to arrive. I'm being brave. I take a deep breath, I'm really doing this. There are a lot of people in this carriage, I'm not used to it. Someone catches my eye. This man; bearded, grubby, unkempt and presumably inebriated, he staggers amongst the commuters, uncomfortably brushing against their finery with his grimy trench coat. I sit, in a prized seat I suppose, and watch his dirty hand slip discreetly into the wool coat pocket of a lady stood swaying on the aisle, her arm raised above her holding the rail to steady herself. I assume he's a thief, but he takes nothing from her and I reckon her pocket must be empty. He's an opportunist, trying his luck wherever he can. His appearance and demeanour is a genius disguise as his presence is ignored; everyone averting their gaze, denying his existence. It's weird that no one makes eye contact here, nobody acknowledges anybody, but it's magnified in this guy's case. He moves closer, then stops in front of where I sit, stabilising himself on the handrail above our heads. I'm eye level with his crotch. Expecting his hygiene to be questionable, I hold my breath as long as I can, turning my face away but surreptitiously eyeing him and clutching my rucksack tight to my chest, just in case he should attempt to rob me.

I watch his shaky fingers delve into his grease lined pocket, from which he pulls out a pen, and then, taking the pen in between his teeth, he ventures back in, eventually pulling out a small piece of paper. The tube stops, and in that brief time he takes the pen from his mouth, and trembling, begins to write upon the scrap in his hand. The train starts up again, and I press myself back into my seat, creating as much distance as I can from the man, but he lurches forward and drops his pen onto my bag, from where it rolls to the floor, rests against my shoe. We make eye contact. Shit! I retrieve his pen, quickly pass it back. Please just get the fuck out of my face! He looks surprised, and I know I've committed a city faux pas. He doffs an imaginary cap, completes his scribble, then shuffles sideways, positioning himself in front of the man sitting beside me. Again the train slows, and awkwardly the guy next to me stands to leave, avoiding as best he can any physical contact with the bum. It's futile, as the drunk grabs his arm and stuffs the scrap of paper into the man's hand. Horrified he scarpers out the open door. The vagrant snorts a laugh and drops into the now vacant seat beside me. It was awesome to watch, but like everyone else I try my hardest to ignore his proximity, and when the tube stops again I rush off as quickly as I can, dismayed at the realisation that this dipsomaniac has exited behind me.

I walk along the platform, nowhere to go, and stop at an unoccupied bench. The wino has settled some way away, sliding down the wall he sits on the floor, pulling from within some hidden compartment of his coat a half bottle of vodka. Confident that he has no interest in me now, I pull my sketchbook from my bag, feeling the need to occupy my hands and mind for a time while I consider my next move. I don't know what else to do.

Man, I'm out of my depth. Why am I here again? I'm shaking, I need to centre myself. I find a pencil and, unsteadily, I start to draw from memory the shape of a woman, wobbling precariously on high heels, arm aloft holding a rail to steady herself, a long wool coat swishing around her calves. I relax, slightly at least, I'm absorbed in my work when I feel warm, acrid breath on the back of my neck. I slam shut my sketchbook, alarmed, and that's when he speaks;

'You a runaway?

Too young to be here alone.

Got no place to be?'

Tense and unsure how to respond, I say 'No.' He continues,

'Looks like you're new here.

I can help you if you're lost,

I know this City.'

'I'm fine, thanks.' I force my book back into my bag. He shuffles around the bench, parks himself beside me, again.

'Where are you from boy?

What brings you to The City?

Streets ain't paved with gold.'

'I'm aware of that,' I respond. He seems less threatening now, and I'm surprising myself, interacting with a stranger. 'Looking for a place to stay, going to find a job or something.'

'Well good luck with that.

Like I said I can help you…

You got money boy?

'Payment is simple,

Tobacco and alcohol,

I'm at your command.'

At this point I realise he's speaking weird. All stilted and measured.

'I'm not eighteen yet, and I don't have any ID, so I can't buy anything.' I don't want to get my wallet out and risk him assaulting me or something, not that there's much in it; the money from Grandpa is stashed in a pair of socks at the very bottom of my bag.

'Well then you are screwed;

Not eighteen and no ID?

You'll never find work.'

'I'm eighteen in a couple of days,' I feel a bit panicked now, because it occurs to me again that I have no fucking idea what I am doing here. Shit, I don't even have a bank account. That's enough right? I pull my tobacco out my pocket, roll myself a cigarette. Feeling vaguely charitable, I offer it to my companion, who near snatches it from me, so I roll another for myself. 'Can you maybe tell me where I can find somewhere cheap to stay?' He's shaking his head.

'I told you the price.

You don't pay then I don't say,

Nothing comes for free.'

But I just gave him a cigarette! Whatever. I light my smoke, and hold my lighter out for the hobo.

'You promise to help?' The man nods, and I slip my wallet out my jacket pocket, pull out a tenner. 'Here, for booze or whatever.' He near snatches it, smiles, stained teeth. He declines my light, instead holds out his vodka to me, grins,

'You can't smoke in here,

Since two thousand and seven.

Eighty quid fine boy!'

Shit, yeah, I forgot. I mean, I know you can't smoke anywhere these days, but it wasn't really enforced where I'm from. I stub it out on the arm of the bench.

'Let's drink together

And marvel at the bustle

Of these people's lives.'

I don't want to marvel at the bustle of people's lives, Jesus. 'You said you'd help? Point me in the right direction?' Fuck these people's lives! They all have some place to go, I want to see what I'm dealing with here. I need fresh air, and a smoke. And I'm not drinking from that bottle either, God knows what germs this guy is harbouring in his spit. Besides, I've never tried alcohol in my life. I stand to leave, feeling fleeced. What a great start.

'OK, what's your name?

I'm a man true to my word,

Somewhere cheap to stay.'

He rises from the bench. I'm slightly placated, 'My name's Joe.' I tell him.

'My name is Tom

A.K.A. The Haiku Man.

Let's get out of here.'

And so, probably against my better judgement, Tom and I walk the steps up out into The City. I relight my rollie as soon as I'm in the open air. Haiku Man? We did those poems at school. I ask him about it, figure out that he'd been writing one on the train.

'I'm from a small town,
But I had gigantic dreams
And left to conquer.
'It never happened
I became jaded and drunk.
Poetry remained.
'I offer poems
To those in need of wisdom,
Or just a kind word.'
I say, 'Fair enough, but do you have to speak Haiku all the time?'
'Speaking in Haiku
Was difficult to begin,
Now it's all I have.'
It's kind of annoying already.
'Are you homeless?' I ask.
'You cheeky bastard!
I am not a vagrant, boy,
But I've been called worse.'

He looks homeless, but actually *I'm* the homeless one. I'd asked for directions to a cheap part of town. I'm happy to make my own way now, I mean, what the fuck am I thinking asking this weirdo for help? I could probably find a Citizens Advice Bureau or something.

'Let's find you shelter
And maybe something to eat.
It is getting late.'
We walk for ages, I'm just following, God knows where. We pass a guy holding a cardboard placard, like one of those The End is

Nigh guys from the movies, except his placard reads KILL YOUR TELEVISION. Tom still talking in Haiku,

'This guy here, he knows,

The media are poison,

They disguise the truth.'

Whatever, I shrug. I don't tell him I didn't have a TV back home. Grandpa would agree about the media. Tom stops dead in his tracks then.

'You know what I need?

A filthy fucking burger

With cheese and ketchup'

I'm hungry too, and begrudgingly I buy us both a burger from the joint we're outside, because he says to me,

'I can't go in there,

I'm banned. Get me a meal deal?

Diet Coke, no ice.'

We walk and eat. He asks me to hold his burger while he pours vodka into his coke.

'It's got ice in it!

You paid for frozen water?

I told you, no ice!'

'I forgot.' Jeez. I hand the burger back and then chewing he asks me,

'What you gonna do?

Do you want to study here?

Art college maybe?

'I saw your drawing,

I'm impressed, you have talent!

Do something with it.'

'Thanks. I don't know, not college though.' He shrugs, acknowledges my opinion and tells me,

'Be self-didactic
Like Batman and da Vinci
Bowie and Lovecraft
'Hemingway, Hendrix…
You'll be in good company
If you follow them.'
He continues, spitting crumbs of cheeseburger out with every sentence.
'There are so many!
Charles Dickens, Marlon Brando
Never finished school.
'And Tarantino,
John Lennon and Walt Disney,
They turned out just fine.
Abraham Lincoln,
He left school when he was twelve,
Became President!
Universities,
Full of privileged arseholes
Who don't know better.'
I'm reminded of Grandpa again. But I am no da Vinci, Batman or Hendrix. Kurt Cobain never went to University either. It occurs to me that all except one of those people he mentioned are dead. He tells me,
'We're not far away,
Two brothers, good friends of mine
Will give you a room.'
I feel slightly encouraged, just hoping these brothers are nothing like the Haiku Man, and that they're not going to pimp me out, molest me or harvest my organs or something.

Of all the people in all The City, Joe finds this guy. You couldn't make it up!

# Youth And The Doors It Opens

The City starts to quieten as people make their way home from work. I'm tired, my bag feels like it's full of bricks. The façade of the buildings has changed, no longer imposing, grandiose structures filled with business and industry, we're now wandering down narrow streets with shitty looking shop fronts and bars. I'm less intimidated. We reach a corner and Tom stops outside a pub or a club, I don't know. The sign above reads *The Queen's Head*. It has a picture of the actual queen, but someone's spray painted 666 on her forehead and a red streak across her neck like her throat's been slit. I'm no royalist, but shit. The sign's high up, they must've used a ladder or something? Seems like a lot of effort.

There's a group of people outside smoking, all bright haired, pierced, young, and confident. They're looking at me and looking at Tom, and I'm just thinking I'd look so much cooler if Tom wasn't with me and I wasn't carrying this humongous fucking rucksack.

Amongst them, this pretty blonde girl in shorts and tank girl boots calls out, 'Hey, what's up Haiku Man?' They know each other. Tom responds,

'Is Bob here tonight?

My boy Joe here needs a room

And maybe a job.'

'Yeah he's inside. No sign of Pete, so your boy Joe might just get some work too, if he's lucky.' The girl smiles in my direction, drops her cigarette to the floor, stamping it out with the toe of her boot. She's looking me up and down with a self-assuredness that near fucking kills me.

Aw, look at him now; so brave, I feel proud. Blushing, so young, naive, and cute! All skinny and nervous, but he's a lovely looking lad. Yes, beauty is in the eye of the beholder. But! Joe has symmetry. Joe has heart. Joe has no existing health conditions. OK, his family seem to have some predisposition to the cancers, but as I already said, it won't get Joe, and he won't be breeding. Just appreciate him as he is now, that dark floppy hair, those dark, pretty eyes. The courage mixed with innocence and vulnerability. If I were human, I'd totally be crushing on him. I love awkward.

Tom motions for me to follow him inside. Glad not to be the subject of ridicule any longer I follow. It's much bigger than it looks from the outside, and quiet, just a few stupidly cool looking people drinking at the tables that are dotted around the edge of the place. There's a band setting up on the stage on the far side of the room.

Posters, gig adverts pasted all over the walls, and I feel like such a fucking nerd, completely out of my depth; I'm not even old enough to be in here. At the opposite end of the room is a pool table. The bar itself spans the entire length of the back wall, all antique wood, and olde-worlde shelves stacked with spirits and glasses, contrasting with the neon signs and the beer fridges and pumps.

I haven't been inside a pub since I was a small boy, must've been at least ten years ago. I was out for dinner with my parents, and a memory comes back to me now, playing in the beer garden, my dad angry for some unknown reason, he storms off to the car, drives away, wheels spinning, leaving my mother and me behind. She took me inside to get some crisps. I don't remember what happened then, if he came back. I just remember the hostility of his company.

Seriously, this is new to me. Is this where normal people go? There's a man behind the bar, couldn't guess his age but he's weathered looking. He's tall and lean, with a face full of piercings, a bright green Mohawk with an Anarchist symbol tattooed on the side of his head. Punk as they come. Various other tattoos dotted all over his arms, his neck, a random faded, mish-mash of images and words, a spider web on his elbow like that guy out of Rancid, inked knuckles, and I wonder if this guy's done time. I don't know where to look and I literally couldn't feel more intimidated. Tom speaks;

'Bob, meet Joe. Joe, Bob.

Joe's new here, he's got money.

Can he get a room?'

I'm actually grateful for Tom now, because there's no way in Hell I could've walked in here, approached this guy and asked for a place to stay.

'He needs work too, so

If your brother doesn't show

Joe will earn his keep.'

Bob glares at me, belligerent, his face like an eagle; but it quickly softens into a wide toothy grin, I see the glint of gold teeth, and he's suddenly welcoming. And loud. His voice booms across the bar.

'Well, pretty boy, you barely look old enough to work here, but I'm fucking desperate for staff tonight. My brother wandered off yesterday, and it's just me and Kitten behind the bar. You worked a bar before?'

I have to be honest, 'No.' I struggle to look at him directly. I think of what Grandpa said about standing tall, head up and shoulders back. I try my best. Try to look less pretty too.

'Ah well, you can learn then. This place will be bouncing in a couple of hours, you'll need to collect the glasses, bring them round and get them in the washer. Make sure to empty the washer when it stops and start over. Empty bottles go in the bin under here. When it's full, take it out back to the recycling bin. Prices are on the wall. All the bottles are £4. Single shots are £4, double shots are £6. Mixers are £1. Stay the fuck away from the pumps, that shit takes practice. You want a room too?'

'Er, yeah.' Nothing he just said sunk in. I remove the bag from my back now, my shoulders ache and I'm exhausted. This is overwhelming, I'm not sure I'm up to working here, I don't think that was my suggestion. I could cry, thinking about my bed in my room back at Grandpa's.

'For how long?'

'I don't know, I just got here today, haven't made any plans yet.'

'Well £70 for a week, nothing is included in that except a room with a mattress. You can't wash or cook here, and don't fucking smoke inside.'

'That's great, thanks.' because what else can I say? I don't feel like I can back out now. Bob stands there, waiting, gesturing with an outreached hand he says,

'Money upfront.' Is this cheap? I don't know.

My wallet in my pocket only has about £40 in it, and now I'm thinking I'll have to rummage into the bottom of my bag, pull out that balled up pair of socks, and get the rest of the cash out. I don't know or trust anyone in this place, and it's just going to make me look like a loser.

'Can I see the room? My money's in my bag, like, right at the bottom.' I look around, indicating that it doesn't feel like an appropriate place to unpack.

Bob looks at me and my bag, and after a moment of consideration, agrees; 'OK, follow me.'

He walks down the length of the bar, and while I heave my bag over my shoulder, Bob lifts the hatch to allow me through. Leaving Tom behind, and the gaze of every punter in the place, I follow him through a door and up a narrow staircase, stark, stained, the floor groaning and creaking. It smells strange, pungent, but I can't identify the scent, it's just weird. At the top is a corridor, an open door with a toilet and sink, filthy and of indeterminate colour. In fact the whole upper floor seems indiscernible in design or colour; just bare walls, dirty, scuffed, graffitied in places. I mean, Grandpa's was a house entirely in shades of beige and brown, untouched since the seventies, and not clean by anyone's standard, but this is a whole different level of filth. Aside from the toilet, there appears to be five other rooms, another two at the back, three at the front. A long corridor stretches down to a fire escape.

Bob's chatty, laughing, 'So you just got here today, huh? You poor fucker, how in fuck's name did you end up with The Haiku Man? Old bastard's crazy.'

'He kind of latched onto me at the station,' I say. 'Said he could recommend a cheap place to stay.'

'Well, here it is, kiddo.' He pushes open a door, next to the toilet, and shows me into a small room, same dirty bare walls as everywhere else with nothing in it except for a suspiciously stained mattress and a small window with a view of brickwork of the opposite building. A single plug socket. He did warn me. To be honest, I'm horrified by the squalor, I wonder if I'd be better off sleeping rough. I still have my key for Grandpa's house, perhaps I should just go home?

'Well, will it do you?' Bob asks.

And I'm like 'Yeah, it's fine.' I'm too tired to consider looking elsewhere. I drop my bag onto the bare floorboards, and start to pull stuff out, my sketchbooks, a hoodie, I'm circling my arm around the bottom trying to find the money socks without Bob seeing what I have, so whilst inside the bag I'm peeling the socks apart, revealing the bundle of cash to myself only, and subtly trying to count out £70. I say, 'I won't stay long, just a few nights while I figure out what I'm going to do.'

'Don't blame you, I wouldn't stay here long either, it's a fucking shithole!' Bob says, cackling as I hand him the money. 'Those three doors opposite are out of bounds; mine and my brother's rooms and our bathroom. Stay out. Don't make noise. If you're not here before we lock the bar, you don't get in.'

'Right, get yourself downstairs as soon as you can and I'll show you the ropes.' And with that he turns and leaves me in my new accommodation.

I take it all in, it really is a shithole. Wondering what the fuck I've done, I slip off my jacket. The room is cold, the window a single pane, damp with condensation, a small crack at the corner. I look out and down below; to accompany the opposing brickwork,

I have a view of bins in an alleyway. I'm replacing my jacket with the black hoodie from my bag when it occurs to me that Bob hasn't given me a key. I look back at the door, and there's no keyhole. On the inside of the door is a small latch and bolt lock, allowing me to lock myself in, albeit not securely, but no lock on the outside, meaning that if I go anywhere I'm going to have to leave my belongings unsupervised in an open room. All the other doors up here except the bathrooms have proper locks. Fuck! Everything I've pulled out my bag gets stuffed back in, save the money sock which I pull out, remove the cash. £4000 in tens and twenties makes a pretty sizeable wad, but there is no way I'm going to leave it here and go downstairs. I'm a perfect fucking target for robbery. I split the notes, hide them in my jeans pockets. I swap my high tops for the boots in my bag, and wedge smaller bundles of notes inside them, and some inside my socks. I take my hoodie off and put my jacket back on, my wallet in the pocket bulging with cash, and every other pocket holding too. My bag repacked, I step out of the room closing the door, and apprehensively make my way downstairs. I don't think this is going to work out.

# On First Job And First Fight

I haven't been upstairs long, but the pub is busier now, and that pretty blonde from outside is behind the bar serving drinks to the guys who'd been setting up the stage. Is it offensive to refer to her as a pretty blonde? I don't know, probably, but she's both. Maybe it's misogynistic to measure a girl's value by her appearance but I've nothing else to go on.

'Hi Joe, I'm Kitten.' She passes me smiling on her way to the till. Bob's behind her,

'Right, come on kiddo, look alive, there's punters waiting.'

Kitten? What sort of name is that? I could die. The Haiku Man sits on a stool at the bar, glass tumbler in front of him. Some customer comes up, pats him on the back, buys him another drink. He winks at me, smirks.

Most people are drinking bottles, which is easy. I don't know how to use the till, and while both Kitten and Bob are initially patient with me, as the place gets busier I can tell I'm stressing them out with my lack of employment skills. I try my best, and as the night goes on, I get into it, feeling important being barside. As instructed I keep clearing tables. The band start playing around nine, they sound fucking terrible but the crowd seem into it. I can't see The Haiku Man anymore. It's rowdy, everyone in here looks tougher than me, even the girls. Especially the girls.

Despite my earlier tiredness I get my second wind. Between serving and clearing and generally feeling useful I barely take my eyes off Kitten. It's so busy we hardly speak, but I watch her flirt with everyone she serves. Guys buy her drinks, give her tips. No one tips me, we're a long way off from equality. The band finish and another set up. They introduce themselves as The Haemophiliac Blood Clots, which is creative, I think. They're marginally better than the guys before. It's getting rougher in here, and every time I go to collect bottles and glasses, I get knocked, shoved, and elbowed by drunk, sometimes merry, sometimes aggressive clientele. My eyes search for Kitten again and she's behind the bar, leaning over, looking kind of pissed off, talking to some guy whose back is to me. I've watched her smile, twirl her hair, pout her lips at guys and girls all night, but she's not flirting now. She looks angry. Arms full, I beat my way back to the bar, dutifully dropping the bottles into the bin, and start loading the glass washer. Kitten has moved on to serving someone else, but that guy she'd been talking to is still lingering, leaning over his bottle of beer, eyes not leaving Kitten for a moment. He's taller than me, not huge or anything, but brawny, all arm and shoulder definition, and confident, wearing a white vest. I see Bob has clocked him, his cheerful demeanor replaced by a scowl. Bob says something to Kitten and she shakes her head in response. I serve a couple of people, and that guy doesn't move from the bar, still watching Kitten, but she doesn't look back, is clearly avoiding him, concentrating her efforts down the other end of the bar. Eventually he moves away, and I see him within a group, looking serious, still staring at her. They obviously have history. I'm not so overtly masculine to deny he's attractive, all muscular and young, strong jawed, a bit white trash, but then, everyone here is. He has an eyebrow ring and tattoos, I think he looks cool as fuck. I think to myself I might get a haircut the next day, consider a facial piercing. Man, I'm so easily influenced.

It's noisy and messy, smashed glass and spillages, the place feels out of control. I soldier on. Bob says not to worry about the spilt drinks, they'll dry out of their own accord, and fuck the broken glass until the end of the night. The band carries on, playing stuff I've never heard, it's proper punk rock in here and I realise I don't know this scene. I see Kitten, wrong side of the bar, engaged in conversation with that guy from earlier. His whole stance is dominating, his arm propped next to her head on the wall she's leaning against. He's a handsome fucker. She doesn't look happy, he looks aggressive. She's rolling her eyes, and I see her try to walk away, when he takes his free hand and, gently, pushes her back to the wall. She submits, and I'm feeling oddly protective, looking around for Bob who is overwhelmed at the helm, alone. Is she OK? I don't even know her. Should I attempt to rescue her?

Bob's struggling and I want to get back to the bar to help, my arms are full again. So I dump the bottles on the counter, lift the hatch and get back to serving. The till is slammed with cash, way more than I've got hidden about my person. It's a weeknight, do these people not have jobs? Or college, something? Bob glances at me gratefully, shouts to me, 'Where in fuck's name is Kitten?' Using my eyes, I direct him to where she's being held captive. She looks a little more relaxed now, but Bob does not look impressed. We continue, the two of us, until the serving is under control, and I slip back through the hatch, looking for bottles and glasses again. I'm still watching Kitten. Her arms are folded, her body language screams distress. I see her attempt to get away, and this guy literally pushes both his arms against the wall, trapping her. She tries to sidestep, but I watch him grab her wrist, and I'm close enough to hear her as the music lulls, 'Get the fuck away Tyler, leave me alone!'

I've never been comfortable at male displays of power; using their strength and size to intimidate or dominate a female. It reminds me of my father, and it makes me feel angry, powerless. I'm not a violent person. But at that moment I can't help myself, I feel the need to intervene, so I walk up, eyes on Kitten,

'You OK?' I ask. They both turn to look at me, he's still holding her wrist, actually, both of them now.

'Yeah, I'm fine.' she says, but he, he looks at me with such indignation, and condescending too, says,

'Who the fuck are you?' I ignore him, cut off eye contact because I'm shitting myself, and say to Kitten,

'Bob needs you behind the bar.' The guy turns his attentions to me, releasing Kitten from his grasp, he's right up in my space, I can't avoid him, and I stumble backward, uncomfortable and scared, he's puffing his chest out, bumping himself into me.

'I said. Who the FUCK are *you*?' He spits it out in my face, I'm terrified now, and before I can get away he draws back his arm, and momentarily, I notice his fist fly towards my face in slow motion. Too late for me to do anything, and oh my God, I feel my face crumple, my whole body jerks back and I fall to the floor. No pain when it happens, just shock and embarrassment. The pain does come though, lying there on that floor, my eye! I feel warmth dripping from my face, my hands which I've belatedly tried to protect myself with, wet with red, with my blood. Fuck! My eye! My face! Lying on the wet floor I prepare myself, expecting to get kicked in the head; he's standing above me, I can see his mouth moving, no doubt insulting me. My ears are ringing, I've no idea what he's saying, but vaguely lip read obscenity.

I glance towards the bar, my arms up around my head still, and I see Bob vault the bar, like an Olympic athlete, focused and determined, he flies towards us, and before I can move or do anything, I see him above me, forehead colliding with the offender's nose; his blood literally rains down on me. I hope he doesn't have hepatitis C. Or anything else I could contract from blood spatter to my mouth, which is agape at this point. I scramble backwards, into a crouch, I'm on my feet. All Hell has broken loose! The guy is stunned, pissed off, but Bob's not taking any shit and is dragging him in a chokehold towards the door.

Others are getting in on the action; one of the guy's friends cracks a bottle over Bob's shoulder, and Bob, he's got grit, still gripping the offender, erupts, his head swings back, his eyes are crazy wide. Kitten's shouting, even the band stops playing, but the level of noise doesn't reduce, everyone's congregating. Someone grabs the bottle guy in a headlock, punching him in the back of the head for good measure. Bob's continuing to the entrance with the help of a couple of others. Then, I see someone burst through the front door; he sees Bob, surveys the situation, and barging past him plants himself in the middle of the fight. His head is shaved, he's small, wiry and toned, of course, tattooed. A rasping wail omits from him, like a war cry, and I swear he's smiling, bouncing around looking for something or someone to smash up. I watch him bound towards the pool table, grabbing a cue from the wall rack, he's straight back in the crowd, swinging that stick around like some crazy Kendo master. Holy shit! I'm upright now, backing away. I see Kitten, flinching, also working her way backwards from the carnage. There's blood, broken glass, I have no idea who's trying to help or who's not. I think Bob needs security working this place.

Within a minute, it's calming down. There's a lot of people outside, I've pulled myself into a chair, I'm nursing my wounds. My eyebrow is split, I can feel it, my eye, swollen half shut, full of blood. And fuck, my cheekbone feels like it's cracked. My mouth's OK I think, three years of NHS dental brace work preserved, though blood is dripping down my face into it, confusing me. The people still inside are wired, excited, though thankfully the violence seems to have moved onto the street. Kitten's beside me now, all like 'Oh My God, are you OK? Jesus, your face!' Not exactly reassuring.

'I think I'm alright.' I muster.

That crazy, wailing, stick-wielding bastard comes back in through the door, sans T shirt; I didn't even see him go out. He's laughing maniacally, a trickle of blood dripping from his nose. Bob follows and slams the door behind him, bolting it shut top, middle and bottom. He turns to the now hushed crowd inside. 'Everyone fucking calm the fuck down!' To be fair, his presence at this moment has done exactly that. 'Finish your drinks and you can fuck off home for the night!' and then, to the nut job with the pool cue, 'Where the fuck have you been, you wanker?'

'That's Mad Pete,' says Kitten, gesturing towards who Bob's confronting, 'His brother.'

She leaves me, walks back to the bar. Bob looks furious, possibly the most scary I've ever seen anyone look in real life, he walks up to where I'm sitting, making me wince because maybe he's going to punch me too.

'What the FUCK was that boy?' He booms, specks of spit flying at me. More hep, I think.

'I, I'm sorry?' I offer. I'm so lame. Kitten's back, with a bar towel full of ice, and she holds it to my eye, 'Fuck, ow!' It really hurts. The F word is contagious.

She's says, 'Hold it, stop it swelling,' to me and then, 'Go easy Bob, he didn't do anything!' I take the wrapped ice and gently rest it against my eye and it hurts so much. I've never been hit before.

'Well kiddo, you're not looking too pretty now are you? For fuck's sake, know what battles to fight, boy! That was fucking stupid.' Mad Pete appears behind him, wiping his bloodied nose on his  bare arm, laughing at me, still looking totally psycho. Bob turns to him, and says 'Pete, meet your replacement!' Pete stops laughing, looks quizzically back at Bob. Bob shakes his head, and looking at me says, 'Get cleaned up. What a fucking mess. And it's only Wednesday.'

Later, once the crowd outside have dispersed, the band have packed up, and the last of the revellers inside have the sense to get out quietly on their best behaviour, I still sit here in this chair. Kitten has wiped the blood from my face, and the makeshift ice pack melts down my T-shirt beneath my jacket damp with a combination of blood and water. Bob's laughing now, sweeping up the broken glass from the floor, 'Well Joe, that was some first night for you, eh? Fucking student night, mind. Those kids are our fucking future!' Still full of fucks, he's guffawing at the ridiculousness of it all, leaning on the brush. Kitten has spent the last twenty minutes explaining how I'd only come to her defense, that Tyler was being a twat.

'Sorry Bob, seriously, it was all Tyler, Joe just got caught up in it.'

'I saw what happened Kitty, I was fucking watching,' says Bob, he's definitely not angry anymore. 'You want to go home yet, Joe?' he starts laughing again. Then, 'Ah Pete, you fucking legend, talk about timing,' he turns his attention to his brother, 'You love a scrap mind, don't you, eh?'

Mad Pete's a complete nutcase, no doubt. Bouncing about on a bar stool, still bare-chested, he looks so pleased with himself. Kitten says I need to rest but she's worried I might have a concussion. I'm exhausted. Bob tells her I'll be fine, my pupils look fine, stop treating me like a pussy. Kitten looks offended but doesn't say anything. Instead she looks at me and says,

'Listen, I can take care of myself OK? Don't do anything like that again. I'm a big girl, seriously,' and then, smiling with what looks to me like fondness, 'Idiot.' I can't help but smile, despite my pain, I feel suddenly heroic. Not that I did anything. I mean, Kitten could undoubtedly kick my arse, she doesn't need me. Bob's behind the bar, hands me a shot glass.

'Have this boy, a painkiller.' It's vodka, I'm aware, because I just saw him pour it. I've never tried vodka. But in that moment of pride and bravado, I throw my head back and pour the liquid into my mouth, swallowing the whole lot in one gulp. Bob cheers with approval. It tastes like fire.

What a start for Joe's adventure in The City. Poor little mite! A day and night of firsts. First time in The City, in the few hours he got his first job, his first black eye, his first alcoholic drink, and his first friends. Overwhelming to say the least.

Bob walks me upstairs, 'You got a sleeping bag kid?' I don't, I shake my head. It never occurred to me that I would need one, I didn't have one at home anyway. Muttering, he goes across the corridor and returns, throws me a sleeping bag and leaves, pulling shut my door. I take my boots off, careful not to let the cash inside slip out, climb inside still clothed and I sleep like the dead.

# Finding Wi-Fi

I wake the next day, momentarily confused until everything comes flooding back. Yesterday, what a day! The right side of my face throbbing, my eye sore and bruised. And my back, my shoulders are in agony; guess I hit that floor hard. I check my watch, 10.20am. Dying to pee, I unzip the sleeping bag and venture quietly out into the corridor, to the toilet next door. Fuck, it's filthy in here. I take a piss, and assess my face in the dirty mirror above the sink. My eyebrow has split, dried blood has caked in the hairs. My eye's swollen half shut, the whole ocular socket discoloured, I have a proper shiner. It hurts and I have the worst headache ever. I run the tap, rinse my face and hands with the cold water, wetting my hair, scraping it back from my face. Blood rinsed away, I look OK. I have faint stubble growing in, I like how it's making me look older. I could do with a shower, but remember Bob said I wasn't allowed to wash here. What's that about? Why not? I feel filthy and only left home less than twenty four hours ago. Back in my room, I can at least get changed. I take my jacket off, then my T-shirt, which is crusty with blood around the neck. It's black thankfully. I start thinking about how I'm going to wash my clothes, feed myself, the stuff I took for granted back home. I'm starving but have only crisps and chocolate in my bag; I'd do anything for a bacon sandwich.

I feel better in clean clothes. I transfer all my money into my new outfit and put my boots back on. I plug my phone in, there must be some free WiFi around. Not here, the network is secured. I faintly hear noise from downstairs, the sound of glass on glass, doors opening and closing. I'm nervous about going down there, like an unwanted house guest. I sit quietly, allowing my phone to charge and I demolish a bag of crisps while I wait. I reach for my jacket and fish out Grandpa's letter from the pocket. I read it again. I still don't know what he wants me to do, but surely this is not what he'd imagined for me? I fold the letter, stuff it in the front compartment of my bag. I roll a few cigarettes, and consider smoking one but I can't be bothered to go to the fire escape. So instead I take out my sketchbook. I think of Kitten, of last night, everything. But I can't draw, my head aches, my back too. I attempt it, working on the sketch from the day before, the lady from the train. My heart's not in it, I should be seeking experiences or whatever, so I leave my phone charging, pack everything else into my bag, pull on my jacket and venture downstairs. The bar's empty, but I can hear Bob's voice through the door that leads into the back of the building. I don't want to just walk in, so I knock the door, not knowing if I'm welcome, despite the fact I spent half of last night lugging boxes of bottles through there to the bin out back. The door behind the bar leads to a kitchen. To the right side of the kitchen is an office of sorts, with a desk and a safe. To the left of the kitchen is the store room. At the back of the kitchen is the rear exit, which leads to the alleyway behind this row of buildings. Silence. I tentatively knock again. Bob pulls open the door,

'It's you! Fucking hell, boy, you're giving me the creeps, what you knocking for?'

'Er, I didn't know if I should walk in or not.' He's looking at me perplexed,

'Well come in if you want to. Nice black eye you got there.' He beams at me then, 'What do you want?'

'Nothing, I'm thinking of going out, getting something to eat. Is it OK to leave my bag upstairs?'

'Jesus boy, yeah, you're paying for the room aren't you?' shaking his head, 'You working here again tonight?'

'Uh, yeah, if you want me to.'

'Well yes, I need staff! Be in the bar by six.'

'OK. Um, will I be able to get back in later?' Bob begins to look mildly irritated,

'We open at four. You want a key? That what you're saying?' Pete appears from the storeroom, sack trolley stacked up with pallets of beer, he looks at me vacantly.

'Alright, kid?' He says. Bob takes himself to the office and comes back with a key, hands it to me.

'Do us a favour, buy your own fucking sleeping bag will you?'

'Yeah, I will, thanks for that. Um, is there WiFi anywhere around here?' I know I'm pissing him off.

He says, 'Well *we* have WiFi. But it's not free. This ain't a hotel Joe,' and then, sauntering back into the office, 'Try Starbucks.'

I go upstairs and get my phone, back downstairs and out the front door. I've no idea where I'm going, but within a couple of minutes I find Starbucks. I go in and order a coffee.

'What size?'

'Uh, large?

'Grande or Venti?'

'Grande.' I've no idea what either means. I sit down and connect to the internet. After half hour of pissing about on twitter and looking at memes I Google 'camping supplies' and click on maps. The nearest store is a mile away. I vaguely make a note of the route and leave.

Outside I check I'm headed the right way and I think I can do this. I recognise street names from my search and I find it, an outdoors shop; windbreaker-wearing mannequins and tents in the window. I'm seriously pleased with myself, all independent and shit! I go in, buy a thirty quid sleeping bag, which I think is a bit steep, but I have money so whatever. I realise I don't know the way back to Bob's bar, but I retrace my path successfully, buying a bacon and egg roll on the way, and I'm back outside within twenty minutes. I've got this! I let myself in.

Bob's there, behind the bar. He sees my shopping. 'Good lad, a sleeping bag.' Feeling unusually confident now I take a seat at the bar and say,

'Thank you for everything. The room and the work. I don't know why I'm even here. Sorry about last night.'

'Ah kid, you're alright. That Tyler's a fucking wanker. We've had worse nights. Far, far worse. Fucking student night, Jesus Christ.' he titters to himself, 'And none of us know why we're here boy. Such is life, we soldier on.' He's laughing. He's seems to flit between merriment and psycho-stern, but I like him. I don't know why but I decide to tell him about Grandpa, his letter. He listens in a way I imagine barmen are accustomed to.

'Well Christ boy, that's a lot to take on board and a shitty deal you got. How old are you?' I tell him I'm eighteen tomorrow, that I'm sorry, I should've told him I wasn't old enough to work here.

'Well you know what, boy? I'm not surprised, thought you were younger to be honest. But I think you're brave, you got guts, well done, lad. Reckon your Grandpa would be impressed.' He carries on busying himself behind the bar. I ask him about Kitten, how old she is. 'Older than you. Soft on her are you? She's a pretty girl, but she's not for you, Joe. Believe me.' I feel indignant. I know she's out of my league, but he didn't have to confirm it. 'You're young, I'm not sure you should be here, kid. But listen, you got a place to stay, yeah? I'll pay you your time and… you really got nowhere? No one?'

'Nope,' I say, 'If I go back they're going to kick me out, put me in a hostel, I might get a flat eventually. There's nothing there for me.'

'Well what you think you're gonna find here?' he asks. He grabs two beers from the fridge, cracks the lids, passes me one. It's only midday and I've never had a beer. I think he feels sorry for me. I don't know, I'm just doing what Grandpa suggested. I came to The City. Now what?

'I don't know,' I say, 'I'm supposed to be seeking experiences. Doing the things I love.'

'Well last night was an experience for you, eh? What do you love doing Joe?' I shrug, sip the beer, not keen to be honest. I like drawing but I don't say that. 'Ah I don't know lad. People say weird shit when they're dying, maybe you shouldn't take it to heart. But, you're here now. Worse places you could be I reckon. You might want to find a better place to stay mind you.' He swigs his beer. I mimic him. I ask him then,

'Why can't I wash here?'

'Well, you only got a toilet and sink Joe, you've seen it!' Yeah, he has a point. He sighs, 'You want a shower?' I really do.

'Well it's just there's blood in my hair, and my clothes got really dirty, It's OK, but I don't know where I can go to get cleaned up…'

'Hmm, well as a one off, you can use our bathroom. Fucking clean up after yourself though yeah? I run a tight ship here. Don't piss or wank in my shower! It's a one time offer, mind, you best start looking for somewhere with better facilities. This ain't that kind of place.' He's grimacing. I don't think the offer has come easy to him.

'Thanks, Bob, I mean it.' I really do. I manage to look him in the eye when I say it, just for a second.

Bob's bathroom is pretty nice, cleaner than I expected. I feel a million times better after a shower. While standing in the water I rinse my T shirt, slightly concerned about the pinkish liquid that dribbles from it as I wring it out. I rinse my boxers too, but not my jeans. I don't even think about wanking. To be honest I'm not used to doing it without the internet, but I do have a pee, he'll never know. The running water does that to me, can't help it. I brought my shower gel and make sure to rinse everything afterwards. I tidy the bathroom after myself.

There's no radiator in my room, so I lay my T shirt hanging off the windowsill, and hang my boxers off one window handle, towel from the other. Despite my initial refreshment from the hot water, I'm freezing now, and quickly dress into clean clothes, skin still damp. I brush my hair. Plug my phone in again. It's coming up to four o'clock, I still have a couple of hours, so I eat some crisps and biscuits from my bag, and I lie and think. I wonder if anyone's noticed that I've left home yet. I reckon Mrs. Parks will have been around with food, will have wondered why I haven't answered. Can't lie, I wouldn't turn down her pork chop dinner right now.

Five to six I head downstairs. Bob and Pete are behind the bar. Pete makes me nervous, I can only think of him last night, waving that pool cue around, that howling laugh, primed for war. He's staring at me, his eyes are fucking crazy, like he's looking right through my head at something behind me. There's no warmth about him like with Bob, just a cold, spaced out glare.

'Who's that?' he says.

'Uh, I'm Joe, I'm staying upstairs?' What the fuck, he saw me this morning. And last night. Bob chimes in, with mild exasperation,

'Pete, stop messing with him, you're fucking frightening sometimes,' and then to me, 'You alright Joe?' Pete seems to snap out of whatever, looks at me more focused.

'Yeah, alright Joe?' A faint smile. I just try to look like I belong here.


That might've been me Pete was talking about. Pete's weird, his brain is wired all wrong. He's not done himself any favours over the years, taken too many drugs and too many knocks to the head, too often restricted oxygen to the brain (he has a penchant for auto-erotic asphyxiation, but we won't go into that now). Childhood trauma. Regardless, he's always been a bit off, it's disconcerting encountering his sort. In defense of his violent tendencies, he's not a particularly bad person, but surprisingly loyal and trustworthy, despite outward appearances.


Bob says, 'Right Joe, it'll be quieter tonight, no bands, so it's an easy one, OK? If it's quiet you can bugger off by ten.' Kitten comes over.

'How's your eye, Joe? Nice little scar you'll get there,' she touches my eyebrow smiling, 'you'll look badass.'

'It's fine.' I say, smitten. She looks hot, all winged eyeliner and red lips, wearing a tight Twenty One Pilots T-shirt with those cut-off denim shorts, and I wish I knew anything about Twenty One Pilots so we could share some common ground. Two geeky guys? I couldn't name one of their songs. I'd Google them if I had data. I remember Casey saying I was so nineties and she's right; I've no musical or cultural knowledge of anything current. I really should know more.

The night is uneventful compared to yesterday. Still busy, but not rough, just the jukebox, pool games. The Haiku Man turns up, sits at the bar, Bob pours him a vodka. I haven't seen him pay for a drink here yet. I'm getting the hang of the till tonight. At some point, this guy comes in, lugging a full carrier bag, looking a little out of place, different to the other customers in here. But he's not a customer; he lifts the hatch of the bar, and with an obligatory nod at Bob, walks upstairs.

'Who's that?' I ask him.

'Forgot his name, he's staying upstairs, next door to you.' I shrug,

'Hadn't realised there was anyone else staying here. How come he gets a proper lock on his door?' I'm being bold, but Bob makes me feel that way and he doesn't seem to mind.

'Cos he got here first boy! First come, first served, he got the presidential suite!' He starts cackling. 'He's a bit fucking weird if you ask me. Quiet though, no trouble. Unlike you.' I grin at him. 'He's been here over a week, he's paid up. Goes out during the day and locks himself upstairs the rest of the time, doesn't drink down here. Don't know his story, but he turned up in fatigues and a military rucksack like yours. Reckon he just got out the army. I didn't ask questions.' I worry again about my bag upstairs, but at least I have my money on me. I found an empty coin bag on the table out the kitchen earlier, slipped it in my pocket. Transferred all my cash into it and it's in my boot. The Haiku Man shakes his head, he's been listening, says,

'Something about him,

He reminds me of our Pete,

That thousand yard stare.'

He has a point, I'd noticed that. Those blank eyes.


The Haiku Man's right, there is something about the young renter, something troubling. And Bob's right too, he is military and he is weird. The guy just came back after his second tour of Afghanistan…no, it's not peaceful there yet. Haunted by what he's seen, what he's done. Horrifying scenes beyond your comprehension. A normal kid once, deconstructed and rebuilt as a government killing machine; his brain isn't working normally anymore. What started out as guilt and remorse has twisted into paranoia and indifference. PTSD and AWOL. Feels disconnected from the rest of humanity. Numb, he'd say himself, with a tinge of anger. He can't sleep anymore. Has issues with his sexuality. Thinks the economy is collapsing, martial law is imminent, is certain there's a class war about to start as well as a race war (he's not far off, there's potential for both those happenings). Maybe this is why Joe's here. Don't want to give too much away.


Around nine thirty Bob says I'm done for the night. I ask, 'Is it OK to hang out down here?' Because what else do I have to do? He says, yeah, but to get out from behind the bar, he's not paying me anymore. So I sit on a stool, a few seats down from The Haiku Man. Bob tops up his glass again.

Mad Pete's playing pool. I can hear his mood elevating, he's erratic and angry and I pretend I don't notice, look the other way. I guess he just lost the game. Pete's not big, shorter than Bob, maybe 5'9, same height as me. And he's not wide either, the opposite, all lean and sinewy. Despite this, he's giving some guy twice his size shit, demanding a rematch. Bob bellows over at Pete's rival, 'You don't wanna piss off Mad Pete mate, he doesn't like losing.' Bob's jovial, and I can tell that he's experienced in diffusing the fires of Pete's unpredictability. It's also a warning, to the giant who won. Mad Pete decides to walk away,

'Ah fuck it, cheating bastard!' He sits between me and The Haiku Man, still antsy, twitching and rubbing his face. The Haiku Man says,

'Calm the hell down Pete,

What the fuck is your problem?

Take some valium.'

Mad Pete scares the shit out of me. Bob gives him a beer and I go to bed.

# 𝔜ou 𝔄re 𝔅eing 𝔓rogrammed

I wake early, immediately aware I'm eighteen today. Officially an adult. It's Friday. Bob said last night that Friday's are the busiest night in the bar, though I have a hard time imagining it could be any worse than the day I got here.

I miss Grandpa. He always made a big effort on my birthday; we'd have cake and he'd wrap my presents. Call it childish, whatever. I'm just suddenly aware of my pitiful existence, how I've reached this milestone birthday alone. It's not normal. And this feeling, missing him, I suppose it's grief? It's physical, like an actual pain deep in my chest, my heart, I don't know, but it's an ache so crushing that it takes my breath away. I just lie awhile until it subsides.

I stretch, my back still hurts. I unzip my sleeping bag, go for a pee. I chuck some cold water on my face, my eye looks a bit better, and I go back and dress. It's only 8.20am, but I feel like I should get out, explore The City, and I have that excited birthday feeling, which is ridiculous because I have nothing to feel excited for. I eat the sandwiches I bought yesterday; they're stale but my stomach is grateful nonetheless. Then, checking my money's in my pocket, I creep downstairs, aware that Bob and Pete are not up yet. The front door is triple bolted on the inside so I quietly slide the locks open and let myself out. Where should I go? Nothing's open, I just walk the streets, trying to find my way back to the grand metropolitan landscape that greeted me on the day I arrived.

Twenty minutes of wandering, I find it. It's breathtaking; there are people everywhere, rushing with purpose to work or wherever they're headed. Shops are beginning to open. I see that placard guy I saw when I arrived; today his sign reads, YOU ARE BEING PROGRAMMED. Whatever, I avoid eye contact. I don't know why I'm here but I like it. It's so big and different and I know I've led a limited life to feel so wonderstruck by some crowds and tall buildings, but still, I'm impressed. There's free WiFi everywhere. I buy a coffee at a Starbucks and sit in the window and check twitter, see I have a DM from Casey.

*Where r u? My mum's worried, she called police! They broke into ur house!*

Should I respond? I decide no, I don't owe her or anyone an explanation, compelled as I am about the cops breaking my door down, I've done nothing wrong. I'm an adult now and can do as I please.

I feel invisible, in a good way, no one's looking at me like I'm weird or anything and I put down my phone for a moment, to people-watch. It's better than television, there's just so much energy and diversity and beauty. I know it sounds cheesy but I feel renewed, a part of something bigger; I feel free. I watch this woman, she looks perfect, not a crease on her skirt or blouse, everything about her looks expensive. Her makeup is flawless, her nails manicured and glossy, her hair a mane of tumbling golden curls, some killer heels that she walks in with no perceived difficulty. Then, across the street, a man catches my attention, he's a male equivalent of the lady; tailored suit and inflated confidence, his chin held high with an air of arrogance, bragging I imagine loudly, into his mobile, weaving through traffic with zero regard for safety, like he gets precedence over vehicles. I see young lovers holding hands, he's kissing her neck and whispering into her ear, her mouth is beaming with delight and, sincerely, it's the prettiest smile. There's an old man, presumably homeless, he has at least three pairs of trousers on, filthy and bedraggled with a black bag hanging at his side, he's shuffling, parting the crowd like he's Moses. I have a realisation suddenly that everyone who passes by the window, young and old, rich and poor, they all have their own varied and intricate lives, incredible and terrible stories, perfect loves and devastating losses. There's a word for it I remember, sonder. I learned it in English class. The sudden awareness that every passerby is living a complex and vivid life, filled with their own complicated thoughts and experiences, hopes and dreams and tragedies, all intertwined with others whose lives in turn are just as intricate and elaborate. I perceive the city as a galaxy, these people the stars. I am awed. I am insignificant, and I think it's the most beautiful feeling I ever had.

Finishing my coffee I decide I'll just wander around, follow my feet. I feel like everything's OK, I don't need a plan and I like it here a million times more than my hometown. I miss only Grandpa, and he's no longer there; I hope he'd be pleased for me. I sort of have a job and a place to stay. There's not really any good shops here. I think I'll go home. My new home.

Later, at the bar, I'm keen to work because I have nothing else to do. Kitten comes from out back, she smirks and greets me with a 'Happy birthday, Joe!' I can't contain my delight at her acknowledging my birthday, and shyly smile a thank you; Bob must've told her. The place fills up fast, there's a band setting up already and it's only six o'clock, and even with three of us behind the bar we can barely keep up. It calms down after the initial rush and before long the first band starts to play. The Gum Butts. Again, a cool name, but they're truly fucking terrible, not that anyone seems to mind. I don't care, I'm in a good mood, I feel grown up.

The Haiku Man turns up, gets in the space of the girl who is sitting on his usual stool until she and her friends are repulsed enough to move. He claims his seat and Bob arrives with a vodka. I go out, collect the bottles and glasses, come back and load the washer. A minor scuffle breaks out, resolving itself before anything happens, and I'm standing next to Bob and I'm feeling ballsy, so I shout to him,

'You think security might be a good idea here?' Bob bursts out laughing,

'Haha, fucking hell, Joe, we got Pete!' He has a point. Pete's out in the kitchen, but wanders in from time to time, serves a couple of people and disappears again. Once the first band have finished, I hitch up the box of bottles under the bar, and shove myself through the door to take them to the bins out back. Pete's sitting at the table in the kitchen, looks right through my head again. Mouth slightly upturned he says,

'Alright, Joe? Busy out there?'

'Yeah,' I say dropping the box of bottles on the table, I readjust myself.

'Well, give us a shout if you need me. Not fussed on the noise these days y'know?' He's sitting there playing with a lighter, which everyone knows is stereotypically a thing that crazy people do. He's freaking me out again. I slide the box off the table and say,

'Yeah, it's loud.' He just laughs, still amusing himself with the lighter, and I lug the box, barging through the back door outside. I don't rush back in, instead savour the cool, fresh air. Although I haven't drunk anything, it's sobering, and I quickly roll a cigarette and take a moment to think about the last few days. I'm coping. I've got this.

Back inside and later on, after the last customers leave, me, Bob, Kitten, Pete and The Haiku Man are hanging around the bar.

'Well that was an alright night,' says Bob, 'Good job,' he pours us all shots of vodka, and says 'To you Joe, Happy Birthday, at least you're fucking old enough to be in here now.' It's not my birthday anymore, we're into the early hours, but I'm indulged anyway. Everyone raises their glasses and we drink. I don't like the way it tastes but I guess that's not the point. Pete approaches the jukebox.

'Let's play some fucking tunes! What'll it be, eh? Any requests?'

'Joe likes Nirvana,' says Kitten, 'It's his birthday, let him choose.' Nope, too much responsibility. I never told her I liked Nirvana, but I have their T-shirt on.

'Really Pete, you choose,' I say. 'I don't mind.' I smile at him.

'OK, on it,' he says, 'Happy fucking birthday, Joe!' and with that, *Smells Like Teen Spirit* kicks in. It's not my favourite, but it's a classic and I'm grateful for the acknowledgment. Pete pogos around a bit and we laugh at him. Kitten shouts to turn it down. I ask Kitten what kind of music she likes, apart from Twenty One Pilots. Her face lights up,

'Oh I love them! But I like lots of stuff…My Chemical Romance is my favourite. Like, ever!'

Bob sniggers. 'Gay.' he mutters. Kitten shoots him a disapproving look,

'You saying that as an insult or literally? Because either way you're a dick.' Then, rolling her eyes back to me, 'Yungblud. I'd marry him, I literally love him.' Yungblud? Eh? She's on her phone, 'He's my screensaver. He's beautiful right?' She shoves the screen in my face.

'Huh.' This is Yungblud? That can't be his real name. He's attractive I suppose but I don't say that. I'd rather go back to My Chemical Romance, I vaguely know them. The singer writes comics and I feel smug for knowing this. I doubt he's Stan Lee, Garth Ennis, Alan Moore, or even Frank Miller, but I'm still delighted to find some common ground with Kitten.

The Haiku Man interrupts, looking over my shoulder and shaking his head,
'This Yungblud fella
looks like a hot lesbian.
It is confusing.
'I ain't no faggot,
But those boys blurring the lines
With eyeliner and shit,
'Blowjob lips and hair
Sweeping over pretty eyes…
Any hole's a goal.'

He grins at that last statement. Bob creases laughing, and he's contagious, I laugh too. Now Pete says, 'Gay!' Bob snorts and high fives him. Kitten looks unimpressed.

'Gay is not an insult!' she says. I just smile, but shoot Kitten a sympathetic look. Yeah, so what? Doesn't denigrate talent. Not that I know if he's talented or not, just saying. Like, who gives a fuck about being gay or not? Bob and Pete are funny, I get it. Not burning bridges, I just don't think sexuality matters. I presume no one my generation does. She's offended, but only momentarily, because again she's smiling, 'Let's do another shot!'

# Our Elite Little Circle Of Trust

Bob, like a toastmaster, dings his glass and says, 'This occasion calls for a Queen's Head initiation!' I'm officially drunk. Everyone's drunk. I feel great, this might be my best birthday ever. Kitten's squealing with excitement and Mad Pete's disappeared into the kitchen with an air of purpose. The Haiku Man sits beside me at the bar, laughing. I've no idea what's going on.

'Don't freak out now, Joe,' Kitten says, 'You're joining our club right?'

'Am I? I mean yeah, but what do you mean?' I'm laughing, contagious as it is, but I feel uneasy. Kitten's literally hopping up and down. Mad Pete returns with a small silver box; a mini metal case which he places on the bar beside me. Bob's pouring another round of shots.

'Right now, quiet.' he says, and then at me, 'Anyone lucky enough to enter our elite little circle of trust and friendship must first, as initiation, get the tattoo.'

Tattoo? Fuck off. Mad Pete's opened the little case now and shit, there's a tattoo gun in there, packets of needles, little bottles of ink. Some tracing paper?

'This tattoo is for the select few, and upon receipt of it, your allegiance to this place and these people is sworn. Understand?' I'm not laughing now, no one is, but Kitten and Pete are still grinning. Bob looks scary serious.

'If you agree to it, our allegiance to you is also pledged. I'm serious.' There you go, Bob just confirmed the seriousness of it. They're all watching me expectantly.

'Uh, I don't know, I don't think so.' No fucking way. They all watch me still, willing me with the power of their stares to change my mind. 'Like what? What tattoo? Why?' Each of them make a fist, revealing their middle finger lightning bolts. Just a small black outline, I'd seen Kitten's, but hadn't noticed the others; Bob and Pete are pretty heavily tattooed anyway; Bob has something inked on every finger, every knuckle. I'd noticed the PUNK on his left hand the first time I met him. Even the Haiku Man has it, but his hands are filthy so I'd only ever noticed the dirt before. Kitten looks hopeful.

**Go on Joe, fuck it, do it. Nothing is permanent, certainly not skin.**

'I don't know. Does it have to be on my finger?' I don't want to render myself unemployable. I remember Grandpa saying no one should ever get a tattoo where a judge can see it. I feel so uncool.

94

Why do I have to question everything? Could I not just lose myself in the moment? All of them in unison,

'Yes!'

'Does anyone else have one? Other than you guys?'

'A few friends.'

'What's it for though, why a lightning bolt?' I ask, trying to put it off.

'Cos it's fucking cool, that's why!' says Bob. 'Jesus boy, yes or no?' I thought there might be some symbolism. No, no, no, I think. Mad Pete's in the box. He's got an extension cord, he's plugging in the gun. Why is he plugging it in? I'm not agreeing to this. The whole thing seems dangerously unhygienic. I wonder when Pete last washed his hands.

Shit. It's definitely a terrible idea and will almost certainly end with infection and possible amputation. But, being drunk and a little in love with my new friends, I warm to the idea. It's good to feel included. I'd never been in a club or a team or anything before and I can't deny it's a great feeling.

'Fuck it, let's do these shots and get this over with!' The four of them cheer, and Bob slides me the shot, raises his own and says,

'Happy Birthday Joe.'

The Haiku Man says,

'You'll be one of us

And earning our loyalty

Requires this emblem.

'A rite of passage!

You're too pretty anyway,

This'll do you good.'

My right leg starts shaking uncontrollably, I try to suppress it. I have doubts about Mad Pete's capability, but Kitten draws it onto my skin.

'Flatten your hand, keep your fingers straight.' she says. Pete simply has to ink over it. How bad can it be? I'm watching Pete unwrap a needle, fixing it to the end of the gun.

'Shouldn't you wash your hands first?' I say to Pete, 'Shouldn't I wash mine?' They're laughing at me again.

Pete says, 'Fucking grow a pair, Joe, will you?' Bob's still holding the vodka and pours some over my hand,

'There you go boy, nice and sterile.'

'Right, hold still,' says Pete. He flicks the switch and the gun starts buzzing. I feel sick. He grasps me tightly by my wrist, 'I mean it, hold still.' I close my eyes tight, brace myself, they're crowding around to watch. The needle hits the skin, it feels like bee stings and cigarette burns. I'm holding still, I don't want him to fuck it up. I open my eyes, the pain is bearable and Pete's doing OK, he's focused, steady. Halfway through, he pauses, wipes away the blood that's beading.

I say, mainly to distract myself, 'Can I get another vodka after this?' Bob's on it, topping up everyone's glass, they all look at me so warm. Before I know it, it's done. Pete wipes it again,

'Pour a bit more on it Bob?' he says, and Bob tips the vodka over it again. It hurts like fuck but it's finished. I feel really fucking cool. Bob raises his glass again.

'Cheers!' he says, and we all throw back our liquor. Kitten's got her phone out,

'Let me take a photo of it Joe, I'll tag you on Facebook and Insta.'

'I don't have Facebook,' I say, letting her take a photo anyway, 'Or Instagram.' The Haiku Man says,

'You don't have Facebook?
But you're eighteen for fuck's sake,
I was on Myspace…'

Kitten laughs, heartily, 'Myspace, wow Haiku Man, you're really down with the kids huh?' Everyone's laughs, me too. I've never heard of Myspace.

'I have Twitter?' I suggest to Kitten. I wish I did have Facebook. Huffily the Haiku Man continues,

'At the library

The internet was free!

The world my oyster!'

He shakes his head,

'All those little girls

 Just whoring for attention

And more followers.

'Gave up on it then,

Librarian kicked me out

For the drink and porn.'

It starts to get blurry after that. Kitten's all over me, arms draped around my neck, gazing into my eyes, which despite my drunken confidence makes me blush and hide behind my hair because I don't know what to do. She says,

'Come back to mine tonight Joe, don't stay in this shithole.

'OK.' I say, hazily smiling. I'd do anything she asked. I remember pulling on my jacket, us going outside, the cold air making my head spin, she's holding my hand. Giggling and wobbly, I let her guide me through the streets back to her flat. She's talking constantly, about nothing and everything. We reach the steps that lead up to her door and she's all,

'Shhh Joe, my roommate might be home.' She's being way louder than me. We go in and she says, 'We're alone! You want another drink?' She's already in the fridge, pulls out some wine, but I tell her, maybe I slur it,

'I can't drink anymore. You trying to kill me?' She laughs, abandons the bottle, walks towards me.

'Are you a virgin, Joe?' she asks. Fuck, I don't know what to say. I let my hair fall over my face again.

'Uh, I've done stuff, you know, just not the actual sex bit.' I'm a fucking embarrassment to mankind. She's laughing, but she's got her hands up inside my T shirt, stroking my sides, my back. I pull my stomach in, puff out my chest, feign masculinity. She lets go of me and without taking her eyes from mine, pulls off her T-shirt. Wow. Am I allowed to touch her tits? Do I need to ask permission?

'Well, Joe, let's do the actual sex bit.'

I think I might die.

# Uterine Matters

Afterwards we lie side by side in her bed. I'm feeling self-conscious naked under the duvet, about my pale boy body and lack of biceps; I know she's out of my league. I'm already semi-hard again just looking at her, hair knotted and wild, her eyeliner all panda like, lipstick long faded. I just keep thinking how I'm not a virgin anymore, and I want to do it again. It was pretty awesome, can't lie. Thinking about it, I definitely could've done it with Casey before, but I didn't know what to do, and didn't have any alcohol to make me brave enough. Had I known about liquor's proficiency for making me feel like I don't give a shit about anything, I would've started drinking years ago to be honest.

So anyway, she's giggling and stroking the hair from my eyes, literally kitten-like, all stretched out and purring, maybe even content; I'm feeling like a fucking king, when out of nowhere she's suddenly melancholy, and I recall reading something about how some people get depressed after sex. So, clutching the duvet around my puny pectorals, I tentatively ask if she's OK.

She sighs, 'Yeah. Fine.' She's clearly not. For fuck's sake. She sits up, pulling the duvet up with her, unfortunately, to cover her tits. 'You want to hear something about me, Joe? Something secret?'

I'm like, 'Yeah, sure I do'. She takes a minute, deciding if she wants to share with me or not, but then, with no caution or introduction;

'I had an abortion last year.'

'Wow, that's a big deal,' I say. Great. This is just wonderful post-coital conversation. Girls are fucking weird. 'What happened?' I face her, leaning on my elbow, holding my head up. I try to look grown up and concerned, sober.

'Well, it was Tyler's. You know how much of a dick he is, and I had nothing you know? Still don't. Just this shitty little flat and my shitty little bar job. I'd dropped out of uni and I was a disappointment to my family, so there was no fucking way I was gonna go back there. Tyler said I should get rid of it, and I agreed.'

I have no experience of this kind of feminist issue, but I know it's not my business to tell any woman what she can or can't do with her body. I'm not equipped for this exchange, I don't know the right thing to say is, so I tell her,

'I don't know what to say.' Really fucking mature.

She continues, 'Let me be clear, I have absolutely no regrets about it, whatever Tyler thought, I know it was the right thing for me to do, yeah? You get me? But, the whole experience sucked. D'you know anything about abortions, Joe?' Obviously no. This really is a shit conversation.

'Er no, I don't. But I'd say I'm pro-choice,' I offer. Jesus Christ I'm cringing internally, I sound fucking pathetic.

'Well, I went to my doctor, told him I was pregnant and needed an abortion ASAP. He asked me why, so I told him, no stable relationship, no stable job, no stable home etcetera. They don't just dish them out y'know, you have to have a reason? I had to do a pregnancy test there and then, peeing into a test tube in the waiting room toilet. Anyway, the doc confirmed it and I got an appointment a few days later at a clinic. I asked Tyler if he wanted to come with me but he didn't.'

'What a prick.' I say. *I* sound like a prick. I feel bad for her, even though she's trying to sound all empowered or whatever, and I'm glad she had options and stuff, but shit, it's not a situation I'd want to be in. Maintaining my sobriety, 'What happened when you went to the clinic?'

'Huh, there were a ton of girls there. Abortion is popular! Women and girls. Some had partners. People who looked like they had their shit together too. I avoided eye contact with everyone in that waiting room, because I don't know, it just felt so shameful. My name got called out and I followed this nurse into a room. The doctor, she asked me why I wanted an abortion again, because, apparently, two doctors have to agree it's in your best interest, like, whatever! *I* know what's in my best interest, right? I told her the same as before, I was practically begging, please help me, just do it already! Know what I mean?'

I don't know what she means, I can't begin to imagine the feeling of a life growing inside me, a responsibility so huge and life changing. I know I'd be fucking terrified. I tell her,

'I'd have been frightened.'

'Oh yeah, I was really scared. Scared of what the abortion involved but even more scared of a baby, you know? I mean, I don't even like kids, they're disgusting. Nappies and shit and snot. Anyway, this doctor and the nurse told me to lay on the bed, they did an ultrasound. I didn't see anything, the monitor was facing away, but I heard the nurse say "There it is." She told me I was about ten weeks gone. I wanted to see, but they didn't offer so I didn't ask.

'The doctor gave me a choice; because there's more than one way to abort a baby, you know? Medical or surgical. I chose medical, because it sounded like you just take some pills and have a really bad period, whereas surgery meant they put you to sleep and suck or scrape the baby out.'

My semi has well and truly faded at this point, my dick could literally not be more flaccid. My balls have almost retracted to a pre-pubescent state. My thighs clamped together, I am wincing at the thought of periods or vacuuming vaginas. Scraping? Jesus Christ. Fuck having sex ever again. Kitten continues regardless, 'And I was obviously nervous about anaesthetic, people die sometimes you know? I chose the pills. I went to the hospital three days later and, get this, I sat in a waiting room full of beaming, glowing pregnant women. Like, what the fuck? They put baby killers in the same room as expectant mothers? I could spot the others like me though, heads down, mostly alone, sheepish. I did the same, eyes to the ground. When my name got called I was taken to a room and yet another doctor asked me some questions, gave me a pill. I had to take it there. He told me it would stop the pregnancy hormones or something, but that I could still change my mind if I wanted to. I swallowed that pill before he'd even finished speaking. He told me to come back two days later, and they would admit me for the day to finish the procedure. I swear I couldn't wait.'

Can you imagine this shit? It's horrifying. I don't know if I'd be embarrassed or desperate or what. I'm speechless. Girls have to deal with some major shit. 'I had to take pyjamas and stuff. Pack an overnight bag just in case. So anyway, the morning came. Bob was a sweetheart and gave me the time off, I'd had to tell him what was happening. I cried and I guess he freaked out a little, he told me to take a couple of weeks to get myself back to normal.'

'Yeah, Bob's a good guy,' I acknowledge, nodding. I can imagine Bob's horror, presumably matching mine at this point. 'What happened when you went back?' I don't really want to know but I'm trying to come across as adult or interested or protective or sympathetic or some combination of all those things? I don't know. Right now I don't even want to have sex with her again but weirdly still feel the need to impress her.

'I was taken to a ward, there were three other girls there, all of them young. I thought I'd get a room of my own at least but no. One girl was sitting there on her bed doing sudoku or something, the TV was on in the corner, fucking Phil and Holly. It was surreal, Joe. Our little ward of shame. I pulled the curtain around my bed and changed into my pyjamas. I was not gonna open that curtain again, I wasn't there to socialise right? Anyway, ten minutes later a nurse came into my cubicle with a trolley full of stuff. She gave me five pills from a pot, holding them together, stacked up. She said I needed to insert them into my vag, to push them up as far as I could. I was like, holy shit! I thought I'd just have to swallow a tablet or something, you know? No one had mentioned shoving tablets into my vagina! Did you know that?'

Of course I fucking didn't. I didn't know tablets could work that way. I shake my head, no. 'She could see I was shocked, and she said she could assist if I should need her to. I was like, "Er, no thanks, I got this." Even then I was still absolutely certain I was doing the right thing, Joe, 100%. She passed me the pills, telling me, keep them stacked tight between my fingers. Next she squirts some hospital lube over them, tells me to lay on the bed and get on with it. She's standing there waiting for me to do it; it was fucking horrible!'

Fuck yeah it's horrible. Also, hospitals have their own lube? I am so clueless, so fucking naive, I can't take anymore, I'm alarmed at the reality. All I can do is look at her and nod.

'So I shoved them up as far I could, embarrassed to be fingering myself while this nurse watches. The nurse said I should just lay down, relax, and in a couple hours I should start to feel some cramping and pain, like period pain. Sounded easy enough. And when I did, I should go to the toilets across the hall, and expel what I could into these cardboard kidney bowls she handed me. They were all initialled and numbered in biro on the side. She gave me a big stack of them! Then she said whatever came out into the bowl I should take into the sluice room next door and leave on the side for them to check.'

What the fuck do I know about periods? What's a sluice room? I feel so uncomfortable now, but I just feel so shit for her too. She's so pretty and young and sweet, and man, she let me ejaculate in her half hour ago. I think she even enjoyed it. Why is she telling me this? I pray she's on some kind of birth control. 'So anyway, some time passes. I had a couple of magazines, my phone. I could hear a couple of the other girls on the ward with me, pacing, someone was moaning. Half hour ago it had been like a fucking party out there, all swapping numbers and laughing. Not now though, shit was getting real. And I started to feel it too, just like really bad cramps, nothing unusual. I figured it was starting, so I took a bowl and went to the toilet.'

Kitten obviously sees me grimacing because she looks a little defensive and says, 'Truth is, Joe, periods suck. They hurt, and you can literally feel your uterine lining tearing away from the womb, sliding out your hole all bright red and lumpy-clotted. That's the reality! Every fucking month!'

**Yep, that's the reality folks.**

I sick into my mouth a little at this, but I put on a brave face, suppress the grimace and swallow my vomit, swap it for concern. She softens again. 'So I'm in the toilet squatting over this bowl, but not much comes out, a bit of blood. I clean up and take the bowl into the sluice room next door. There were other girls used bowls in there already, laid out on the counter, I tried not to look too much. I went back to my bed and the cramps got worse and worse, and I got this urge to push, like I was in labour or something? I guess that's what it must feel like, giving birth you know? More painful, obviously. So I went back and forth to the toilet a couple more times, these crazy cramps and spasms, when this huge chunk of stuff just slid out of me into the bowl between my thighs. I saw it then, Joe.' Oh fuck, what did she see? I'm looking at her, my forehead knit encouraging her to carry on. Almost a whisper; 'I saw the baby! It was tiny, but it stood out amongst the bright blood, it was all firm and pale and it was a fucking tiny foetus! My actual baby. I sat there on the toilet for a while longer, the bowl right up in my face, I couldn't stop looking at it. I prodded it, looking for signs of movement. It was the weirdest thing, but I felt I should get to know it somehow, what I had done. Do you understand?' I don't, but I nod anyway. Hesitating now, she says, 'What are you thinking about all this, Joe? Do you think I'm a terrible person?' I don't, but I think it's awful, every damn detail is terrible. Fuck being female. It's not all pillow fights and feeling up your own tits.

'No, I don't think you're terrible. You just did what you had to do right? I'm sorry though, it sounds…traumatic.'

'Yeah, it was traumatic alright. I cleaned myself again, took that bowl into the sluice room. It was so undignified, walking into the corridor with a bowl of blood and waste and foetus. I told the nurse at the desk outside the ward that I thought it was done and went to lie down. I was still getting cramps, I felt like shit, but relieved too, you know? Nurse came and said it wasn't over, there would still be more tissue to pass. Said to carry on as before and I should be able to go home in a couple more hours.' She pauses again, lies back on her pillow and closes her eyes.

'Jesus Kitten, I'm so sorry you went through that, it's just so sad,' I can't find the right words but I try, 'Thank you for sharing it with me, can't be easy reliving it like that.' She's opened up her soul to me and I want her to feel OK about it all. But she isn't done yet.

'I kind of wished I'd had it vacuumed out at that point. At least I wouldn't have seen everything. Two of the girls on my ward got discharged. I emptied the rest of my womb, took it into the sluice room again. And you know what, Joe? On a little shelf above the worktop there were four tiny labelled bottles, I saw my name on one. I knew what was in there, and I picked it up, and there's my tiny little baby inside, floating around in some clear liquid. I looked at it for a while, I looked at the others too. Four little lives over before they'd even begun, four little hearts no longer beating.' She turns back to face me now. I force myself to look at her, I feel embarrassed, I don't know why. 'The abortion was no secret, Joe, but I did something else, and nobody in the world knows but me.' Oh man.

'What? What did you do?'

She looks at me long and hard, then leans back, reaching over to her bedside table she opens the top drawer. She rummages awhile, and pulls out this tiny clear bottle, leaning back to show me. I can feel my stomach preparing to propel that earlier vodka back up out my mouth.

'I took my baby. I didn't know what they were going to do with it so I took it. It's mine right? I put it in my dressing gown pocket and then hid it in my bag. They sent me home an hour later, not before they gave me a contraceptive injection though. They didn't want me back there y'know?'

I don't want to look, but I have to, she's holding it out to me. It's just this titchy greyish bean-like blob, about an inch or two in length, like a little alien toy or something. It's got black dots for eyes on its oversized little head. It is repulsive and fascinating and macabre. It doesn't look real but I know it is.

'You can see its little fingers and toes if you look real close!' I decline by doing nothing. The hospital sticker is on there, I read it. HALL, Katherine Paige, her date of birth and hospital number. I muse to myself, Katherine huh? I ask,

'Didn't the hospital realise? That it was missing?'

'I don't know, nobody said anything. Maybe they thought they'd misplaced it or something? It's not like they were going to tell me they'd lost it.' I don't want to see it anymore. I close my eyes, I don't feel well. I say,

'Kitten, this is the most fucked up thing I've ever seen or heard. I'm not saying you did anything wrong, you didn't, but I just don't get why you'd torture yourself by doing that, taking it with you.

'You DO think I'm a terrible person then, Joe?' I open my eyes,

'No! I don't! But why would you bring home a reminder of something so sad?' She shuts her palm over the bottle, clutches it tightly. Like she's closing the door to her heart.

'I don't know. Penance or something?' I can see her eyes filling with tears, she puts the little bottle back in the drawer and shuts it. I know she's regretting telling me, showing me. I lean over and stroke her shoulder. 'I'm tired. You?' She lowers herself back under the covers.

'Yeah.' Not really, I'm wired now, my brain's gone into overdrive. I still feel nauseated.

'Please don't ever tell anyone OK?' I promise I won't. She closes her eyes and I guess she's done talking, and she falls asleep a little later. I feel like shit, this girl bared her soul to me, trusted me with something so uncomfortable and private, and I didn't know the right way to behave. I slide my arm from under her, get up and puke my guts up into the toilet, sick and sweating until there's nothing left inside me.

# Things Are Looking Up

I wake the next morning, another unfamiliar room, feeling like my brain is trying to push itself out my skull. It actually throbs, which I didn't know a brain could do. I start to recall, this is Kitten's room, her bed, and the torrent of last night's events suddenly stream through my mind. I had sex! The thrill of that memory is somewhat dampened however, because I have the worst headache ever. I'm so thirsty and my mouth tastes like a bin. I recall more, the throwing up, dressing and then laying on the bed beside Kitten while she slept. I'd wanted to leave but also didn't want to abandon her, and besides I'd been too ill to do anything other than pass out at that point. There's no sign of Kitten now, she must be up.

Alcohol is weird, because while I initially remembered hardly anything at all, little details keep floating up to the surface of my thinking, and within a minute or two I feel like the entire jigsaw is complete. The sex! The Haiku Man, Bob and Pete, the shots, the tattoo. It's actually real! I hold my hand up, gaze upon this scar. A little concerned, Grandpa would have a shit-fit. But, Kitten holding my hand, lifting her T-shirt over her head, the sex…the fucking aborted foetus in her drawer. I remember everything. It was a pretty epic eighteenth birthday. I step out of Kitten's room and she's sitting on the sofa, playing on her phone. She looks up at me and smiles,

'Morning Joe, how's your head?' She looks beautiful. She could have a collection of dead babies, a museum of death and sadness, and I'd still think so.

'Wrecked. I feel like shit.' I actually feel better for seeing her. She laughs and gets up,

'You want a coffee?' and walks over to the kitchenette, flicks the kettle switch. I flop down on the sofa and watch her get the mug from the cupboard, she spoons a heap full of coffee in, asks if I want sugar.

'So eighteen now huh? What's next Joe? You got your whole adult life at your feet!' She's cheerful, hands me the mug.

'I don't know, I just want to feel human again.' She giggles, it's really cute. I wonder if she's my girlfriend now?

'You'll be fine, drink the coffee, give it a couple of hours.' But her face turns real serious then, 'I just want to say, let's never, ever talk about last night again OK?" I'm not sure if she's referring to the bottled baby or the sex, but I nod in agreement,

'OK.'

'OK good! Now, I gotta ask Joe, where'd all the money come from?' Oh, shit. 'Did you rob a bank or something?' She throws me the money bag with the cash bundled inside. It must've come out of my boot.

'It's mine,' I say, 'My Grandfather left it to me, told me to come here.' I stuff it in my pocket but it's too late to keep quiet.

'Come where?' she looks at me quizzically.

'The City,' I say, 'He died, but left me a letter telling me to come here.'

'What for?' She asks.

'I don't know.' I say.

'Well what's the point in that?'

'I guess he thought there was nothing worth staying there for. He said I should do something, enjoy myself, seek experiences.'

'Oh, right, well how's that working out for you?' She looks amused, interested. 'Tell me about your family, Joe.'

'There is none,' I say, 'Grandpa only died last week. It was just me and him. My mother died, I don't know where my dad is, there's no one but me.' She gasps, and a look of sincere condolence crosses her face. I'm unprepared for such sympathy.

'Aw Joe, last week? Seriously? That's sad. I'm sorry.' I don't need pity. But next she says, 'Right, this is what I think you should do today. You go back to the bar and pack up all your stuff, bring it here. You can stay awhile. I don't mean in my room, don't get any ideas like that OK, Joe? Last night was just a birthday present. But you shouldn't be staying in that fucking dive, nobody should. You can sleep on the sofa, or my floor depending on when my roommate is here. I mean it's not much but I have a cooker and a fridge and stuff, a shower. I'll help you find somewhere better. It'll be a good start for you, your new life.' Well I guess she's not my girlfriend. She's looking at me for approval, still smiling. She's so damn pretty, seeing her now without all that eye makeup on she looks so different. I'm grateful, anything is better than that room at the bar. Kitten's flat is tiny, but a palace in comparison.

'Are you sure?' I asked, 'I mean cool, but it's OK if you think I'll cramp the place up.'

'Nah it's fine, Joe, and it's temporary, right? Tidy up after yourself and we'll be fine.'

'Your roommate won't mind?'

'No, it'll be OK, she's hardly here anyway, let me deal with it.'

'Cool, thanks. Would it be alright if I have a shower?'

'Sure, use the blue towel. That's mine. Mind the tattoo.'

The shower is the best I've ever had. I stand there in scalding water letting it slap my face and chest. I examine my tattoo again. I feel proud. I use some girly looking shower gel that sits on the edge of the bath. My head still hurts but I'm ready to function and face the day. My clothes are, again, pretty grubby, but I dress and examine my face in the mirror. My eye's a nice shade of yellow with purple edges. My teeth need brushing so I just squeeze some toothpaste out from the tube on the edge of the sink, rub it onto my teeth, swill it around with water from the tap. I use a hairbrush from the windowsill, smiling to myself, Jeez, make yourself at home, Joe! I properly had sex last night. It was everything and more than I could've imagined. Not like porn or movie sex, but normal, natural. I know it was probably really basic and clumsy, but I think I did alright. Kitten didn't laugh or anything. And when I came, man, that release! She was gasping all breathy in my ear, it was so fucking hot. My dick's hardening at the thought… so much for never having sex ever again. Kitten's way too attractive, too cool for me, and despite all that weird abortion shit last night, I still want her. But she said that was just a one off, a birthday present. I've been friend-zoned. I push all sex thoughts to the back of my mind and gather myself. I hang the towel on the back of the door, rinse the sink of my toothpaste spit and open the door feeling like a man. Kitten tells me to hurry up, she has to go to work soon.

'At the bar?' I ask.

'No, I work another job in the day. You think that wage alone could pay my rent?'

Huh. Guess not.


Fucking go, Joe! Another night of firsts! Got drunk, got a tattoo, got laid, and I'm pleased for him, I really am. Because things are going to start going downhill from here on in. At least he got a good couple of days under his belt. He has the biggest smile on his face this morning, a newfound confidence. Boy's done well.


I bounce back to the bar, a spring in my step, a smile on my face. I'm a real life cliche. I found my way back here easily. I forgot to get something to eat, but I'm nailing this! Haiku Man greets me, sitting on the low step of the doorway. I'm pleased to see him, his filthy, ugly familiar face, the one who brought me here, master of my fate. Nothing and no one could bring me down right now. I grin at him, and he stands, creaking and sighing. He says,

'Have you got a key?

No one's answering the door.

I need some vodka.'

Feeling playful I fish out my key and say, 'Are you allowed in?'

'What you smiling for?

Got laid last night did you, boy?

Yes I'm allowed in!'

I unlock the door, still beaming, push it open and the Haiku Man follows, shutting and bolting the door behind him.

'You look like someone

Gave you a million quid

And loads of blowjobs.'

He's laughing and wheezing, I chuckle too. He takes his seat at the bar. I didn't get any blowjobs but I feel like a million dollars.

'Get me a drink boy,

Quickly, before I'm sober;

Not a pretty sight!'

I do as I'm asked, the smell of alcohol momentarily turning my stomach. He raises his glass in imaginary cheer and I tell him,

'You know what? I'm feeling good today. Thanks for bringing me here. I think I'm going to be alright, I can do this now.' He shakes his head and serious he says,

'Do what exactly?

Work at this fucking shit hole?

Choose a proper goal!'

Whatever, I'm high on life, I don't give a shit about tomorrow or the next day. I just want to enjoy the moment. I tell him,

'Stop bringing me down! I'm happy!' Shrugging he says,

'Just don't waste your time.

Don't forget why you came here,

There's more to explore.'

I don't know if he's genuinely trying to offer me some wisdom or if he's meanly attempting to dampen my high spirits.

'Yeah, OK' I say, rolling my eyes to myself. And I remember what I came back here for, my things. 'See you later.' I exit the bar and up towards my room.

# Head Shot

Forget the Haiku Man, I only came back to collect my bag. For the first time in forever I'm feeling positive.

Reaching the top of the stairs I notice my door is open; I thought I'd been methodical about shutting it tight, but last night is hazy, so much happened and I was drunk. I don't remember if I came up here at all, or if I shut the door tight when I left. I had my money on me, so I knew everything would be OK. Bob and Pete wouldn't screw me over.

Still, I've got a bad feeling. With hesitation, I push my door fully open. An uneasy creeped out suspicion as I walk through, things are not quite right, the hairs on my neck prickling. Before I can register anything else, this guy, it's the weirdo from the room next to me, he pounces on me from behind the door, waving a fucking gun in my face. A real fucking gun! I lose my breath.

Everything slows down.

'Who the fuck *are* you?' He hisses, 'You looking for me?' God no. I cannot think straight, I cannot speak, can't even look at him properly, the barrel of that gun pointed at my head. Oh Jesus fucking Christ. I recoil, trying to remove myself from the threat, and it takes every ounce of my being not to crumple to the floor, which in the interest of self-preservation might be the right thing to do, it's hard to think logically when you're held at gunpoint.

I muster a 'No!' Instinctively my arms are raised, palms open. 'Please no, I'm sorry, I was just getting my stuff and going, I swear, I'm sorry!' I somehow stutter this out, a lump forming in my throat.

'Quiet!' he stage whispers, and I realise both Bob and Pete are across the hall. Should I call out? I can't, he'll just kill me, I know it. I begin to shake. 'What's with the bag?' he rasps, momentarily side eying my rucksack, 'You fucking military?' I can barely hear him over the thump of my heartbeat.

'No, no, of course not! It's just my bag, it was a gift!' He looks suspicious, I can visualise cogs turning in his head as he decides whether to believe me or not, surveying me, looking me up and down.

'Don't make a fucking sound,' he says, then, 'Turn around.' I truly think this is it, he's going to shoot me in the back of the head, and I shut my eyes tight, anticipating the worst. Oh Jesus Christmas, mother-fucking God, I can't believe this, fuck! But then I feel the gun between my shoulder blades; my shoulders still really hurt I realise, which is not important, but my brain registers it anyway. And seriously? Do I look like I'm fucking military? I definitely don't, I'd laugh if I wasn't so terrified. 'Walk,' he growls, 'Next door.' I do as he asks, slowly and measured, my hands still raised in front of me; I know his finger is poised on that trigger and I don't want to give him any cause to blast my chest open. Oh God, please don't, my heart's doing a fine job of bursting out on its own. I hear him pull my door closed behind him, and then silently and carefully we walk the few steps to his room. His door is shut, and I daren't move or attempt to open it so I just stop right there, my face inches away from the panelling, I lay my hands slowly against the door. Without relaxing that gun in my back, he reached around me and slides a key into the lock, pushing against me as the door creaks open. His room is full of junk, like he's a proper hoarder considering he hasn't been here long. Bags full of God knows what, bottles, boxes. In addition to a shitty bare mattress, he has a chair and a table, both of which are laden with more bags.

Still nudging me forward, I enter, shuffling and stopping only when I can go no further from the obstruction of all that fills his room. I feel the pressure against my back relax, and in turn I breathe as carefully as I can, not moving, and hear the door close behind us. He says, 'Do not move.' I don't, I won't. I hear him sliding bolts. What the fuck? What does he want from me? What did I do? My mind's filled with more thoughts than I knew possible. Memories, encounters, random shit that I can't figure out why my mind has stored…that time an ice cream van passed my window and I couldn't have one, the time I woke in my orange bedroom and there was a butterfly on my wall. That time I swallowed bubblegum and thought I'd die. That dream I had about the giant who was going to eat me, from that terrifying story book. My mother's face, my father's face. That kid at school on my first day, who pointed and laughed because I went to play with the doll house. And just unmitigated fear. I don't want to die. I have nothing to live for, but I don't want to die yet. Please.

I say it, quietly, a whisper, 'Please…I'm sorry, I just wanted to go.' I don't know what I'm apologising for.

'On your knees, hands behind your head,' I'm shaking so much that I don't think I can drop to the floor without steadying myself. I turn slightly to allow myself some space, slowly, and one knee at a time I manage, because my life depends on it. I pray, inside my head, to God. Even though I didn't think I believed in him or her or them, right now it's worth a shot. I pray, beg for my life; *Please God I'm sorry, don't let me die, I swear I'll be a good person, I'm sorry, please God, please help me, save me, please. Please save me, I'm not ready, I'm sorry, I am sorry, please help me, please God help me, I don't want to die, please.*

Fucking Hell man, moments like this are the worst. I'm sorry Joe, but please don't mess this up. Don't die. Not now. Come on, keep your cool. Poor boy has no idea what he's signed up for. Sweet, innocent Joe. My metaphorical heart breaks for him now. Hold it together kid. You see this all the time though, begging to God when you're desperate. You might've never given God a thought before, but presented with actual fear of death, you all beg, you all pray.

He says to me, 'Who the fuck are you?' I plead,

'No one! I'm just staying here, I *was* staying here, I'm leaving now, today.' He walks around to stand in front of me, pushing the gun into my temple, and says with absolute sincere ferocity, his voice low,

'I swear to God you better tell me the truth, I *will* fucking kill you…were you looking for me?' His eyes are piercing, he's staring right into my soul, or through it, I'm trying to look back at him and can only hope he sees my honesty.

'No I swear, I don't know you, I've been working here, I don't know you, I'm sorry, I promise!'

'That rucksack, it's the same as mine…you fucking with me?'

'No, my Grandpa gave it to me, honestly, sorry.' I don't know how many times I can declare it, the truth, how to make him believe me, how much I can apologise for being in the wrong place at the wrong time.

'Your fucking *Grandpa*?' He starts to laugh, a maniacal, unhinged laugh, still hushed. The gun leaves my head. 'You joking, kid?' I look at him then, get a real good look. My hands still on my head, my arms aching. I'm incredulous; why am I fucking here? He's insane, his eyes are gone, the gun still waywardly waving about my head. He looks worn and damaged, yet there's a determined sharpness about him, a cause.

'I'm not joking, I mean it, I promise, I swear!' My eyes plead with him. How much can I beg? I know I'm repeating myself. I'm amazed at my mind's capacity to survive, it's all I want, I'll do anything. 'I just wanted to go!' I wish someone would help me. Anyone. God, Bob, Haiku Man, Grandpa, anyone. I am so alone.

'You freaked me out, kid,' still sniggering, 'I saw that fucking rucksack and I cracked! You understand?' I don't, but I nod frantically,

'Yes, I'm sorry, I'm nobody, sorry.' What the actual fuck?

He looks at me, he's mulling shit over. I don't move my hands from my head, and I'm still shaking. I need to pee. I might piss myself. I can feel my knees shuddering against the bare floorboards, I'm trying so hard to stay calm.

'Take your jacket off,' I do, slowly, and drop it on the floor beside me. 'And your T-shirt.' I hesitate,

'Why?'

'Just fucking do it!' Gun right in my face. I slip it over my head, drop it. Why? I've never felt so vulnerable. With precision, he slides the barrel of the gun across my face, and pushes it into my mouth. I can't breathe. He pushes it right in and I whimper, I'm so frightened, and resigned now. 'Suck it,' he says, and my eyes, I know they beseech him, I'm so sorry. I'll do anything.

I feel it now, the sting of tears. It's been so long, so many years, and I can no longer suppress those emotions, the sadness and feeling of so much time, water brims from my eyes, and I begin to sob. I blink and I suck and I sob, I'm so sorry, I'm so sad. Tears pouring hotly down my face, I'm trying to be quiet but it's been so long. I want to close my eyes, just submit to death. 'Suck it!' He's louder now, and I suck as best I can, on the barrel of that gun, just waiting for the shot, the end. I hope I don't know it's coming, I pray it's quick. I have given up hope of rescue. Licking his lips he says, 'With some enthusiasm, kid! Don't hold back! I can tell you like it.' He looks so intensely at me and I try harder. Suddenly, I'm outside myself, looking down; disembodied, I see me, eyes wide, humiliated, pathetic and powerless, sucking on that gun like it's a fucking ice lolly. I wonder if it's done, if he already killed me. He hasn't, I know, because I'm still so frightened, so scared to death. I'm back inside myself. I will give up. I pull myself away from the gun, and shut my eyes tight. Sobbing without discretion, I can't communicate anything else. I'm so sorry I give up. I discover there's some strange relief in crying. It's been so long. I remember my father and why I never cry. I suddenly feel so much, everything, a lifetime of melancholy and grief. I can't contain it any longer; I'm sorry, I'm sad, I'm nothing, I lack ambition and I'm alone and unloved, I'm cursed and I lost everybody and everything, I'm not needed or wanted. I'm pointless and insignificant. Just do it, I don't care anymore. I allow myself to cry and brace myself, my eyes screwed tightly because I don't want to watch. My head gets thumped, hard on the side of my temple, and although I tensed myself in preparation, I hit the floor, and it hurts. A lot. Momentarily I presume I've been shot, quickly realising it's not the case.

'Quiet, I said, fucking quiet!' My head throbs and I open my eyes, push myself up from the floor back onto my knees. I'm quiet. I whisper,

'I'm sorry! Just let me go, I'll never come back, I'll never say anything.' My eyes beseeching, tears silently dribbling down my cheeks.

'I can't just let you go,' The gun's back in my face. It's sobering being confronted with that power. 'You fucking little prick, fucking shit up for me,' He's seething, continues, 'If I just let you go you'll fucking turn me in, you'll fucking tell, you bastard little shit!'

'I won't, I swear, I don't know anything! I just want to go!' I've pissed myself, I don't know when, maybe right now, it isn't a conscious decision. I'm aware of the wetness on my jeans, pooling around my knees. I glance down, acknowledge the incident, ashamed and embarrassed, appalled with myself. He looks down too, sees the mess I've made, and he's furious.

'You fucking little bitch! Pissing on my floor!' He's waving his arms around now, the gun haphazardly gripped in his hand, when, unanticipated, it slips from his grasp, and in slow motion we both watch as it drops towards the floor in front of me, and I don't know why but I reach out for it, I want to catch it, or take it, just anything to remove the threat, the control, the terror. It feels like a race, and I have it, I have this gun in my hands, the weight surprises me, and then fuck, it fires. It's so inconceivably loud and I worry that I've blown off my fingers; there's moisture, there's blood, I feel it speckle on me. Fuck, he can have it back. I never saw or touched a gun before. I look up, in time to watch him fall, heavily without grace to the ground. Oh shit. Oh fuck, fuck! His face. His jaw is half gone, bone, teeth, flesh and blood, his eyes rolling, and he smashes to the bare floorboards. What have I done?

# I'm Fucked

The silence is obscene. Nothing but my breathing. I regard the scene before me, blood is pooling around his head, the gun still in my shaking hands. I place it carefully on the floor. Fuck he is dead, he is dead. My ears hurting, I hear Bob across the hall, his door opens, Pete's opens,

'What the fuck was that?' he says to his brother.

Bob bangs the door, bellows, 'Open the fucking door! Now!' I am frozen, horrified. Then I hear footsteps pounding up the stairs, the Haiku Man,

'What the fuck was that?

Someone shoot a gun up here?

What is going on?'

'Wait,' I cry, towards the door, 'Wait!' and still crying I scramble to my piss soaked feet, fumbling at the bolts on the door, my hands like I got Parkinson's or something, it's a struggle. My body feels like jelly and lead at the same time, and still sobbing, I am spooked. I can hear Bob, his confusion.

'What the fuck? Joe?'

The door is open, and I'm confronted by the three of them, and them with me; stripped to the waist, the blood, the dead man, the piss, the gun and the blood, so much blood, spattered all across the room, all over me. I just showered half an hour ago. Mouths agape, they each assess the situation, this scene of horror and gore. Without warning I vomit, just to add to the bodily fluids that have collected in the room, I puke my coffee and bile down my bare chest and onto the floor. I can't stop shaking.

'What the fuck?' says Bob quietly, then louder, 'What the actual FUCK is this?' Heightened, angry and questioning. It's warm in here and blood smells. As does piss and vomit. I don't know what to say. I drop back to my knees. 'JOE!'

'It was an accident, he had a gun!'

'Did *you* do this?' Incredulous, still in the doorway Bob sweeps his arm across my situation.

'No! I mean, he had me at gunpoint, I think he was going to kill me; I only came up to get my bag.' The Haiku Man has seen enough; I watch his colour drain, revulsion on his face, he turns away, disappears back into the hallway. Pete's morbidly fascinated, his eyes thoroughly scrutinizing every detail. Sweating and sobbing still, I dry heave, my stomach painfully contracting, I feel dizzy. I close my eyes again, I can't look back and I can't explain to Bob, my mind and body surrendering to shock.

'Oh Shit...' says Bob, 'Shit, fuck, balls, what are we going to do?' Despite what he's confronted with and his profanity he seems amazingly calm, I hear him but I can't look. 'Joe fucking STOP!

SHUT UP! Tell me what's going on, what did you do? What did he do? Start fucking talking boy!'

I try to control my wailing, sniffing back the snot dripping freely from my nose, wiping it onto my bare forearm.

'Call the Police!' I plea. I open my eyes now, in time to see Bob above me, grabbing me disgustedly by the back of my neck, a handful of flesh and hair, pulling me up from the floor.

'Fucking listen, you better start explaining this fucking bloodbath, we are not calling the police, you hear me? Not a fucking chance. Just talk!'

'Why, why not?' I'm frightened of Bob now, he's incensed, still gripping me by my neck and I think *he* might kill me.

'Did you do this or him?'

'It was an accident, he dropped the gun and I caught it, it went off by itself!'

'Why's he got a gun? Why are you in his fucking room? Why are your clothes on the floor?'

I can't impart the information quickly enough because my brain can't make sense of what's happened. Bob's rationality is admirable. I manage to scrape a coherent sentence together.

'He was in my room; I came back and he was behind my door with the gun, he was crazy!'

Pete's in the room too now, having a good look around. There's not much space and Bob shouts at him,

'Get out, Pete, it's not a fucking exhibition!'

'Alright, give me a minute,' and he crouches down to pick up the gun.

'Don't fucking touch it, you idiot! Leave it! Get out!'

'Jesus, keep your hair on,' Pete stands and does as he's told. Shrugging he says 'But we're gonna have to clean this shit up.'

Bob says, 'Joe will be fucking cleaning this up!' Looking fixedly back at me. I don't want to argue but there is absolutely no way I can clean this up. The police will clean up, right? I'm still shaking so much, trying to stifle my crying. Bob assesses me with distaste, the blood, the piss, the puke, the snot, and tears. 'Wash yourself, you're covered in blood and sick. And piss, for fuck's sake. And get dressed, Jesus Christ Joe, you're fucking disgusting.' and pushing me towards the door, he releases me from his grip.

Pete steps aside from where he leans in the doorway, and wobbly I shuffle through. The Haiku Man sits against the wall in the hallway looking nauseated. His face is grave, his eyes following me, he says nothing. I hear Bob say to no one,

'What the fuck *is* all this shit in here?'

Pete says, 'What are we going to do with the body?' and I'm wailing again, I don't know how to cope with this. I go down to the end room, splash my face with cold water over and over until I'm sure the blood has gone, then I head to my room, open the door, still blubbering like a baby. The simple act of putting clothes on seems absurdly difficult, I can hardly function enough to breath, but trembling, I fumble through my bag for clean clothes. My boots and socks are piss-soaked, I pull them off, and remember I put the money in my jacket pocket this morning when Kitten threw it back to me. But my jacket is still next door.

I hear Bob, 'Get some black bags.' I change everything, my skin clammy from sweat and urine, I'm trying my best. The tears still fall, but I'm quieter now, calmer. The implications of what's just happened are creeping into my consciousness. Oh my fucking God, I just killed a man. Am I a murderer? It was an accident. I'm a good person, I've never hurt anyone, I wouldn't. I'm sorry. I want to call the police, my phone's in my jacket, why can't I call the police? They'll understand, I'll tell them everything. I'm horrified, I can never go back in that room, I don't want to see it again, I can't ever erase what I've seen. His eyes were open. Broken flesh is pinker than it is red. Pete has gone downstairs, I heard him muttering as he went, and I hear him come back. I don't know what to do and I don't move. I need my jacket, I need my money and my phone. I stand in my room, half my filthy, bloodied clothes in a pile beside me. I'm cold and shuddering still. Will the tremors ever stop? I feel like this might be my permanent state of being from now on.

**The tremors will stop Joe, chill.**

'Joe? JOE!' Bob's calling. I jump, I'm too frightened to reply. 'JOE!' Shit.

'Yeah?' A half-hearted answer.

'Get your fucking arse out here!' I pull on my hoodie and gulping back dread I open my door. He's standing there, hands me a black bag. 'Put your clothes in here.' He looks solemn but composed, like he deals with this shit every day. My jacket and T shirt are already in there.

'My phone's in my jacket, my wallet.'

'Well get them out then.' Taking the bag I rummage through my jacket pockets without pulling it out, the money, my phone, my tobacco, a lighter. I pull them out, slide them into my hoodie pocket. I scoop up my ruined attire, drop it into the bag. There's moisture left behind on the floor. Bob bellows backwards, 'Pete! You'll have to go shopping.' Pete appears behind him, and Bob carries on, 'Bleach, a shitload of bleach. More bags. Fuck, I don't know what else...' He's suddenly drained. I fumble for the money bag in my pocket, slip it into my rucksack on the floor. Bob turns back to me.

'Why can't we phone the police?' I ask him timidly. 'I'll explain everything.'

'Shut the fuck up, Joe, you brought a shit ton of trouble to our door, I'm fucking livid with you! You will shut up and do as you're fucking told you hear me? There will be no police, YOU will clean this mess.'

'But if we phone them they'll...'

'No Joe, no! For fucks sake, we do not involve the pigs in anything, we don't need them. Pete has sixty fucking plants in his room and we are not bringing the cops here. Do you think this place is legit, boy? Do you think we are adhering to FUCKING REGULATIONS??' His mood is climbing again, he looks like he wants to beat me. Plants? 'Come on, this is your fucking mess, we are not doing this shit for you, get the fuck out here.'

I am still shaking, it won't stop, but I've stopped crying. Unsteadily I step out through the doorway to follow him. I drop the black bag on the floor of the landing. The Haiku Man's on his feet, outside next door's room, and looking solemnly at me he distressingly says,

'You fucked up big time!

I curse the day we met.

Shouldn't have helped you.'

I know he's right. I can't bring myself to look in that room. He shakes his head, absolute solemnity,

Well Jesus Christ boy,

You shot his fucking face off!

What a fucking mess.'

I am amazed at his ability to continue his haiku mottos at a time like this.

'I didn't shoot him,' I attempt, 'It was an accident, he dropped the gun, I didn't do anything!' The Haiku Man carries on,

'Don't know what I've seen.

If he was gonna rape you,

You could just tell us.'

Rape? No! Is that what was happening? Shit, I don't know if that's what he was thinking, I thought he was checking me for a wire or something, like they do in the movies. I feel embarrassed at the suggestion.

I say, 'No, no rape. No! I don't know. I think we should just call the police, it's all on me, I'll tell them everything...' I'm a mess.

'NO!' says Bob, 'Fucking no, *listen*!'

The Haiku Man says angrily,

'We don't talk to cops.

Police? Are you fucking mad?

Want to go to jail?'

OK no, I don't want to go to jail, but they'll understand if I tell them, I'm sure of it. Pete is back in there, he has a black bag open, I can hear him whistling through his teeth, he says 'I think this fucker was making bombs and shit, you see him bring all this stuff in here?'

I recall the full carrier bags, the suspicious eyes when I saw him, alive, just yesterday.

Bob says, 'I ain't been watching him! What the fuck you on about, bombs?'

I'm avoiding the room. I stand outside, between mine and his, the Haiku Man blocking my way. Pete continues, 'Who the fuck *is* this guy?'

I hope Grandpa can't see me now. I know this isn't what he had in mind for me when he wrote that letter. I think of Kitten, smiling and waiting back at her flat. I can't see a way forward from this. Bob exits the room, exhales, he looks sick. Looking at no one he says,

'We need to think about this. Pete! Get out here, let's go downstairs.'

I'm grateful I don't have to go back in there and see him on the floor. I won't ever sleep again, I'm traumatised. Am I supposed to go down too? The Haiku Man waves the way, and numbly I follow Bob and Pete downstairs.

OK, I realise how awful this is. Why didn't I intervene you wonder? Why did I allow this to happen to my protégé? Well actually, this is Joe's purpose, his calling. Mission accomplished. One of them anyway, he still has some work left to do before it's over. But this, he nailed it, job done. And besides, I don't have much influence, remember? It's limited, only so much I can do. Joe has his free will just like everyone else. I can only observe and hope for the desired outcome, I will it with all my might and hope he hears it.

# Shit Ideas

We sit at a table in the bar. 'Pete, make us some coffee?' Bob instructs. The Haiku Man says,

'I don't want coffee.

Get me something stronger please,

I can't deal with this.

'It's worse than the time

Pete crushed that kitten you got

With a crate of beer.'

Bob snaps, 'This is way fucking worse! For fuck's sake!' I say nothing, daren't speak, I'm quietly crying again, I can't stop the tears.

'It was pretty grim,

That cute kitty face all squished,

Its guts spilling out.'

'Enough, Jesus.'

While Pete is in the kitchen Bob asks, 'What's the plan of action then? What the fuck do we do? Where do we start?' He is looking at the Haiku Man, not me.

'Sorry, I'm leaving,

It's nothing to do with me.

Just came for drink.'

Bob sighs, 'Nothing to do with you? You fucking brought him here! At least give us some advice?' The Haiku Man responds whilst side eyeing me,

'Don't fucking blame me!

Didn't know he'd bring trouble,

Felt sorry for him.

'I'm not going down,

Accessory to murder,

Whatever it is.'

Bob's silent, his eyes blank and staring at the table. Pete comes back, three mugs of coffee, he puts one in front of me. I don't think I can drink it, I'll vomit again, but I'm grateful not to be ostracised. He goes back behind the bar, grabs a bottle of vodka and the Haiku Man's glass, brings it over. Pours him a large shot. Pete's crazy, no doubt, but right now he seems to me a pillar of stability, of kindness and sensibility. Placing the bottle down on the table, he says,

'We're going to have to dispose of the body.'

Bob replies, 'Yeah, fucking genius, how?'

'I dunno. Remember that movie where those people have to get rid of a body and they cut it up with a saw and bury it in a shallow grave? They smash the teeth out so the cops can't trace the dental records.' Please God no. The Haiku Man downs his glass in one go,

'We're not chopping him!

I hope you're not serious?

You fucking psycho!'

Bob chimes in, 'A shallow grave is a shit idea, we want a deep fucking grave! We don't want anyone to find him! I just know I want him the fuck out of here, today!' Bob looks at me, 'You got any ideas boy?' I don't. I want to ring the police. I tell him so.

'Oh for fuck's sake, get it through to your thick fucking skull! We are not bringing cops here.'

'Why not?' I ask quietly, I'm timid, submissive, I remain deferential.

'Because! I fucking said so! Pete's got a fucking pot farm upstairs! Pete's not going to jail for you! *I'm* not going to jail for you!' I had no idea. Explains the weird smell though.

'What about water?

The river is deep enough

If we weigh him down?'

The Haiku Man has given in to involvement. For Bob and Pete's sake, not mine. No one answers, but Pete comes up with something,

'We could take him to the countryside, burn him? Or we could get some acid and dissolve him?' Bob's not impressed, he's shaking with rage.

'Shit ideas, Pete, for fucks sake this is not a movie!' Where the fuck we gonna get acid from, eh? Eh?' Pete shrugs and says,

'At least I'm coming up with something, unlike Joe here.' They all look at me for an idea.

'I can't, I don't know… I'm sorry, I can't do it!' Bob leans across the table towards me, lifting from his chair and angrily pointing his finger inches from my face, and tells me,

'You *will* fucking do this boy. We will all do this, and if you fucking dare try to leave here without my say-so, I will find you and kill you too, then you'll be leaving us with double the shit we already have to deal with! You hear me? You're doing this!' I'm silent, my bottom lip quivers. I bow my head, hunched in the chair. Bob drops back, that outburst calmed him a bit. He gulps some coffee. 'We'll need to wrap him up, get him in the car. I don't know where to take him, but we need to do it soon. Before we fucking open. Something quick! The river's a good idea, but we'll never be able to do it without being seen unless we take him right out of town. But I don't know any deep rivers out of town. Fuck!' He's frustrated. We sit quietly for a minute, contemplating. I'm just watching the three of them, hoping for the best. Everyone drinks their refreshments apart from me.

Pete pipes up, 'What about train tracks? We could put him on the tracks, let a train cut him up?' I wince, that's horrific. Bob looks like he's entertaining the idea.

'Hmm, yeah. Actually yeah, that could work.'

Pete says, 'It'll look like a suicide or an accident right?' They're both insane. The Haiku Man shakes his head gravely,

'No, bad idea,

There's a bullet in his head,

Think they won't notice?'

Bob doesn't give a shit, he's not hearing any opposition.

'Well it's the best option so far. We only have to get him there, we'll dump the gun in the river. Clean up. Saves us digging or burning or whatever. Yeah Pete, go out, get a shitload of black bags. Get bleach, rubber gloves. Hurry the fuck up! We'll need to burn everything we use afterwards, get some petrol too. And gaffer tape. Look discreet, wear a cap. Pay cash.'

Pete looks pleased with himself, 'Saw it in a movie.' he smirks. Bob is organised, focused. The Haiku Man reasons,

'How will you get a

Dead body into the car

Without being seen?

'There's CCTV

Out back down the alleyway,

Can't go out the front.'

Bob's rubbing his forehead, gets to his feet knocking the table, my still full coffee mug splashing.

'I don't fucking know! I'm trying my best here, so if anyone else has a fucking brainwave about what to do, I'm all ears! Anyone. Anyone? No? Didn't fucking think so. It's almost eleven o'clock, we're opening in a few hours, we need to sort this shit out now. Pete, fucking go, get some money from the safe and go.'

'Uh, I have some money.' I offer, I figure it's the least I can do, maybe soften Bob a bit.

'Oh yeah? Well, fucking hand it over then, it's the least you can do.'

'How much?'

'How much you got?' I realise then that it's no longer in my pocket or my shoe.

'It's upstairs,' the tears start again, 'In my bag. I, I can't go back up on my own.'

'Oh for fuck's sake, Joe, go and get it, don't be such a fucking pussy.' rolling his eyes.

I slide my chair back, reluctantly stand, and hesitantly make my way towards the bar. I'm shaky still, but a numbness has also befallen me; I don't know why I'm frightened to go upstairs, I don't believe in ghosts. I look back at them, hoping someone will offer me company. They just sit there, glaring at me impatiently. I gulp. I don't have to go back into *that* room, I just need to get to my bag. At the bottom of the stairs I pause and listen. I don't know what for, but there's silence, so I go up, and at the top I bolt to my room, grab the money bag and stuff it in my hoodie pocket, rushing back down as quickly as I can. I could feel the presence of death up there, heavy and warm. My heart thumping I stop at the bottom, and before I go back into the bar I pull out my money and count out a hundred. More than enough. I stuff the rest back into my pocket. I can still hear my heartbeat as I push through the door, and Bob is there, the other side of the bar, hand outstretched.

I hand over the notes and he says, 'Jesus Christ, Joe, nice one!' gives it to Pete.

'I'll be off then.' says Pete, spinning car keys on his finger. I didn't know he had a car.

'Hurry the fuck up, time's getting on.' says Bob, and Pete's out the door.

Bob turns to me and says, 'Well boy, you better hold yourself together today, we got a lot of shit to do. First we'll go and wrap him up. No need to wait for Pete, we've got enough bags to make a start.' I take some deep breaths, try to regulate my pulse. The Haiku Man is still sitting at the table, he's topped up his glass again.

'I can't believe this,
I'm not helping you out but
I'll keep my mouth shut.
'Does anyone know
Who he is or where he's from?
It's a shit idea.
'The cops will be told
Straight after the train hits him,
Might trace him back here,
'And we won't even
Have time to clear his room out.
Christ, think about it!'
Bob snaps, 'Give it a fucking rest. And never bring anyone here again. Ever.' To me he says, 'Come on, upstairs, there's some bags

up there already. We need to check if he's got ID and get rid of it,' I'm reluctant. 'Well come on then, Joe, I'm right behind you. Get up there!'

I push open the door and walk. Bob's behind me as promised. At the landing I stop, and taking a deep breath I muster up the courage to say, 'I can't go back in there Bob, sorry, I can't do it, I can't see it.'

He responds by shoving me against the wall. Pure ferocity oozing from him, and my cheeks still wet, I'm taken aback. So much violence in these last few days.

'You WILL help. We will help you. You understand me? There's no fucking getting out of this, boy, this is your fault. I wasn't joking when I said I'll kill you, I swear it! You have to do this.' I am pinned, terrified. He's desperate. Cooling off slightly, 'Come on.'

I let him go first. His distaste is palpable, it stinks in here, and I want to shut my eyes and I want to be sick again. I'm retching, bile burns my throat. I breathe through my mouth, look towards the blood spattered ceiling, using Bob as a shield against what lies on the floor.

'Oh fuck, look at all that fucking blood! You got a towel? Get a fucking towel, shit.' Any excuse to not be here, I back out, to my room, my only towel still hangs by the window. It makes me think of home. I take it back and hold it out to Bob from the doorway. He grabs it, crouches to the floor, I don't look. He says to me over his shoulder, 'Check his pockets, has he got a jacket? Find his wallet.' I look around, for a coat or bag or something. I can't check his pockets, but my peripheral vision suggests Bob's doing that, and he comes up trumps, 'Got it, his wallet.' Relieved, I stay where I am. Bob stands, opens the wallet. A British army identity card sits in a clear sleeve inside, I see it, his photograph, his head intact. I'm not close enough to read his name. Bob pulls it out, along with a driver's licence and a bank card. 'We'll burn these. Actually we'll burn the whole thing. Fuck, we need gloves, we can't be touching shit in here!'

I bring myself to quickly glance down, and oh my God, the blood. Bob has lifted dead guy's head and dropped my towel onto the pool beneath it. Bob's hands are stained red and he's standing in the dampness of my piss. He pulls out two twenties from the wallet, stuffs them into his pocket along with the cards and hands it emptied to me, 'Put that in the bag with your clothes.' I do. There's nothing left in it save a few coins. I see my jacket inside the bag. I love that jacket, it cost a lot of Grandpa's money and it is my identity. I'm devastated about getting rid of it but I have no choice; it is tainted with blood and corruption. Bob pushes past me, to the toilet. I hear him running the tap. My phone in my jeans pocket starts to ring. I pull it out; Kitten, I already knew because no one else has my number. Only Grandpa. No one else ever asked for it. Bob sticks his head out the door, 'Don't answer it! Who is it?'

'Kitten,' I say, 'I told her I'd be straight back. She said I could stay with her, I came back here for my bag.' I'm holding the phone aloft, looking at Bob pleading.

'Don't answer it! And if you think you're going anywhere, you're having a fucking laugh! You stay here until this has all blown over, you hear me?' The phone stops. I'm not going to argue. But I can't possibly stay here ever again. Bob goes back, turns the tap off, and with clean hands steps back onto the landing. A text message comes through. I read it;

*Where r u? Call me! Had to go to work but I've left a key under the mat 4 u x*

My heart lifts momentarily, that x at the end. I know text kisses don't mean shit but whatever. The feeling is fleeting because, well, everything, this mess.

'Don't reply. More important shit going on.'

'She might worry if I don't.'

'No.'

'I could just text, say I'll see her later?'

'NO!'

Defeated I sigh, 'OK.' I slip the phone back into my pocket. I need to charge it but now doesn't seem like the right time.

'Look, we can't do anything until Pete gets back, we need gloves, I don't know shit about DNA and that, but we can't risk it. I don't know, what do you reckon? I want to bag that fucker up, quickly.'

'I'm scared, Bob. I can't look at him.'

'Scared of what? You think *I* want to look at him? You think *I* want to see this shit? No one fucking does. Come on, it can't wait, let's bag him.' He goes into the room, and I hear him breaking a bag off the roll. 'Come on then, fucking help me.' he shouts. Taking a deep breath I shuffle in, my eyes on Bob, nothing else. He opens up the bag, shaking air into it, and then crouching he pulls the open end over the guy's head, 'Help me Joe, lift him up a bit. For fuck's sake, why am I doing this? You should be doing this, come on!'

I'm going to start crying again, but I move forward. I think about running, downstairs and out onto the street, running for as long as I can and calling the police. I don't. Instead, avoiding the blood and everything else I attempt to crouch, my eyes screwed almost closed, and I try to help him pull the bag down over his shoulders. This dead guy is not a big man, but the bags are designed to line bins not bodies. It's catching on the furthest shoulder, and I'm not very strong and he's heavy.

'Right, on three, lift as much as you can and I'll pull the bag down. Actually, no, I'll lift, move out the way, you pull the bag down.' Thanks, Bob. Thanks, God. I shuffle myself over, making room beside me. Bob moves around, and '1,2,3…' he lifts his chest and I pull the bag over his shoulders. Bob drops him down, onto the bloody towel.

'Right, good. Feet and legs next, then we'll worry about the middle. Bob reaches over, grabs the roll of bags and rips one off, hands it to me. 'Go on, bag his legs.'

I do it, his legs are like lead weights, but I slip the sack over his boots and lifting each leg one at a time, manage to pull it up as far as it goes. The bag only reaches his thighs. I'm squirming the whole time.

We stop, it's exhausting. Bob says, 'Well, it's a start,' Another text message. I can't retrieve my phone without standing up. 'Don't fucking think about it!' and I don't. He stands up, I follow. 'We need tape, we're just going to have to wait. Let's go downstairs, but open that window first, it fucking stinks in here.' I step over the mess and reach over the table, push the window open, and Bob's already gone, so I run out after him, not wanting to be left alone. I pretty much fall down the stairs behind him.

The Haiku Man is still in the bar, still drinking. Bob's not saying anything, ignoring me while he wipes down the bar like there's not a bleeding corpse upstairs. I pull my phone out of my pocket, read the text.

*Everything OK? You at my place?*

No kiss this time. Bob goes out back, and I quickly reply,

*No, sorry, something came up, see u later x*

Bob's back, stocking up the fridges. I sit at the table opposite the Haiku Man, my cold coffee still there. He looks me in the eye, concerned and disturbed.

'Let me tell you boy,

Life will never be the same.

I'm sorry for you.

'So young, with promise,

ruined in a split second.

I wish you the best.'

He raises his glass, takes a big swig, slams down the empty glass. I want to defend myself, and I protest,

'I didn't do anything wrong, it was an accident, I swear. I'd never hurt anyone on purpose.'

'Well, what's done is done,

You cannot let Bob and Pete

Pay for your mistake.'

Bob acknowledges my existence again. He says, 'Come on, Joe, I got an idea. It's shit, but it's an idea. Upstairs.' I follow Bob upstairs, what choice do I have? He opens the door to his room, and I'm shocked because it's nice in here, spacious, neat. He has everything, widescreen TV on the wall, leather sofa, artwork. The big sash windows make it seem like some New York loft, it's pretty sophisticated which surprises me; I don't know what I expected but it wasn't this.

'Right, this rug. I fucking like this rug. But we have to get that body into the car. I can't think of anything else, other than rolling him up in it. We can't take him out in black bags, it'll be fucking obvious right?'

The rug is a huge patterned Persian type, it looks expensive, laid under the sofa, a coffee table and two mismatched chairs.

'Yeah, I guess,' I think carrying him out in a rolled up carpet is just as obvious to be honest, but I don't want to piss Bob off anymore. But without me displaying any doubt, Bob has a change of heart.

'Ah shit, we'll have to burn the rug too. Forget it, we're not using it, it's full of my DNA and everything. Can't chance it.'

He sucks air through his teeth, clearly at a loss. Should I say anything? I don't need to. 'I think we're better off sticking with the bags, it's less to get rid of. Just need to make sure we're not seen.' I see tears in his eyes. In his weakened state I can only offer,

'I'm sorry.'

We go back downstairs. I sit at a table while Bob wipes the bar again. I ask about Pete.

'Why is Pete called Mad Pete?' Bob sighs and stops grabs two beers from the fridge and lifts the hatch, comes and sits beside me, beers for us both.

'This beer's coming out of your wages, mind.' he says. And then he tells me the story of Mad Pete.

# The Story Of Mad Pete

'What happened was this, Joe. Sometime back in the 90s, me and Pete were going to a rave  in some rural part of the county. Raves weren't our scene, but drugs and promiscuous girls were, so we were in. Wanted to score some drugs for ourselves obviously, because frankly, the music's shit without it. So along with a bagful of E we scored a load of weed and acid.'

I always thought raves were mythical. Bob must be really ancient.

'Anyway, LSD is cheap as chips back then, kids buying it with their lunch money. We buy a load, figuring we can sell it at the rave and make a profit. We score a full sheet of tabs.'

I'm lost. Full sheet of tabs? Like a bed sheet? What's a tab? And a bagful of E? I'm picturing a Tesco carrier bag, full of tablets. Hoping for some clarification, I say, 'A bagful of E? You mean ecstasy?' I'm not stupid, I know these things exist.

'Yeah, Joe, a load of pills.' OK, a bagful sounds like a lot.

'And a sheet of acid tabs? What do you mean?' Bob laughs, heartily, I'm embarrassed.

'Where are you even from kid? You serious? Acid tabs, you know, perforated blotting paper, soaked in LSD? You break a square off, slip it under your tongue? Cartoon elephants on them or something. All the rage back in the day.'

'Oh, right.' Nodding. Nope. Elephants?

'Yeah, a full sheet of tabs is usually a hundred tabs. We're selling for £3 a hit, and we paid a hell of a lot less than that. Whatever Joe, just know it was a shitload.'

I try to look like I understand. Bob asks, 'You know what else makes a profit at raves?' No. I shake my head. 'Water.' he says, 'Alcohol is not a great bedfellow for ecstasy Joe, it makes you dehydrate, so water is key because otherwise you risk getting really ill or an OD or something. That shit kills people. We'd bought ten cases of bottled water, each bottle working out to cost 20p. The intention was to sell them for £1 a go. Not big money, we were only kids, and it's a free night out and we may as well make some cash right? And we had the drugs to sell. We were onto a nice little earner, looking forward to our night.'

Well, entrepreneurial if nothing else.

'So, we're on our way, only a vague idea of the route. And I reckon we're like ten minutes away when a cop car starts tailing us. I'm driving, I make some joke about smelling bacon, but Pete's getting nervous, totally paranoid because we've just shared a joint. I toddle along this country lane trying to look normal and law abiding, but to no avail, because the coppers flip their blue light switch and sound the siren. We're both like fuck, fuck, fuck, we've got a load of drugs and a bong rolling around the back!' This sounds terrifying. Bob continues, 'I say to Pete, "Let's hold it together bro,

I'm gonna have to pull over." The car's insured and taxed, totally legit, a present from the old man after passing my test. The drugs are the only issue we've got. I don't know what to do at this point, Joe, I'm shitting myself, Pete's spazzing out, "Shall I lob the drugs? What the fuck do I do, Bob?!" Looking to me for guidance. He's already wound the window down, baggy full of pills ready to drop into oblivion. I tell him, "No, don't throw the drugs! I don't know, let me fucking think a minute!" Lay-by coming up, no more time to think; Pete folds the sheet of acid tabs and secures them inside the sweatband he's wearing around his head. Stupid fucking thing, black with smiley faces on, he said it seemed like appropriate rave wear. Made him look like a right twat, Joe, but he didn't give a shit. Anyway, Pete swallows two pills dry from that bag, stuffs the rest in his jeans pocket. He still has the weed too. Says to me, "Fuck it, I'm gonna run!"

I slow the car into the lay-by, and before I stop, Pete has opened the door and jumped out, leaps over a fence and runs, full-pelt through a field full of sheep as fast as he can. I'm left in the car, all fuck bro, go! Run like the wind! I feel proud, Joe!'

He pauses a minute, reminiscing and smiling. Takes a swig. I'm rooting for Bob and Pete now. Fuck the Police.

'What happened next?'

'The cop car behind me; one of the pigs makes chase on Pete, but Pete's a wiry fucker, youth on his side, he's got a good head start; the copper behind him is a chunk and no spring chicken. The other one, straight to my window, giving me shit. Pete runs as if his life depends on it. His cardiovascular system clearly supreme in comparison to the aging copper, because he glances back and sees him red and huffing on his knees, collapsed in sheep droppings. I see it too, suppress my mirth. Pete's on a high, leaping across the farmland, giggling. I watch him from the roadside, willing him on, laughing internally while the other cop is checking my pockets, but I've got nothing, and am civility incarnate. "Yes, sir, no, sir. No I don't know him, just giving him a lift, seems like a right nut-job if you ask me." Pete's still going strong, he's legendary. He can see some kind of fallen down barn up ahead and figures he'll drop the drugs there, hide for a bit and see what prevails. He reaches the old barn and drops behind a wall, his lungs bursting. The cop gives up.

'Meanwhile, the car gets searched, but there's nothing except for an empty bong and cases of water. I end up with a request to produce my documentation at the station within seven days.'

Fucking hell.

'The cops wait until I get on my way. I drive around a while, thinking I'll go back to the lay-by soon, wait for Pete to come back. And Pete waited against that barn wall for a while, but it's beginning to get dark. He can hear the low thump of bass drifting through the air. Irresistible! He makes his way through the fields, following the noise, forgets about me, and miles later he makes it to the rave. He's feeling pretty fucking crazy, the pills have kicked in. I drive around for hours. Fucking twat!

'Anyway, The rave is mental apparently, white gloves, bomber jackets, glow sticks and girls in bikinis. He's completely alone, but welcomed. Everyone's friendly, he goes with the flow, ends up having a good night. He's dabbing amphetamine like sherbert from some guy he's hanging out with, all safe, bro, fucking safe! He takes another pill.

'Of course, I wasn't there, it's just what he told me. And he's long ago forgotten the sheet of acid he's got stashed in his headband; unaware that he's been absorbing LSD through his skin for the last five hours. He's dishing out the pills, got some girl hanging off his arm. He's feeling a complete and utter love for his fellow man, he's jittering and chewing his cheeks and his limbs are completely out of control. The night continues, pure bliss.

'That's the best thing; there's no hostility at raves, with ecstasy. It makes you able to talk to anyone, strangers. You're not shy, or tongue-tied. You're suddenly sociable, you develop an eloquence with no awkward silences or not knowing the right thing to say. The words pour right off your tongue!'

Well, get me some of that shit.

'What happened, after that?'

'He lost the girl. Across the horizon the faint glow of morning creeps, it quietens, the crowds dispersing, just a few hardcore ravers remain. But Pete's feeling like shit and totally spinning out; the people are not looking human anymore, more like some kind of vampiric alien hybrids, everything's suddenly hostile. Coming down off X is no fun Joe, but that's not all Pete's contending with. Unbeknownst to him, he's now potentially absorbed some hundred tabs of acid through his sweaty forehead. Pete wanders off, he needs space. Passes out. Wakes up, God knows how long later. The music, speakers, lights, generators gone. Sun high in the sky, burning his eyes, and Pete does not feel good. Tears in his eyes, he's dribbling, and he's pissed himself too, miles from anywhere he recognises as familiar.

'Takes him a whole day and night to get back to the bar, he walks in at half six in the morning, filthy, stinking of piss. No word from him in almost thirty-six hours, I'd been lying awake worrying, thinking of reporting him as missing, imagining him beaten and dead in a ditch. I was livid Joe, I'm all like, "Where the *fuck* did you GO? I fucking waited for you!" Old man is furious too, but I'm worse. "Thought you were fucking dead or something!" I'd figured Pete was a big boy, could look after himself, he'd turn up back home later, though he really wasn't and couldn't and didn't.

'Pete still hadn't come down, God knows what happened, no drugs left, no money. He was still wearing that fucking headband though, and after our minor spat, retired to his room and collapsed into bed. I checked on him later, I clocked the headband, Joe, pulled it off his head, and there's a mush of paper stuck to the inside, some of it fused to his forehead; the acid, unrecognisable, all disintegrated. Pissed me right off, what a waste. But that was nothing, because when Pete eventually woke up, his brain was fried. He told me, nothing looks the same as it did before. He was anxious, nervous and shaking, scared to leave his bed. Light was weird, dark was weird, sound was weird, people were weird, even pissing and shitting was weird; there were creatures everywhere he said, spider-like, spiky, sneaky, twitching evil creatures. Vampires, disembodied eyeballs, deformity everywhere he looked for days after. Can you imagine that? A victim in the horror movie of his mind Joe, he couldn't escape it except in sleep, and even then he was fitful and moaning.'

'Wow,' I say, not knowing how else to respond. 'You think it was the acid?'

'I *know* it was the acid. Listen, as far as anyone says, it's pretty much impossible to overdose on acid. And it's been said that it would be impossible to absorb it through the skin. But, I know what I fucking know, Pete came home different. Maybe it was the pills, the speed, or everything at once. But he's never been the same since.'

'He was normal before?'

'He's not a fucking alien, Joe, he's still normal. Define fucking normal!' Bob's defensive, but the whole point of this conversation was to establish why Pete's mental.

'I just mean, everyone's calling him Mad Pete?' Bob sighs, remembers himself,

'Yeah. Headfucked, Joe, take drugs in moderation. He always had the crazy eyes after that, sees stuff no one else sees. Our mates started calling him Mad Pete, it stuck. Lucky our old man left us this place, because fuck knows where Pete would be otherwise.'

We finish our beers in silence, then Bob leaves me alone, wanders into the kitchen. I think I've lived a sheltered life.

# Our Fearless Saviour, Pete

Some time passes, we just hang around not talking. Pete gets back and Bob is full-pelt again,

'Come on Pete, upstairs, what you got?' Bob signals to me, points to the stairs, I don't protest. Pete follows us up, carrier bags in hand, he's smiling as he plods the steps,

'I've got this!'

He's done well; disposable gloves, black bags, gaffer tape, shoe covers, plastic aprons. 'There's a load of bleach in the car, couldn't carry it all in. Parked in the alley right out back. Let's fucking do this!'

Pete's positivity and energy at this moment is notable, I'm genuinely glad he's here, he's the only one of us unfazed and he'll get us through this. He's bouncing, ready for adventure, clearly enjoying a project to focus on and I admire him right now. Pete glances into the room, 'Made a start did you? Let's finish wrapping him.' He actually grins at me. What a psycho.

We put on the shoe covers, gloves and aprons. I unravel the black bags, and Bob and Pete lift the body from either end while I lay a bag underneath his middle, then they lower him and Pete gets the gaffer tape, starts sealing the bags to one another. We (they) decide to double up, do it all over again, this time starting with his middle, and then bagging either end. Tape it all up again. Me and Bob take off our shoe covers, gloves and aprons, put them in the black bag with my clothes and the towel. We don't talk much, it's just mechanical; we (they) know what to do and do it quickly and efficiently. Bob puts fresh gloves on but doesn't hand me any. We go downstairs, out back to the alleyway, where there's a battered old black Ford Focus parked right outside the door. Bob pops the boot. It's not very big, and I doubt the body will easily fit, not without some manipulation anyway and I'm not fucking doing that. The fresh air is cleansing. I feel like I've barely breathed the last hour or so, I'm taking in huge gulps of oxygen now. As expected, there's six large bottles of bleach and a can of petrol. Bob moves the fuel to behind the driver's seat while I take the bleach into the kitchen. Back outside Bob unravels more black bags and we line the boot, covering every part of the interior that we can. Assessing our work, Bob says to me,

'There's no cameras pointing at us here, except for mine, and it don't work anyway. Tell the Haiku Man he'll have to come out and be lookout, while we get him down here.'

I walk back into the bar. The vodka is finished and the Haiku Man has still not, as far as I can tell, moved a muscle. He looks reflective and surprisingly sober, acknowledges my presence with a nod. I say,

'Bob's saying you need to be our lookout for when we bring him down, make sure there's no one around. The car's out back.' He replies,

'Why should I help you?

This is your fucking shit storm,

You should sort it out!'

Bob comes through the door, 'Get out there, Haiku Man, we'll be down in a couple of minutes.'

The Haiku Man, reluctant, huffing and puffing, gets to his feet. How can he even walk after all that vodka? I follow Bob upstairs and ask,

'What do I do now? Am I coming with you?'

'Of course you're coming with us.'

I look at the time on my phone, it's almost half past one, the bar opens at four.

'Will we be back by opening time?'

'I fucking hope so, boy,' Then, 'Aw, for fucks sake, phone Kitten and tell her to be here to open up, just in case. Tell her we're sorting something out and might not be back in time. DO NOT FUCKING TELL HER WHAT WE'RE DOING!'

I still have my phone in my hand, and when I get to the landing, I get her number on the screen. I'm no good at talking on the phone. It makes me feel uncomfortable, I don't know how to act, what to say. Can't Bob call her?

'Shall I just text? She's in work.' I'd be more comfortable with that.

'No, fucking ring her, make sure she'll be here.' He turns his attention to Pete, 'I told you to fucking leave that gun alone! Christ, don't go killing yourself, put it down!'

'Shall we keep it?'

'No, definitely not, it's the murder weapon you knobhead. We'll get rid of it. Point it the fuck away from you and me, see if you can empty it, or put the safety on it, whatever. Fuck it, I'll have a look. Put it down, Pete, carefully!' I can't see Pete, but Bob is standing in the doorway and has his hands up in submission, and I know Pete's waving the gun around like a nutter. He must put it down because Bob drops his arms and turns to me, 'Ring her then! Time's getting on.'

Murder weapon? I did not murder him, it was an accident. I press call on my phone, I feel nervous but really this should be the least of my worries. It rings a few times before she answers,

'What's up, Joe? Thought you were dead or something. Everything OK?'

'Yeah, hi, everything's fine.'

'Well you didn't come back so, I had to go.'

'Yeah sorry, something came up. I'm helping Bob and Pete out with some stuff and we have to go somewhere. We might not be here for when the bar opens. Bob wants to know if you can be here, just in case we're not back?'

'Yeah, I'll try, where you going?'

'It's not important, just be here to open, yeah?' I try to sound as nonchalant and relaxed as I can. I think I'm doing alright and it's not difficult speaking to her, she makes it easy for me.

'Right, yeah. You sure everything's OK? What are you guys doing?'

'Everything's fine, see you later?'

'This is weird, Joe, but OK. See you later.'

'Cool.' I hang up. 'Kitten'll be here,' I tell Bob.

'Good. Right, take that bag down to the car and come back, we're going to bring him down.' Oh fuck. I take my bag of clothes down, out to the car, throw it on the back seat. The Haiku Man is standing in the alley, waiting.

'Hurry up will you?

Haven't got all day you know,

Other shit to do!'

I go back in, upstairs. Bob and Pete are both in his room, I don't want to go in, it's a mess in there despite the body being all neatly wrapped, there's a shitload of blood and human debris left behind. It smells.

'Haiku Man's waiting.' I shout.

'OK, come get this.'

I venture to the doorway, and Bob hands me the gun, it's wrapped in a shoe cover.

'Point it at the fucking floor OK? Don't go anywhere near the trigger. Take it down, put it in the boot. Then come back and hold the doors for us.' Pete's in there grinning in his plastic apron and bloodied gloves. It's fucked up, I wonder if he feels anything.

I'm nervous but I take the gun, vigilantly aware of the barrel and the trigger. I'd rather carry this than the body. I nod at Bob, take it out to the car. The boot's shut, but I open it with my free hand and gently place it down to one side. I don't think I breathed the whole time, because as soon as my hands are empty I gulp for air, lungs screaming. I leave the boot open and go back in. Bob and Pete are at the top of the stairs waiting,

'Hold the door, Joe, we're coming through!'

I hold open the door at the bottom of the stairs, feeling grateful. They lumber down, Bob first, Pete behind. As they get through the doorway I spring ahead, pushing open the door to the kitchen, and as they struggle through I run and open the door into the alley. 'Check there's no one there,' Bob grunts.

'We clear?' I shout to the Haiku Man. He gives a thumbs up, and I wave them through. Bob's face is red, the dead weight taking its toll on him. Pete looks fine. They're outside, and Bob drops the soldier head first into the boot. Pete hangs onto the legs, unsure how to fit them in.

'Jesus, trust me to take the heavy end. How the fuck we going to fit him in there?' Bob's leaning against the back of the car, breathing heavily, looking anxious, 'We need to do this quickly. Fuck!' Pete's trying to shove the body in, and surprisingly, he manages to bend the legs, the black bag stretching and tearing slightly, but with brute force, he crams him in.

'He's not too stiff!' exclaims Pete, 'Easier than I thought.' He chuckles. I feel sick. They remove their gloves, chuck them in with the body.

'Close the boot,' says Bob. And Pete does, he tries, but the dead guy's knees are too high. Pete perseveres until the lock catches. 'Get back in there, Joe, make sure his room is shut tight. Bring the gloves. We'll deal with it when we get back.'

I do it, I go in and I run up those stairs, and quickly, not looking, grab the box of gloves and shut the door to his room. His key's still in the door, so I bring it with me. Back to the car. Bob and Pete are already sitting up front, so I climb in the back. Bob's driving. He starts the engine and through his open window says to the Haiku Man, 'Stay here? Wait for Kitten? For us? Don't say shit to anyone!' Haiku Man accepts with a bow of his head, and Bob reverses out the alley and onto the road. We're doing this.

**Joe's so brave.**

We drive at least forty-five minutes, through the city, through suburbia and into the countryside. No one says much except for

Pete who fiddles with the CD player, but when Bob says no to music, Pete just cheerfully hums to himself like a weirdo. Eventually we get to a layby in the middle of nowhere, and Bob pulls in and stills the engine. Sighing, he says,

'There's tracks just over there. It's Saturday, the trains are regular. Shall we do this now?' He looks from Pete to me for approval.

'Yeah, come on, let's get this over with. Reckon if we put his head right on the rail, they'll never know about the gunshot.' This is Pete's contribution. He hands out the gloves.

Shaking his head, Bob opens his door, 'Come on, let's not fuck about.' We all get out. Pete's opening the boot, saying rationally,

'Shit, we can't leave these bags on him, should've brought scissors!'

'Fuck it, let's get him out,' says Bob, 'Beside the tracks, and then we'll get the bags off. Joe, fucking keep an eye out for trains. Trains, cars, people, sheep, cows, everything. Seriously!'

Indebted, I oblige. They act quickly, running from the boot to the side of the tracks, dropping the body, and Pete tears at the bags, ripping them apart. Bob interrupts, 'Careful, we don't want to leave anything behind,' and then he's helping, peeling the bags away. I stand guard, until Bob shouts, 'Joe, put these bags in the boot.' I fetch the ripped bags, I'm looking around, checking for signs of anyone and anything. I'm worried a train is going to come before we can do this and the driver will see us, dead body at our feet, cops will come. I will rot in jail.

Bob and Pete drag the body onto the tracks. Pete takes the time to position the head onto the rail. He pulls the legs across the other one. I'm already back at the car.

Bob cries, 'Let's go! Pete!' We're all in, breakneck speed, Bob does a U-turn and we drive. I have my fingers crossed; please let this work, let this be over, please God. But we still have the gun, the bloodied bags, my clothes, his wallet and ID. I see a train on the horizon, we all see it, and I turn away and try to think of something else, forget it. But the thought of a mangled head, legs sliced at the calves, the ghost of a wronged corpse lingering in the backseat next to me is too strong to deny.

Bob declares, 'This was a shitty idea. That's it, the cops already fucking know, and we're nowhere near fucking done! Fuck!' He punches the steering wheel three times, losing control of the car momentarily, but he keeps us alive, regains composure. 'Where the fuck are we going to burn this stuff? Fuck shit fuck, we need to get home. We need to get off this road.'

'Relax bro, we'll be fine, just put your foot down. Worst is over.' Pete offers this comfort, but neither Bob or myself are convinced. I'm waiting for the sirens to come whizzing over the hill. Bob's driving too fast, desperate to get back to civilisation. I check my phone, it's almost three o'clock.

'Seriously Pete, how are we going to get rid of this stuff? Where? I'm fucking done, I don't have a clue, I'm tired. Joe?' I see his eyes in the rear view mirror, cold and desperate, 'You're a fucking arsehole, you fucking twat, this is all your fucking fault and you will take the fall for this, you hear me?!' Before I can say anything, not that I would, Pete interjects with delicacy,

'Stay calm, Bob, I'll sort this, I promise. We'll do this.' He's confident in his declaration and I want so much to believe him. This is not over, not by a long shot.

# Cardiac Arrest Potentially:
## Losing The Gun

Unscathed, we reach The City. We still have the incriminating luggage but we're relieved to be back amongst the faceless Saturday traffic. Bob says there is no way we're taking the gun back with us. We'll have to stop somewhere and dump it, preferably in the river. All the big bridges have cameras fixed on them, so we'll go to a walkway alongside the water, and he says I'll have to take it, throw it in discreetly, make sure I'm far away from the car and make sure no one's looking; Check the buildings and lampposts for cameras, be careful. I grudgingly nod.

Bob finds a side street consisting of tiny yet expensive apartment buildings that lead down to the riverside promenade. He parks the car, turns back to me, fixes me with that intense stare, and tells me,

'You fucking dare make a run for it and I'll beat the living shit out of you. Pete's going to tail you on foot. Come back quickly as you can, keep your head down. Leave your phone here. Go on, boy.'

Nervously I pull my phone out of my pocket, leave it on the seat and slide myself out the car. Head down I walk around to the boot, pull the lever and without opening it fully, reach my hand inside, pick up the gun in the shoe cover, and slip it into my hoodie pocket. I start walking, and Pete hangs out the window, top of his voice starts singing,

*'Hey Joe, where you goin' with that gun in your hand?'*

Oh my fucking God. Looking back, I give him the most desperate of eyes in the hope of silencing him, I see him creased with laughter while Bob is punching him and dragging him back into the car. Fuck! I keep my hands inside, holding the barrel away from me, forward at the floor. I'm terrified. My breathing's shallow, my heart walloping against my chest on the verge of a heart attack. I walk towards the river, and the promenade is busy, cyclists, couples strolling hand in hand, kids on scooters. I walk a while, stopping to lean against the railings; I gaze over the water, subtly looking side to side, looking up for cameras. I don't see any. There are people on balconies above me, drinking wine, tapping on phones, laptops. It's a beautiful afternoon and I wish it would rain and everyone would piss off inside. I clock Pete way up the promenade, we lock eyes and he gives me an encouraging nod. I can't do it, not now, too many people. The water is deep and murky and I reckon if I can throw it in there it'll never be seen again. I'll have to propel it a bit so it doesn't just land on the muddy bank. I have one hand on the gun, ready for when the opportunity presents itself. Too busy. I'm so nervous, and I glance again at Pete who is looking impatient. Even at this distance I swear I can see him roll his eyes, curse under his breath. I turn back to the water. Next thing, I hear Pete, at the top of his lungs,

'MOTHERFUCKER!' I'm startled, I look at him. He's standing in the middle of the path, 'FUCKING GET THE FUCK AWAY YOU FUCKING WANKERS!' I realise he's trying to create a distraction and it's working because everyone's eyes are on him, no one knows what to think. The cyclists have halted, the couples turn and walk the other way. 'YOU'RE ALL FUCKING CUNTS!' The kids on scooters stop and stare.

Now, do it now. Taking a quick look around I gently pull the gun from my pocket, and meanwhile, Pete is along the way, pulling off his T Shirt.

'WHY ARE YOU RUNNING AWAY YOU SHITS? COME AND HAVE A GO IF YOU THINK YOU'RE HARD ENOUGH. COME ON! FUCKING BRING IT COCKSUCKERS!'

I do it, through the railings I project it as best I can, watch it hit the water and sink. The splash is bigger than I'd have liked, but I don't think anyone sees me. I start walking away instantly, towards Pete until I take a right and head back towards the car. Pete calms down, knows it's done, laughing at the fear and confusion he's caused. I don't look back. I see Bob sitting at the wheel, looking concerned. I guess he can hear Pete from where he's parked. I climb into the back shaking all over.

'What the fuck's going on?' Bob questions me, and then Pete's in view, strolling up the street as he's pulling his T shirt back over his head, that crazy fucking grin plastered on his face. He jumps in beside Bob.

'Let's go, job done.' Bob doesn't hesitate, we are out of there.

'What the actual fuck?' says Bob as we pull out onto the main street. Pete laughs,

'All good. Needed a distraction technique, it's busy down there.'

'For fucks sake Pete, what you drawing attention to yourself for? We were supposed to be unnoticed, subtle. You fucking tool!'

'It's fine, all done, right, Joe?'

'Yeah,' I feign a smile to match Pete's. We still have a shitload of evidence to get rid of, it's definitely not all done. It's a relief to be rid of the gun though, and the body, obviously.

Spitting livid, Bob says, 'Have you forgotten about the fucking state of his room back home? The blood-covered clothes, the bags in the back? I've got his fucking ID in my pocket!'

'Alright, alright, calm down. Stop by B&Q, we'll pick up one of them burner bins.'

'You want to get an incinerator bin? Where the fuck you going to do the burning? On our fucking doorstep? Are you fucking real?'

Bob is undoubtedly a true vulgarian. His sustained use of profanity has so far, despite popular concept, never made me doubt his intelligence. I know swearing can be construed as a sign of a lack of vocabulary, but I don't think this is the case. Grandpa didn't think so. This guy runs a bar. Bars are probably the most sweary of places to work, with the exception of oil rigs. I like how he swears, not at me obviously, that's just scary. But it sits well with his personality. No airs or graces, Bob is Bob, coarse and honest. Its use is always effective in delivering whatever emotion he is expressing, be it humour or anger, defeat or incredulity. His cursing just adds weight to every statement he makes. Even though Bob has threatened to kill me more than once today, I still like him, I can't help it.

I have to agree with him on this, burning evidence in a bin out the back of the bar seems like a bad idea, too blatant. Pete comes around,

'Alright, Christ, Bob. Never mind. You go back to the bar and me and Joe will go somewhere quiet and do it. No bin. Find a field somewhere.'

'What about all the shit in his room? Remember his brain is painted all over the fucking ceiling? The blood all over the floor? I want it gone, now. Joe can stay and clean up, you can take it. Seriously Pete, I'm trusting you with this, you need to do a good job. Those clothes, those cards, everything needs to be incinerated to ash, you get me?'

'Yes, I get you.'

'Don't forget all the bags in the boot. It's likely we're going to have to burn more stuff later, but Joe can sort it, he'll bag whatever we need to get rid of. Right, Joe? You listening?' That stare in the rearview mirror again. I'm listening and scared shitless. I nod nonetheless. Bob thinks he's done me a huge favour with this, getting rid of the body, I would've happily told the police. Too late, I'm in deep.

# ﬃalf ﬄ Dozen Bottles ﬀf Bleach

We pull up at the bar and Bob fishes the ID from his pocket, hands it to Pete. We all get out but Pete's not staying, he's off to find an abandoned scrap of land, he'll be back later with an empty car. Might get a full valet afterwards. The place is already open. Bob and me stand in the kitchen, and he says,

'You look a fucking wreck. Take that bleach upstairs, get some washcloths, the Fairy liquid. Under the sink, there's a bucket there too. Pull yourself together. Don't come down, use the sink upstairs.'

I ask, 'How will I reach the ceiling?'

'With a stepladder. I'll get it now, it's in the office.'

I'm going to look conspicuous walking through the bar with a stepladder, a bucket and half a dozen bottles of bleach. Kitten will have questions. Bob, maybe taking pity on me says, 'Come on, I'll help you carry everything up. Grab what you can. Where are the black bags? Did we leave them in the car?' I grab the bucket from under the sink, a pack of washcloths, the washing up liquid. I hook up two bottles of bleach with my other hand. Bob gets the ladder, and I let him lead the way through the door into the bar.

'Can't stop, be down in a minute!' He barks at Kitten before she can open her mouth. I shoot her a half smile, try to look normal. The Haiku Man sits on the other side, looks at me, a million questions conveyed in one glance, but we head straight upstairs, and Bob plonks down the stepladder outside the closed room. I have the key. I hold it out,

'Will you open the door?' I ask.

'What do you think's going to happen, Joe? Fucking zombies or ghosts?' and then, in a loud whisper, 'Did you not see that we got rid of him today?'

'Yeah I know. I'm just spooked. Sorry, I'm scared, and I'm not good with blood.'

'Well tough shit, Joe, I think I've done enough for you. This is the least you can do. You hear me?'

'OK, but open the door for me? Please?' I'm pathetic.

'Right, go get the rest of the bleach. Don't stop to chat, straight back up, yes?'

'Yes.'

I go down, I don't make eye contact with Kitten or the Haiku Man or the customers that are accumulating at the bar. Straight through to the kitchen, straight back up. I hear Kitten as I push through the door to go upstairs,

'Joe? Joe! Are you OK?'

I gallop up those stairs. I'm not OK. I'm aware that she probably thinks I'm being a dick, especially after last night and this morning, but I'm doing what Bob asked because I'm scared he's going to hurt me. I don't believe he will kill me, but I wouldn't be surprised if he gets Pete to give me a pasting if I step out of line. Much to Grandpa's disgust I have an inherent respect for authority figures, even if it is contrary to what I think in my head (Fuck the police! Destroy the system, damn the man!). For some reason, Bob's an authority figure to me now. I'm sure Bob would be disgusted too, by my deficiency of rebellion, my absence of disobedience and lack of punk rock values.

Upstairs, Bob stands inside the doorway assessing my workload.

'Please Joe, help us out, you can do this, it's nothing, just bodily fluids. We all have them.'

I'm close to tears again. He's not even angry anymore, and it's somehow worse. 'Look, when Pete comes back he'll come up and give you a hand. I'm going downstairs, everything needs to look normal. You understand that, yeah?'

I nod, 'OK. I'll try.' A lump in my throat, I'm holding back the waterworks until he goes.

'Good lad,' he pats me on the back. 'I'll pop up in a bit, see how you're getting on. I'm going to close the door OK? Just in case. No one will come up here, but you know, better safe than sorry.'

'I need to get some water first,' I take the bucket to the sink next door, fill it, carry it back, add some washing up liquid, drop in a washcloth. Bob looks satisfied that I'm trying, and with a smile that looks more like a grimace he closes the door gently behind him. Here come the tears, blinding me, my lip quivering. I've cried so much today and it's draining. I feel like I should deal with the half dried pool of blood on the floor first, I start to wipe, but I'm only spreading it around. The water in the bucket is instantly dirty. This will take forever. I wipe, empty the bucket, refill it maybe ten times before the floor starts to look any better. It's not just blood, there are bits too, some hard, maybe fragments of bone, some softer, flesh or brain, and I try not to think about it too much, but when

I empty the bucket in the sink, I notice the bits getting stuck in the plughole. Two teeth. I momentarily consider keeping one, fuck knows why, the same reason Kitten keeps her dead foetus. I pick them out, flush them down the toilet. I surprise myself with my lack of nausea, I'm on autopilot, and I can do this. I'm not crying anymore.

The boards are stained a reddish brown, but hopefully the bleach will fix that. There's piss too, mine and his, comparatively easy to clean. Despite wearing gloves my hands are wrinkled and raw from scrubbing. I'm done with this part of the floor, and I look around, figure out what to do next. The range is incredible. Every surface is spotted with blood. I examine the various apparatus within the room, mostly gathered against the window wall, and recall Pete saying earlier about making bombs. Bottles of peroxide, acetone. Thought they were beauty products, but what do I know? Bags of sugar, salt. firelighters and matches, funnels. Wires, lots of wires, batteries. Most of this is in carrier bags, though there are just as many filled with rubbish, chocolate wrappers and takeaway boxes. Behind a bag of empty beer cans I spot the rucksack, just like mine. I gently tug at the opening, I see clothes, and I know this is one thing we should've dumped a hundred miles from here. It's literally a bag of his DNA. I stand up and scan the room some more, and obscured by so much crap I notice his mobile phone plugged in at the wall. Shit. Again, this has to go, soon. As if Bob could sense my panic, I hear him coming upstairs.

He calls out, 'Joe?'

'Yeah,' I open the door. He looks at the damp floor, seems glad I've made an effort.

'Still a lot to do, look at the ceiling, Christ!'

I point, 'His rucksack is here, and his phone, there.'

'Fuck, get the phone, is it on?'

I reach over the bags, remove the charger. Bob takes it from me between one finger and his thumb, walks out. I follow and he drops it into the sink down the end room, runs the tap.

'It might be waterproof?' I say.

'I don't fucking know, I'm going to try to kill it anyway. Shit!' Fishing it out he smashes it against the edge of the porcelain a couple of times, rips off the back cover, takes out the battery, drops them all back in the water. 'What's in the rucksack?' he asks.

'Don't know, I only glanced inside; clothes? Might be other stuff, I didn't want to rummage too much, there's some weird shit in there. Pete might be right about the bomb thing.'

'You think there's a bomb in his bag??'

'No, but I don't know. I mean probably not. But there's wires and chemicals and other stuff in those carrier bags.'

Bob takes a deep breath, exhales. 'You're doing well, Joe, keep going. Don't touch the bag. We'll deal with it when Pete gets back.'

I go back in, up that ladder and with the bucket precariously balanced at my feet get back to cleaning. It's not as bad as the floor, though it's dried hard and takes some effort. I keep dripping pink blood-tainted water on myself, it runs down my arms and soaks into my clothes, but I'm not getting rid of any more clothes, no way. I'm still pissed off about my jacket. I hear Bob go back downstairs. My phone died a while ago so I have no idea what the time is. I climb down and quietly creep into my own room, dig the charger from my bag and plug my phone in, then I go back to work. I finish the ceiling, start on the splattered walls. The hardest part, other than the gore, is the constant changing of the water, rinsing the cloth, though I'm needing to do it less and less.

Finally I think I'm done. Except for what has hit the bags, which I figure we'll dispose of some other way, the room is wiped clean. The place was filthy dirty in the first place, so if anything I've left random clean patches over the ceiling and walls. Once the room's cleared I'll bleach everything. I'm thinking logically and feel an odd sense of achievement; decide to tackle that stain on the floor. Empty the bucket again, pour in some bleach, dilute it, rinse the cloth. I start wiping. More bleach, and it's clearing.

A little time later I hear Pete chuckling, Bob behind him, on their way upstairs. Pete opens the door.

'Alright, Joe?'

'Yeah, fine,' I actually am.

'Good lad, nice work! Everything's sorted, we'll bag this shit up and dump it around town yeah?'

'Can't just dump it around town, Pete, there's fucking cameras everywhere,' Bob, the voice of reason.

'Where's his phone?' I ask Bob.

'I took a quick walk into town, threw it in a bin, no one saw.'

'Got black bags, let's make a start shall we?' Pete's so enthusiastic, and starts looking through the carrier bags.

'A lot of it's rubbish.' I tell him.

'Yeah, I can see, easy. We'll just bag it and dump it, what about this rucksack? Bob says you're too scared to have a look?'

'Not scared, just cautious. I think it's just his clothes.'

'Let's have a look then!'

Bob warns him, 'Cool head now, Pete, just in case yeah? The wires and shit, chemicals, can't be too careful. Don't blow the place up, don't kill us.' Pete's already dragged the bag into the middle of the floor, pulling out T-shirts, army fatigues, socks, pants.

'It's fine, just threads. Gonna have to burn this shit though.' Me and Bob sigh with relief.

Pete smells of smoke, I wonder where he went today, what he did. Was he careful, meticulous? 'Hang on,' Pete pulls out the guy's dog tags, two little metal discs on a chain, 'There's these...O POS...

Jones?' Pete holds them out to me, 'Nice little souvenir for you Joe? A memento?'

'Don't be a twat, Pete, they need to disappear!' Bob snaps.

'Only fucking joking aren't I? Jesus, lighten up,' He slips them in his pocket.

Bob, shaking his head; 'I need to go back downstairs, it's getting busy. Kitten's suspicious so I'm trusting you both to clear this room. Two piles, one of the easy stuff, the other with anything incriminating. Get on it.'

Pete; 'On it, don't worry.'

Bob; 'I'm fucking worried!'

Bob shuts the door. Pete's already unravelling black bags, hands me one.

'Right kid, come on.'

We fill some bags, then I need to pee, even though I haven't drunk anything all day. I feel ill, I still have a headache and my body aches. I go to the toilet, pretty much piss syrup, and drink around a gallon of water from the tap. Then on my way back I quietly step into my own room, turn my phone on. It's almost half past seven, I have been up here for over three hours. I put my phone in my hoodie pocket, go back to Pete. He hands me the sugar, the salt. 'Pour them down the sink,' I do, then when I return, he hands me the bottles, the peroxide, the bleach; 'And these.'

I worry if I pour them down together they'll cause some chemical reaction, so I take my time, running the tap full blast and slowly pour each bottle away, diluted and safe. Pete's done most of the work. There are two piles, the biggest simply rubbish. The smaller pile contains the rucksack, a box of bullets, the wires and various other weird shit. The bucket of bleach still sits on the floor, so I make a start cleaning spatter I missed earlier that was obscured by the junk. We're almost done. Once we get rid of the bags.

What a fucking day! A terrible day for Joe admittedly, but a great day for The City. Honestly. Unbeknownst to its population, Joe has single handedly prevented what would've been a horrifically violent, devastating event. An event that would've changed the very makeup of the whole country's collective consciousness, would've altered it's politics for the worse (yes, honestly, that's possible!). The death of this one man has prevented the death of 76 human lives; several of which are important to the future of your humanity in turn. 22 children, 28 women, 26 men. Not to mention the countless injured, the limbs lost and the psychological damage (The train driver from earlier needs therapy for life). Now, thanks to Joe, one of those children will grow up to become a visionary world leader. One of those women is unknowingly pregnant with a baby girl who will one day be key in developing an absolute cure for cancer. One of those boys will change the course of history in his work to eliminate poverty and world hunger. Many of those children will grow up to be decent, kind and contributory people. One of them will father the inventor of actual time travel! Yes, for real! No joke! Sons and daughters, lovers and revolutionaries. You had so much to lose in one man's disillusioned and misguided actions, we couldn't allow it to happen. Poor Joe, our pawn, our puppet. He's done good.

That man, soldier Jack Jones, with his sad and twisted ideals, media manipulated, he would've built two bombs. One he would plant at The City's busiest tube station, detonating on a morning when an excited school trip were disembarking on what was for many of them, their first ever train ride. The other, at The City's busiest shopping centre, blowing up just minutes later. The emergency services wouldn't cope, two major incidents in such a short time. Sometimes, perhaps often, you might think you live in a cruel world; terrible things happen every day. But don't forget the kindness, the decency of normal folk, the helpers and the selfless. So much horror and sadness yet so much beauty.  Triumph and goodwill. It's everywhere, always look for it, seek it out.

# Acting Normal

Bob comes up again sometime after eight. We're basically finished. I want to scour this whole room with bleach again, it'll never be enough. A crappy band has started downstairs.

Bob says, 'Good job, well done, really, I mean it, Joe. You up for coming downstairs?'

'I guess. I don't feel too great.' I don't want to go down, I'm fucked, completely knackered, though I daren't challenge his suggestion.

'Yeah, you look like shit. I'll order a pizza. We need to act normal. Pete, you up for getting rid of this junk?'

'Yeah bro, I got this.'

'What you gonna do with it?'

'Dunno. The rubbish is easy, we'll just chuck it in the dumpsters.'

'Not ours!'

'Yeah, alright. The other stuff, I'll burn the rucksack I suppose. Would be nice if it could wait until the morning though, not gonna lie, I'm fucking whacked. The bomb shit, again, I can dump around the place? Looks like nothing on its own, separated.'

'I don't know about the rucksack, I don't want it here. And you know what Pete? Your plants are going to have to go too.'

'What? You serious? I can't just get rid of them, they're not ready, not now!' Pete's alarmed. I think Bob could've waited to drop that on him, but it's not my place to say shit at this point.

'Not tonight, but if we're lucky enough that we get away with today, we need to toe the line from now on. I can't take the stress. I'm so fucking tired, today has nearly killed me. Please Pete, get rid of this stuff tonight. We'll keep you pizza, a cold beer. I'm counting on you.'

'Not the plants though, yeah?'

'Not tonight, no.' Bob looks at least ten years older than he did yesterday.

'Alright, I got this, don't worry, bro.' He reaches out, a reassuring shoulder squeeze for his big brother.

'Thanks Pete, you're a legend. Don't forget the dog tags. Lose them, anywhere but here. Down a drain or something.' Bob's energy is waning. I get it, mine is too.

We all go downstairs, arms laden with black bags, the bucket, the bottles of bleach. We load up the car, and Pete takes off, still motivated and in high spirits. Bob and I sit at the table in the kitchen and he orders pizza through an app on his phone. We don't talk. I have a headache and I'm thirsty but feel awkward about asking for a drink. The bar sounds busy.

Eventually Bob says, 'Well, what a fucking day, eh, Joe? Craziest day I've ever known, and believe me, I've dealt with some fucked up crazy shit in my time. This tops it all though.'

'Yeah.' I say, because it is definitely the craziest and worst day of my life too.

Kitten bursts through the door flustered. She looks at us both, disbelieving and incensed.

'Oh! Having a nice time are you? It's fucking heaving out there, could do with some help, Jesus! For fuck's sake! I'm on my own!' We both look back at her, neither of us know what to say.

Bob shrugs, 'I just ordered pizza.'

'Well, that's fucking wonderful, Bob! Nice one. I'll restock the fridges on my own, you guys just relax, take it easy. We've run out of glasses so I'm using plastic cups, and the band is shit; someone just threw a bottle at the singer and now everyone's joining in…where's Pete?' She's seething, a bit hysterical too. But she takes a moment to inspect us, and she must sense something's off because she thaws a little, asks, 'Is everything OK? Why are you being weird? What's wrong? You both look like shit.'

Bob's got this. 'Everything's fine. We had some stuff to deal with today, nothing to worry about. Pete's out. We'll come and help now. Joe, help Kitten with the bottles, I'll go calm down the crowd.' He shoots me eyes which I translate as *Keep your fucking mouth shut!*

'Yeah, OK.' I'm on my feet, running on empty, I am not up to this but somehow muster the strength, and I give Kitten an archaic smile.

Bob goes into the bar and I go to the store room with Kitten. She looks me up and down.

'You look like hell, Joe, and you stink of vomit. Are you alright?'

'Not really, but I'll be fine. What do we need?' I'm poised over a crate of Budweiser.

'Everything! Fridges are empty. Where've you been today?'

'Nothing much, had some stuff to sort out with Bob and Pete.' I try to change the subject, 'How's the Haiku Man? He drank a lot today.'

'He left hours ago, he always drinks a lot. So what exactly did you have to sort out?'

'Nothing much.' I barge past her carrying two crates, push through the doors into the chaos. The noise and heat is ridiculous. Bob's dragging someone out the front door and no one's manning the bar so I fill the fridge quickly, get to serving. Kitten wasn't kidding, it's heaving, I can't keep up. Kitten's alongside me now, unloading more bottles and cans into the fridges, she shouts up at me,

'You look ill, Joe!' I mishear her initially, hearing the words 'Who'd you kill Joe?' My brain unscrambles my paranoia quickly though, and I nod. Bob's back behind the bar and within five minutes everything is under control. The band stops briefly, and Kitten's on my case again, 'So I guess you're not staying at mine then?'

'I want to,' I say, 'but Bob says he wants me to stay here for a little while.'

'Why?' I shrug, and I'm saved by the pizza delivery guy, who stands intimidated in the doorway.

I swoop out from the bar, go and collect Bob's order, barging my way back through the crowd, realising I'm not frightened by them anymore. Bob sees me, raises the bar hatch for me.

He says to Kitten, 'We haven't eaten, give us ten minutes yeah?'

'Yeah, no worries.' She means it, her face a picture of confusion and concern.

In the kitchen Bob hands me a can of Coke, which I drink in one gulp. Shaking his head he gets me another, and we sit and eat in silence. He ordered two huge pepperoni pizzas and we demolish the first, start on the second, at which point he says while he chews,

'We gotta keep some for Pete.' I'm done anyway, my body shocked at the sudden intake of food and liquid after today's fast. Physically I feel better, less weak. But mentally I'm fucked, my mind replaying over and over the worst of the day: the gun, the piss, the gunshot, the blood, the broken face, the vomit, the stench, the train, the blood, the bleach. I'm desperate for a shower, to scald away the guilt and filth.

I say to Bob, 'I want to bleach that whole room again, but I can't face it tonight. Can I stay at Kitten's?'

Bob's suddenly vocal again, 'No, no way, sorry Joe, no fucking way! Because if the cops turn up here tonight, you're still taking the fall for all this. Because you did it! This is still your responsibility. For some reason that I'm struggling to fathom, we helped you today. Maybe because of last night, the tattoo… maybe because you're wet behind the ears and I feel sorry for you. I don't fucking know. D'you remember what we *did* today? It's not over! You're not out of the woods, boy, nowhere near!'

'It was an accident,' I remind him, 'I didn't actually do anything wrong.' At least, until you made me dispose of a body and destroy evidence and pervert the course of justice. I don't say that part out loud.

'Hmmph. And yeah, agree, that whole room needs scouring. You can do it in the morning, but it's still early and I need you in the bar, at least until Pete gets back.'

'I won't be able to sleep up there.'

'Well, you're gonna.'

I resign myself. I'm not going to sleep, and I decide right then that I will go home to Grandpa's the second Bob sets me free from my prison. I can't do this. I'll go back, get a council flat, a menial job, maybe a girlfriend if I cut my hair and get a car. This is too much, I fucked up this whole adventure. This is not what Grandpa meant and I'm tired and I'm done. What a shitty few days.

It wasn't really shit. Yeah, alright, today was majorly shit. But necessary for the greater good. Honestly! If Joe takes a moment to think about it, he'll realise that it hasn't all been bad; remember all those firsts? The good ones? Bless his cotton socks. He's not going back to Grandpa's, sense and duty will prevail, he will recognise his fruition and will overcome this hurdle. He'll complete his mission.

# Learning About Bob

Just make conversation I ask Bob, 'Why d'you let The Haiku Man hang out here? He looks like a tramp.'

Bob pauses for a moment, looks me in the eyes, all hawk like. He says solemnly,

'If I tell you, you must never tell anyone else. I mean it, you keep quiet.' Yeah, we've been here already.

'OK.' He's scrutinising me. It's scary, he leans in.

'Right. So, mad bastard is my uncle. My dad's little brother. Used to be normal, made bad decisions. Dad left this bar to me and Pete. We let him hang here, give him vodka. He's family.'

Wow. I let that sink in, thinking how to respond.

'Why don't you call him Uncle Tom? He can't have always been The Haiku Man?

'No Joe, once upon a time he was our Uncle Tom. Actually, Tommy Unc. He never used to do the poetry, that's just some weird thing that's developed.' He gets up, grabs us both another Coke, sits back down, 'Let me tell you a story.'

Grateful for the drink and distraction, I'm all ears. I lean forward. Bob leans back.

'Back when I was your age, me and Pete were little shits. No respect for anything. I mean, hardly look like a pillar of civilised society do I? And I'm fine with that, who wants to be?

'I'm seventeen. Dad still alive, my mother not long buried. I was a twat. Stealing cars, robbing shops, burning things, the usual stuff, no reason other than I was bored and thought I was invincible and a rebel you know?'

The usual stuff? I don't disagree, just a half smile.

'People thought I was acting out because my mother died. That's bollocks.

One day, me and Pete, we'd been smoking weed all day, and I'd robbed us a couple of bottles of Mad Dog.' He's chuckling, 'It's lethal Joe, fucks you up, tastes like squash!'

I've no idea what he's talking about. Bob relaxes further into his chair.

'It's a beautiful summer's evening. I say to Pete, "Let's rob a car, go to the coast, find some surfer chicks." Think we'd just watched *Point Break* or something.'

Despite Bob's appearance I had him down as a decent guy, never imagined him stealing cars. Speak as you find, and who am I to judge? I killed someone today.

'Some cars were easier to nick than others. Can't go taking anything too conspicuous, but you want something with a bit of kick. On this occasion it was a silver Peugeot 205; piece of piss to get into. I know drink-driving is bad, but I didn't give a fuck Joe. I'm not that arsehole anymore, OK?'

I'm glad he's not that arsehole anymore.

'Not even two minutes to get that car running. Stoked, we pull off towards the coast. Blasting The Prodigy from the tape deck, windows down, we were the dog's bollocks.

'Sun's shining, girls all in shorts and crop tops. Unfamiliar roads, the beach still a way off, but a tankful of petrol. Almost an hour later, down all these twisty lanes, we make it. The sea on the horizon, sunlight sparkling on the water; it's beautiful, Joe! If I ever retire, that's where I'm headed.

'As presumed, hot surfer chicks everywhere. Yeah, maybe they're into the surfers, but we're there all city boy; we got swagger, an edge, know what I mean? The lads are in the sea anyway, ladies unattended. And we'd kick every one of those rich kid arses. We've got confidence and a ride. Pete's cuter than me, but I've got front and I ain't afraid of girls. We're turning heads Joe, and we zone in on two girls sitting in the sand, giggling, tanned in sandals and bikini tops. We strut up and strike up a conversation. I tell them we're brothers, we spin this yarn about being in a band about to get signed. We weren't even in a band! Just want to take them for a ride, maybe get laid, y'know? Pete and me are a team, we persuade them to get in the car. Say we'll buy them some alcohol 'cos we've obviously lied about our age and they're obviously not old enough.'

I'm not sure I like where this is going. I ask, 'Weren't you worried about the stolen car? About getting caught?' About the statutory rape, I think. Times have really changed.

Bob laughs and says, 'Nah Joe, course not, it was normal to steal cars back then. Anyway, I got this girl up front with me, she's got this beautiful curly blonde hair, freckles, legs for miles, a toe ring, can you picture her? Pete's in the back with the brunette, she's got banging tits but she ain't as pretty as the one next to me. I'm beaming! It's still light and warm, and I'm showing off, zooming down little lanes, acting cool. I don't have a licence. It's fun, we're onto a winner.

'I'm doing maybe 50 or 60 down this country road, and next thing, the girl's rubbing my thigh through my jeans, inching up towards my tackle. I'm excited, distracted. I glance at her and she's grinning at me, and I'm not looking at the road for a couple of seconds. I turn back to check my direction and there's a fucking sheep standing in the middle of the road staring at me! I brake but it's too late, because I smash into that poor fucker, Joe, and I've lost control of the car. The impact is incredible, they're bigger than you realise, sheep!'

Bob's agitated; leaning forward, arms flailing.

'Everything's slow motion. The stupid sheep thrown to the side of the road, car skids to a halt, and I'm the only one wearing a seatbelt. The girl next to me smacks into the windscreen face first. The girl in the back, her head thumps into the seat. Pete's behind me and he's flung into the back of my chair; I feel it, my neck jarred. There's blood on the windscreen, the girl beside me flops back, she smashed the glass! Her nose looks fucked, it's pissing red, dripping down her tits. Her eyes are closed. I'm like, FUCK! I think they're all dead! I'm unscathed and I'm conscious, Voodoo People still blasting on the tape deck, my semi long gone, but all I care about is Pete. He's taken a knock to the head. I'm shouting, "Pete? Pete! You alright?"

'Hesitant he answers, "Yeah." Almost laughing, the way Pete does in ridiculous situations. He's OK! I don't give a fuck about the girls anymore, they're alive, that's enough for me. The one in the back moans and her arm is twisted wrong. I say, "Pete! Get out the car!" and somehow he does. The car's fucked, the sheep's fucked.

Me and Pete are fucked if we get caught. I'm out, he's out, my door won't close. I feel bad about the sheep.

"Come on," I say to Pete, "Let's fucking go."

"The girls?" he says, but he's obliging and steps up beside me. I feel shit but I gotta think of me and Pete. We're off, zigzagging because we took a knock and we've had a drink and I think we'll never get away. We keep walking, far, far away as quickly as possible.

'We look like zombies, Voodoo People still playing in my head. Pete's puking, shaking from shock and maybe the alcohol, his eyes swollen from smacking into the back of me. It looks like he's been stung by bees! His nose is bleeding, clearly broken, but he follows me. Walking through fields, we don't want to risk being seen. We hear the sirens. No mobile phones then. We eventually come to some village and there's a phone box. I don't want to ring my old man but I've no choice.

'So I ring home, and by some lucky twist of fate, Tommy Unc answers. He was *never* around, Joe, but on the rare occasions he did turn up he'd make himself right at home, answering the phone like he owned the place.'

Oh, Tommy Unc, I'd almost forgotten.

'Because he's not dad, and I'm suddenly grateful to be speaking to an actual adult, I tell him we're in trouble. Help! We're in the middle of nowhere, only wanted to go to the beach. Pete's in a bad way. Come pick us up? Please?

'Tommy Unc hears how frantic I am, he doesn't ask questions, says stay where we are. He's there within an hour. We dive into his car and he drives us out of there. He asks, "What happened to your face, Pete?' I answer for him, he got in a fight. Pete's spaced, probably concussion. Tommy Unc asks if we want to go to the hospital. No fucking way, just take us home. We get back here, and he comes in first, distracts my dad. Gets him out the back into the office, and me and Pete sneak upstairs, get cleaned up.'

Bob stops talking. He's tapping his fingers on the table, some rhythmic pattern that indicates stress. A long pause while he calms his breathing.

I ask, 'What then?'

'Nothing! Got away with it. I worried for weeks that the cops would catch up with us. Can't hear The Prodigy without getting flashbacks.'

He stops tapping the table, 'Ah the nineties. Golden times.'

'Were the girls OK?' I'm concerned. It's a bit of dick move to leave two girls bleeding and unconscious in a car while you flee the law and the consequences.

'Fuck knows, felt bad, reckon that pretty one got her face fucked up. Don't think they died or anything.' He shrugs, 'The sheep was a goner though, no doubt.

'Pete wasn't the same after that. I know I said this before, and he always was a scatty bastard but he definitely wasn't right after that knock, had that vacant gaze ever since.'

I'm reassured that the vacant gaze isn't reserved specifically for me. Along with the acid story, it's a wonder Pete's allowed out in the community unsupervised.

'Rarely saw Haiku Man when we were kids. Occasionally he'd turn up merrily drunk, slip me and Pete some cash, regaling us with tales of pseudo success. Always been a drifter. But now, Joe, round here, this City, he's legendary! The Haiku man!' Bob rests his elbows on the table, leans over, 'You and I know he's a stinking pisshead, but he lives the way he wants to. I trust him. Likes to believe he's helping people with his weird poems and shit. People around here like it. I didn't even know what a haiku was Joe, I don't remember when I learned. Whatever. Sometimes it's perfection!

Most of the time it's bollocks, and I reckon he's just counting the syllables in his head, seeing what fits,' He pauses to laugh. 'Not too bad for business though. Some reckon he lived in Japan, trained to be a ninja. Bollocks obviously. Or they think he was a member of the Yakuza, that he has all this Japanese tattoo work covering his body; he was damned by his leader for failing to commit himself to some murderous task, cursed to only speak in Haiku, and that he fled back here, living incognito so they wouldn't find and kill him. He's never left this country, but let's not quell the myth, OK? He's weirdly revered around here. Let it be.'

'Yeah, OK. I was just curious. Does he think in Haiku?'

'I don't know kid, ask him. Just don't extinguish the myth.'

'I won't.'

'Good! Anyway, something to ask you. Did you shag Kitten last night?'

That's a big change in the direction of our conversation. He's grinning, maybe he even looks proud of me.

'I stayed at hers, yeah.'

I'm trying to be gentlemanly, don't want to say we fucked and it was awesome.

'Good night was it?' Still grinning. He has really good teeth.

I'm smiling, forgetting the day for a moment.

'Think she's pissed off with me.'

'Probably. Women are always pissed off.' He chuckles.

# Loud Noise, Ghosts And News

Pete gets back, both me and Bob are in the bar and a new band has started. The music's shit, same noise all the time. It's punk and anti-establishment or whatever, but it lacks depth; if I could hear what they were saying it would help. Yeah, I'm a Nirvana fan, but I've heard nothing with any integrity or meaning since I got here. Maybe it's all about good production, Nirvana probably sounded this shit once. But there's no talent or charisma here.

I'm tired and Kitten is icy cold, ignoring me. Bob takes pity on me and my woeful state, tells me to sit out back awhile, take a break. Pete's in the kitchen eating his promised cold pizza and drinking his beer. I sit opposite him and ask if everything went alright.

'Yeah, sorted, Joe, don't worry your pretty little head.' He's chuckling and chewing, half a pepperoni slice slipping down his chin which he sucks back into his mouth. Watching me he says,

'Got to say, you're fucking weird Joe, you freak me out a bit.'

What? He's calling me weird? There's nobody weirder than Pete.

'Sorry. Like how? What do you mean?'

'I dunno Joe, but it's like there's someone with you all the time, it's hard to explain…feel like I'm talking to two people when I'm around you, know what I mean?' I don't, and although Pete's been a legend today, he's making me nervous, like, what the fuck?

'No,' I shake my head, 'I don't get you.' I'm so creeped out.

'Ah never mind.' Does he mean like a ghost or something? Grandpa? The thought is terrifying and embarrassing in equal measure.

'What do you mean about two people? Like I have a split personality?'

'No, not that.'

'Then what? Like a ghost following me around?'

'Hmm. Nah, don't think so. Forget it, kid, my heads fucked, ignore me.' Great. Today of all days. I'm spooked. I won't let this go.

'But you've creeped me out, at least try to explain?'

'I'm not much good at explaining. I've done too many drugs Joe, I'm talking shit. It's just like now, even though I can see there's only two of us here, I *feel* like there's someone else too, a presence or something,' As he says this, I see him looking over my shoulder, 'And I don't get this feeling with anyone else.' He shrugs. Prickles on my neck, I look behind me, following his gaze, there's no one there. Pete feels bad I can tell, 'It's nothing sinister, don't worry. You're just special, Joe!' he laughs again. I remain unsettled.

'You sure you don't mean a ghost?' Just checking.

'No, fuck off, that's creepy.'

Bob bursts through the door with The Haiku Man behind. Bob's irritated and impatient,

'What's the fucking urgency bro?' The Haiku Man waits for the door to close behind him, regards me and Pete then looks back at Bob,

'That lad from upstairs?

Well, I saw something tonight

In the newspaper.'

He's scrabbling in his pocket,

'He was a soldier

AWOL with a stolen gun,

Should have called the cops,'

He unfolds the page he's pulled from his coat, lays it on the table. His hands are shaking.

'Says he's dangerous,

PTSD sufferer,

Twisted ideas.'

Shit, I'm scanning the page, it's definitely him. Bob breathing over me, both of us digesting the information presented to us. Jack Jones, 23 years old. His parents are worried, want him to contact someone, let them know he's safe. His mother says he's always been a gentle boy but the army messed him up, gave him no support for his PTSD. The police are concerned for his wellbeing and his intentions, appealing for sightings and warning that he might've stolen a weapon before going AWOL. The army are saying nothing. Unstable, apparently he left some letters about his plans and his objectives. No details though, just that he should be considered dangerous as he may be armed and has mental health issues. There's a huge picture of him, clean shaven and smiling, his teeth intact, and there's no mistaking him, the eyes. I wonder how many people will recognise him from here. We're fucked. I'm fucked. Bob knows it too, I can feel him mouthing expletives on my neck, and when he's finished he stands up, declares it,

'Well, we're fucked!'

Pete asks, 'Why, what's wrong?' He hasn't been paying attention, still stuffing pizza. Bob continues to no one in particular,

'Some wanker will say they seen him here, cops will call. We're all fucked.'

Pete remembers something, 'Oh shit, yeah, meant to say, heard on the radio the Western train line is shut 'cos of a body on the tracks.

'Well great. Hardly surprising but still. Pete's scanning the newspaper now, not overly concerned, shrugs, 'He's not missing anymore, they found him on the tracks earlier. Case closed, yeah?'

'Not if someone fucking phones this number and says he's been staying here, you dipshit!'

'Well, if that happens, and someone turns up, we'll just say he came and he left a few days ago, right?'

Kitten sticks her head round the door, 'Some help, please? Jesus, having a party are you?'

The newspaper on the table catches her eye, she sees the solemn looks on our faces and leans over to look. Bob's already folding it away, but too late, 'Is that the bloke staying upstairs? What does it say?'

'No, he's not staying here, left a couple of days ago.'

'Oh, what does it say?'

'Nothing. Joe, go help Kitten.'

'What is up with you all today? You're all cagey and weird and I know something's going on, I'm not stupid!' She's pissed off, hand on her hip.

'Go on Joe.' I get up, feel sick again, and Kitten rolls her eyes at me and walks through the door. I start serving, and Kitten beside me asks again,

'What's going on?

'Nothing.'

'Bullshit.'

I shrug, 'Really, nothing, no big deal.' I carry on, feeling zombie-like. I don't know how I'm managing, this has been the longest day of my life.

'Whatever.' she mutters, and saunters down the other end of the bar, as far as possible, which suits me fine because I don't know what to say. I carry on through the noise and heat, my mind elsewhere. I'll never be able to get past today, it'll hang like a noose around my neck forever.

The Haiku Man exits the kitchen, lifts the hatch and props up the bar. We make eye contact but it's too busy to speak and there's nothing to say anyway. I pour him a vodka. How is he even alive? I can't wait for this night to be over, I will get out as soon as I can.

The evening drags. Bob mans the bar with us, goes easy on me. My head's thumping and I stink, but carry on through my fog of self-loathing and worry. Every time the door opens I expect the police. The band finishes, the crowd lessens, the end is in sight. Pete's about, but he hangs out with the clientele, laughing and joking like nothing out of the ordinary happened today. Kitten goes home first without so much as a glance in my direction. The Haiku Man leans across the bar to me and whispering he says,

'For tonight at least,

I think you are off the hook…

Good luck tomorrow.'

I take the time to examine his face, looking for a resemblance to his nephews. But it's difficult to see beyond the grime and facial hair. He leaves. Just me, Bob and Pete left, and I ask if I can go lie down, I can hardly hold myself up anymore, and although I won't sleep I need to rest my head. Bob looks the same, nods and says,

'Try to sleep, still shit to sort out tomorrow.'

I'm frightened to go upstairs. I do it because I have to, and in my room I leave the light on, take my shoes off, pull my hood up and lie inside my sleeping bag exhausted. I hear Bob and Pete come up, go to their rooms. Sitting up, I roll myself a cigarette, the first since this morning at Kitten's. Feels like that was days ago. I unzip myself and get up, open the window and smoke. Then I roll and smoke another before curling back up in my makeshift bed. Although I try to fight it, my eyes close and I sleep.

# Everything Aches

I wake the next morning with a jolt, yesterday flooding every thought. It wasn't a nightmare, it was real life.

My neck aches, my back aches, everything does. My face is sore from getting pistol-whipped, I still have that black eye from the night I got here. I'm thirsty, hungry, and still frightened. I look at my phone, it's early, 8.15. I'm going to bleach that room again this morning, will see what Bob asks of me today and then I'll go. I lie thinking awhile. Blood, teeth, vomit, bleach. It's not doing me any good so I peel open my sleeping bag, and I smell of pee and sick. I rummage through my bag, find the shower gel I packed, and head to the sink next door. I make do with cold water. I wet my hair, awkwardly holding my head under the tap, I wash my face, my neck, shut the door, wash my crotch. I peel off my socks and lift one foot at a time to the sink, rinse the stale urine away. I don't have a towel because we used it as an absorbent pillow for the dead guy.

Jack Jones, 23. He looked older. A person with a loving and worried family. A person with a past and a future, until yesterday. I've replayed the moment over and over, when the gun slipped from his hand and fell in slow motion, when I instinctively held my hands out to catch it. I ruined everything. What would've happened if that gun hadn't dropped, hadn't fired? What was he going to do? I've thought about it. My cheeks burn red when I remember sucking the barrel of that pistol. They think I killed him.

My hair dripping, back in my room. I'm running out of clean clothes, so decide I'll scrub that room before I ruin anymore of them. We took all the bleach and cleaning stuff back downstairs last night, so I creep down to the kitchen, fill the bucket with warm water, add some bleach. I find a scrubbing brush under the sink, which I could've used yesterday but never mind. I make my way back upstairs, careful not to spill any, and push open his door. I'm proud of myself. It's empty, quiet and smells of bleach, but there's still the stain on the floor, and flecks that I missed yesterday. I don't know where to start, but I do the floor. Three quarters of the way through and Bob sticks his head through the door. I'm so engrossed that I don't hear him coming, and I'm startled when he says,

'Nice one, Joe, bit early though?'

'Yeah, just want to get it done.'

'Good. Good boy. You want a coffee?'

'Yeah, please.'

'Alright, finish up the floor, come down yeah?'

I finish, feeling minorly accomplished, I trot downstairs. Bob's sitting in the kitchen, mug of coffee waiting for me.

'I want to talk to you, Joe,' he says. I take a seat opposite him, take a sip. Bob takes a deep breath, assesses me, 'I'm sorry for you. I'm sorry about yesterday, it was a shit storm of a day and I can't imagine how damaging it must've been for you. Seriously, I found yesterday traumatic and it wasn't me who killed him, I didn't sleep a wink last night. I don't know how you feel, boy, I can't even begin…' he pauses, leans back a little and from his pocket pulls a small bundle of money, slides it across the table towards me, continues, 'I'm no slave driver, so here's what you earned for working. If you want to carry on working here that's fine, great. I need staff. But also, if you have anyone, family, somewhere to go, you should go there. Get out. You're still the guilty party Joe, and I'll turn you in if I'm put in that position. I hope you understand the risk me and Pete have taken in helping you.'

He stops, takes a gulp from his mug, so I tell him,

'I didn't ask for help. I wanted to phone the police remember? I would never have done what we did yesterday, you made me do it! I didn't kill him.' I sound insolent, but it's true. Bob shrugs, looks unconvinced. I carry on, 'And I can't stay here anymore. I need a shower, I need a launderette, a microwave and stuff. And I have nowhere to go. Yesterday Kitten told me I could stay with her, but obviously that's out the window. But I have to go somewhere else.' I'm feeling emotional, my eyes start welling, a lump in my throat, if I keep talking I'll break down. I turn away, stifle the feeling. Bob takes the cue to respond.

'Ah, I'm sure the offer is still open with Kitten. Call her. You want to talk about what happened yesterday? Because I'm still not sure what the fuck went on. I believe you, it was an accident. There's no way you'd have the balls or the crazy to do it, Joe, no way. But what fucking happened? You said he was in your room?'

'Yeah, behind the door with the gun. He thought I was looking for him, guy was nuts. I had the same rucksack as him, he thought I was military.'

Bob guffaws at this. 'You? Military? That's a fucking laugh! How'd you end up in his room?'

'He forced me in there, don't know why.'

'Why were you undressed?'

'He told me to. He had the gun in my face!'

'It looked dodgy.'

'Yeah, I get that.'

'What happened then?'

'I pissed myself. He dropped the gun and I caught it. It went off on its own.'

'Why'd you piss yourself?'

'I was scared, I thought I was about to die!'

That's it for a while, we don't talk, just finish our coffee. Bob makes us some more. I pluck up the courage to ask,

'So I can leave today?'

'Yeah,' Suddenly free I don't know where to go. I never did. 'You can have a shower if you want. We've got a washing machine too.'

'That would be awesome, thanks.'

'Get your clothes, we'll chuck 'em in the washer.'

Indebted I go, change my T shirt, take all my soiled clothes downstairs, and Bob's waiting, pouring powder into the drawer. In case he's changed his mind I check, 'Still OK if I have a shower?'

'Yeah, knock yourself out.'

I scald myself clean. No towel anymore but I didn't want to push my luck so I'll just drip dry. I ponder the day ahead, I'll buy a new jacket. I don't know what after that. I'm in a daze, and no matter how I try to distract myself I keep going back to yesterday. Should I call Kitten? See if she'll still have me? Even masturbation doesn't seem appealing. I'm here alone in the shower, I could. But I'm cold, only blood, only death fills my mind.

After I've shivered myself dry, dressed and packed my bag, I go downstairs. Bob's staring into space in the kitchen, no sign of Pete. It's gone ten.

I say, 'I'm going shopping, I'll be back in a couple of hours.' I'm not committing myself to leaving because I don't have anywhere to go. Also, most of my clothes are in the washing machine.

'OK Joe, see you later.' He doesn't break his gaze from the wall. I let myself out the front door. I head into The City.

# Normality, Sort Of

I reach The City centre, unsure what to do. Where can I get a jacket like the one I had? I've no idea, this place is huge, alien. Anyway, I love the people here, the diversity and purpose of everyone, the way no one notices you, so I walk around shops, regular high street stores, and feel vaguely normal. There are no jackets to replace what I've lost. It's summer, there are shorts, vests, sunglasses. I wander and find a Starbucks, get coffee and cake and connect to the WiFi. Don't know why but I go into my DM from Casey and reply;

*I'm fine, in The City. Had nothing to stay there for*

I press send. I suppose I feel like I need a friend or some familiarity. I miss talking to Grandpa and I miss my bed. I text Kitten;

*Sorry about yesterday. Are we OK? x*

I delete it, start again,

*Sorry about yesterday. U OK?*

I want to say more but can't think what, so I just send it. I'm waiting for my phone to be cut off because no one's paying the bill. Casey responds first;

*Shit Joe, you're alive! The City?!! You coming back?* Emojis; shocked face, smiley face, kisses. I reply,

*No, not coming back*

*Can I tell my mum? She's been freaking out! What you doing there?*

*Yeah tell her. I got a job, somewhere to stay*

I suddenly feel a pang of fondness for Casey. I'm grateful she cared enough to message me. I'm sorry I called her slutty. Truth is, she was my only friend back home, I shouldn't have been so dismissive.

*Wow, Joe, I can't believe it! I'm pleased for you, I mean it! Maybe I can come meet up with you sometime? Hang out? My first uni choice is there* Sunglasses emoji.

*Yeah that'd be cool* Smiley face emoji.

I'm actually smiling. It feels good, until I realise I have no right to smile because I killed a man yesterday.

*Happy Birthday BTW xxx* Cake emoji.

*Thanks*

I'm smiling still. I resist imitating her kisses.

Kitten texts back,

*It's cool. I'm fine. C u later?*

I reply immediately,

*Cool. Yeah, c u later x*

I welcome this distraction; it's good to feel ordinary. I eat my choc chip muffin, drink my caffe latte. No more messages. I scroll through twitter though, catch up. I text Kitten again,

*Can I still crash at yours? No worries if not*

Seems like forever until she responds,

*Yeah I guess, talk later at work OK?*

*OK*

I text her again,

*Where can I buy a new leather jacket?*

*You already have one though?*

*Not anymore. Any ideas?*

Laughing emoji, *We can go shopping tomorrow if u like?*

I send a thumbs up emoji.

No more messages. I Google *Jack Jones missing soldier*. Top of the list links me to the news article from yesterday, nothing else. Don't know if that's a good or bad thing. It's still early. What next? I finish my coffee, and just amble around the town aimlessly, trying to keep my mind off yesterday. I slowly head back in the direction of the bar, I want to talk to Bob, not about anything in particular, I just want some company. There's a church and I've passed it a couple of times since I got here, but today it catches my eye. The sign outside says St. Jude The Apostle Catholic Church. It's Sunday and there are people milling out the door. I know St. Jude is the patron saint of lost causes, because he was Grandpa's favourite. I recall a conversation we had not long ago, when the internet wasn't working.

'Pray to Saint Isidore!' Laughter into coughing.

'Who?'

'He's the patron saint of the internet. Read it in the paper the other day. Catholics have a saint for everyone and everything Joe. Saint Drogo is the patron saint of ugly people! Can you believe that? Hilarious!'

I turned the router off and on again. Grandpa was full of useless information. Although he had long ago turned his back on religion Grandpa still regarded Catholicism with a fond yet bitter sentiment. Even though it was fiction he said, he liked the iconography, the art. He liked how, and I can hear him laugh, you could commit any sin and be absolved of guilt with a couple of prayers. I wonder if it would work for me, now. He said St. Jude was the saint of the damned. If I'm not damned I don't know what I am. I wonder if there's a patron saint of murderers, I'd bet money there is. I remember a comic book I read with the Saint of Killers, a ruthless cowboy condemned to Hell, summoned by an angel to kill, weirdly, a priest. I've never been inside a church and I loiter outside, watch the people leave. Can I just walk in? The door's still open. People do it in movies. I don't look Godly or devout or whatever but I figure anyone's welcome, fuck it.

I enter the vestibule, I'm pretty sure that's what it's called. There's a font and I peer inside. Water, as you'd expect. I dip my fingers in. Holy water, right? What can Holy water do, except repel vampires? I don't believe in God but I feel bad for thinking that while I'm here. I say inside my mind; *Sorry God, I accidentally killed someone.* Just in case, reckon it's best to keep my options open. I venture further, strolling down the aisle, and there's no one here as far as I can tell. And actually, it's pretty cool. A haven of calm within this boisterous city. All stained glass, statues, and candles. The place looks expensive. There must be someone here to monitor all these dangerously unsupervised candles. There must be a priest.

I hear a noise and turn my attention to a confession booth. That's what it is right? A lady leaving, head bowed, no eye contact, she strides past me. The priest is inside the confession booth, should I go in? Confess? Will he call the police? Will he absolve me? Too late, the priest exits the box. Oh man! He sees me, nods, walks towards me, oh fuck. Sorry God, but fuck, why am I here?

'Hello young man, a new face! Can I help you?'

He's almost bald, portly, glasses. His smile is creepy but I'll give him the benefit of the doubt; he's a priest after all.

204

'No, I was just curious. My Grandpa told me about St. Jude. I was just passing.'

'Ah yes... O most holy apostle, Saint Jude, faithful servant and friend of Jesus, the Church honoureth and invoketh thee universally, as the patron of hopeless cases, and of things almost despaired of. Pray for me, who am so miserable!'

Shit. What can I say to that? 'Yeah.'

He can tell he's freaked me out because, to explain himself, he says, 'Saint Jude teaches us that we must persevere through difficult circumstances, through harsh times.' Well, I'm trying to do that. I nod. 'Are you seeking guidance? How can I assist you?'

'I just wanted a look around. It's pretty cool in here, peaceful.'

'Well, yes, peace and comfort are things I would hope you can feel here. You could come to mass this evening, if you like.'

Um Hell no. 'I'm working.'

'Me too.' he chuckles. He holds out his hand to me, says, 'I'm Father Thomas, what's your name?'

'Joe.' I shake his hand. It's cold, limp. Don't know why but I don't like him even though he's nothing but pleasant.

'Joe, a pleasure to meet you. Feel free to stay awhile, you're welcome here anytime.'

'Thanks.'

There's a moment of us standing awkwardly before he smiles, turns, and strides down towards the altar, and through a door and out of sight.

Relieved and alone I take a seat at the back of the church, just for a minute. There's some cool shit in here, if you like this kind of thing. I think of Grandpa, and in my head I tell him I'm sorry I fucked up. I imagine him replying, I can hear him in my mind,

'Get out of that fucking church Joe, it's poisonous! Toxic!'

And so I do, I get up and leave.

Joe doesn't like him, because on some imperceptible level he knows and senses that Father Thomas is not a good man.

Father Thomas has, within his long standing and mistakenly respected position, committed countless paedophilic acts. Predictable eh? The church, and indeed the world in general, is no stranger to such abominations. For a long time, the bishops would protect guilty and accused priests, relocating them to new parishes far away, where usually, the abusive behaviour continued. In recent years, after unrelenting criticism, and damage to its reputation, the Vatican has attempted to mete out punishment for these perverse priests. Some are defrocked, but more often they've been sanctioned with the lesser penalty of a life of prayer and penitence, both of which, I'm sure we agree, are worth nothing. They should be rehabilitated, where it is deemed a possibility, or imprisoned, because let's face it, for some there is no hope of reformation. That's just my opinion.

Yes, I have opinions! Who said I shouldn't? Don't even get me started on child marriage. Listen, I know better than most that paedophilia and pederasty is ancient, how you deemed it normal and acceptable since the beginnings of humanity. I've seen how such behaviour is only recently vilified due to modern sensibilities, and thank goodness for that (thank goodness, not God, because what the fuck does God ever do? Nothing!).

Times have changed. It's taken so long. Now, more time is permitted to develop into an adult. In some places, you allow kids an education. Attitude has shifted; you realise children are not ready for such intimacies and decisions before they are matured, and this is a big step for you guys, I'm proud to witness this. You recognise the damaging consequences of such activity, the trauma and confusion it causes, that robbery of youthful exuberance.

The attention on such abuse has waxed and waned for the longest time; periods of horror and disbelief, then periods of thinking it is of little significance in comparison to the political issues of the moment.

I'm in the mood for expressing, so this is what I think: Consent is key. Not consent gained through authority, or bullying, or societal norms, but consent through mature and informed intelligence. An educated decision, an understanding of the implications and consequences, a reciprocated and permitted act. This is what you should be teaching your kids. You like to differentiate yourself from the rest of the animals, you think you're so smart and superior; start with this. Just saying! Sorry, I'm going off on a tangent. But also, you're no better than the other animals. You are animals. You're not special.

Somehow Father Thomas has slipped through the net. It's not gone unnoticed by us, we know everything, seen the damage he's done. Joe's instinct is one of the reasons I'm here, it's that intuition that makes him so exceptional. His intrinsic sense of good and bad. It's an essential requirement for us.

Joe's crisis of conscience was to be expected. Anyone with half a heart would not cope well with taking another's life. Killing's not good for the soul, even when it's necessary. And finding refuge in a church is not unusual, people turn to religion all the time in the hope of redemption (ineffective but, as I said earlier, whatever makes you feel better). Trauma and radical life changes compel you to reach out for moral instruction, for comfort. I think Joe's coping pretty well, hasn't broken yet. He won't. The resilience of youth.

In the church there, that wasn't Grandpa replying, that was me. Don't want him getting any romantic ideas about that place.

# Getting To Know
## The Haiku Man

It's gone midday so I buy a McDonalds before I head back to the bar. I might as well work tonight because what else am I going to do? Everything's so expensive here. I'm going to ask Bob for the WiFi password, nothing to lose. I take my time, feeling like I'm beginning to know this place, I stop at a shop, pick up some snacks. I get to the bar and let myself in, and the Haiku Man is sitting with a vodka. He looks at me,

'How are you today?

How did you sleep last night boy?

Badly, I'm guessing.'

I don't want to tell him I slept really well because it makes me sound like I don't give a shit about what happened, so I just say,

'I'm OK, thanks. Where's Bob?' Maybe it's the resilience of youth?
I am that shit personified.

'Bob's upstairs with Pete,

Clearing those plants thanks to you,

I'd stay out the way.'

He gestures at the stool next to him. I sit down, setting down
my purchases on the bar. He stinks of alcohol and dirt, a little bit of
wee. I've learned to inhale through my mouth around him.

'Feel shit to be honest. I'm tired, scared, I can't believe it
happened. I slept OK, but only because I was exhausted.'

'You surprise me boy!

I barely slept a minute.

Haunted by his face.'

'Yeah. I'll never get it out of my head, ever. I feel like I'm in a
nightmare. It was an accident, you know that, right? I wanted to
call the police.'

'Then you'd be in prison.

Was he going to fuck you?

You had your top off—'

'No! No. I don't know why I had my T-shirt off, I don't think
it was that.' Christ. Why does everyone think that? I can still taste
that gun barrel, feel it clicking against my teeth. I suppose it was
a possibility. I feel embarrassed, ashamed, I deserve it. 'I shouldn't
have come here, to The City. Everything's gone wrong. I had all
these ideas on the train on my way here…' The Haiku Man lifts his
hand up to halt me,

'Give me a penny

For all my failed ideas;

I'll cry you diamonds.'

He snorts a half-hearted laugh. Then, suddenly serious, searches
my eyes. He's contemplating something. His eyes are intense, and

for the first time I see beyond the filth and ruination and recognise the soul inside. Eye contact doesn't come easy to me but he's forcing me now, and I wonder if I took the time to really look at people I'd be able to see beyond the exterior, the humanity beneath, and maybe I wouldn't feel so awkward all the time.

'Let me share with you

My tale of misadventure,

You might feel better.'

I make it known I'm listening. But it's a solid minute until he starts speaking again, it's starting to feel awkward.

'When I was thirty

I did a terrible thing.

I killed my best friend.'

Shit, OK, I wasn't expecting that. I was thinking it was going to be something minor and he drops this? A tale of misadventure? I'm watching him intently and he can see the look of shock on my face I suppose, because reassuringly he says,

'Let me tell you boy,

I am no stone cold killer,

We both made mistakes.'

Vaguely relieved, I feel like I should say something but I don't know what. I'm interested, I look at him expectantly and he sees my face, understands. Maybe he *will* make me feel better about everything? It seems I'm good at facial expressions because he's placated, carries on,

'Met John back at school

When we were thirteen years old,

We became firm friends.

'I'd caught him throwing

His dirty pants in the bin

Cos he'd shit himself;

'I remember the
Eye contact in the toilets,
My look of support.
'All I could offer.
When he said, "I got the shits."
I nodded, 'Been there."
'This was during break,
Between PE and Science,
Didn't tell a soul.'

I nod. If I'd shit myself at school I would've had a kicking. The Haiku Man's mood has shifted and he's smiling now while he reflects.

'A week or so passed,
Sat next to one another
In technology.
'Our mates were off school
With a bad case of the squirts,
His fault I reckon.
'Didn't wash his hands,
Germs spread like bubonic plague,
As it is with kids.
'Then on, firm friends,
Right through our teens and twenties
We laughed, cried and sinned.
'Girls and rejection,
Cigarettes and alcohol
The parties and drugs.'

Huh, thinking of The Haiku Man as a teenager is weird. Even after everything Bob told me, I find it hard to envisage him any other way than how he is now. I wish I could see an old photo of

him. How does he talk this way? It blows my mind! I tell him, 'I've
never had a best friend.'

'You poor bugger, Joe!
But it doesn't surprise me,
You are a bit odd.'
He thinks *I'm* odd?
'They were sunny times
And you cannot imagine
All the shit we did!
'The years flew by and
We lived in a joyous haze;
Sex, drugs, rock 'n' roll.
'Carefree and reckless
We swore we would always be
At each other's side.'

Sounds a bit gay, but he did mention girls. Not judging, I'm just
trying to figure him out. Guy's an enigma.

'But my family
Weren't happy with my choices,
I was a waster.'

His family weren't happy with his choices? What, a joyous haze
of sex, drugs and rock 'n' roll? Because yeah, that's just what every
parent wishes for their kids. I nod sympathetically.

'My brother, bless him,
Always was the golden boy,
I could not compete.'

Bob and Pete's dad, right? I don't say anything because he doesn't
know that I know.

'It was obvious
I was a disappointment
And they were ashamed.

'I kept my distance,
Tried and failed to be better;
It wasn't to be.
'When my father died
John was there with a beer and
Of course, a joint too.
'My brother did all
The necessary duties
While I lived it up,
'And I masked my grief
With anything that numbed me.
John was my constant;
'Soothed me through,
I was sorry and grieving.
And the guilt I felt...'

The Haiku Man shakes his head. The poetry is monotonous yet captivating. I sort of wish he would speak normally; it'd be easier and he'd get to the point quicker. I try to look compassionate and understanding, I genuinely feel that way, I don't want him to stop.

'I talked to him and
He talked to me. Our bond
Was unbreakable.
'Even my brother,
Even my own flesh and blood,
Was no match for John.'

Having not much experience of friendship, I can't understand what this means. I think it's sad his family were ashamed of him, but I get it. I was ashamed of my father before I even knew what shame was. Grandpa, he was merely embarrassing, yet the only one who had my back.

'We got arrested,

For minor offences. But,
It was just a laugh.
'Youth, misadventure.
If we are lucky enough
We have all been there.
'It was fun mostly,
Until we got addicted.
But friendship remained.'
Surely, getting arrested is never 'just a laugh'. Anyhow, I really
wish *I* had a best friend like that. A lifelong friend where nothing I'd
done mattered, my background didn't matter. I suddenly consider
the Haiku Man blessed.
'A few years later,
We were addicts through and through,
We couldn't break free.
'I guess we were both
As bad as one another,
Just seeking escape.
'We started dealing
Little bit of everything,
Made a little cash;
'There was temptation
To sample the stash we got,
Try the merchandise.'
I can't comment, and I can't decide if I admire it or not. Either
way, still interested. He doesn't care what I think, he's on a roll.
'One night, we're messed up,
Been drinking and smoking crack,
Still wasn't enough.'
I don't even know what crack is.
'He says, "Shoot for me?

I'm too fucked to find a vein."
I did what friends do.
'Those were his last words.
If I could go back to then
I'd suggest a smoke.
'Mainlining's not safe.
Knew that but we'd done it loads,
It was worth the hit.
This was different,
Watched his eyes roll back in bliss
Or at least I thought.
'It was not bliss, Joe,
It was death taking its hold.
Sat with him awhile.
'I hadn't done myself
And if I had I wouldn't be here,
It was a bad batch.
'Rolled a cigarette,
Knowing when I took my hit
I'd be gone all night.
'Watched his colour drain,
Touched him and I knew right then
That he was dying,
'Or already dead.
Did I call an ambulance?
No, I did not Joe.
'His skin turned stone cold,
I realised what happened,
I took his money.
'I got out of there,
The needle still in his arm.

I was fucked up too.'

He pauses. What the fuck, Haiku Man? No ambulance? No attempt to wake him or CPR? I don't actually say this. He looks emotional. His eyes are wet and yellow glassy and gratefully he stares into nothing, reaches for the vodka and takes a huge gulp. I start rolling some cigarettes for later. While I'm searching for words he blurts,

'I'm ashamed of this,
You realise that right, boy?
Don't go saying shit!
'Look at me now Joe.
You can see my suffering!
I deserve this lot.
'Consider this confession
Confidential yeah?
No one really knows.'

I'm intrigued, the poetry still entrancing me. All of a sudden I want to say so much.

'Does Bob know?' I ask, 'Pete?'
'No, keep your mouth shut!
They know I was a smack-head
But this stays with us.
'I've only told you
Cos I've got dirt on you too,
You're no angel boy.
'I must admit it's
Good to get it off my chest.
It's like therapy!'

He laughs then, a laughter that masks sadness, takes another swig from the bottle.

'When the cops turned up

They saw another junkie,
One less waste of space.
'No come back for me
And I count my lucky stars
I'm not in prison.
'I punish myself
More than prison ever could,
I promise you that.
'Think you'll do the same,
don't be too hard on yourself;
Living is penance.'
I feel the need to comment. I tell him, 'But you didn't kill him,
he wanted you to give him the drugs. It was his choice, it's not like
you wanted him to die, it was an accident.'
'Same as you Joe huh?
But yeah, just an accident.
Doesn't numb the guilt.'
He has a point. He's not finished yet.
'At the funeral
I watched his folks grief stricken,
I stood at the back.
'I'd known them well once,
Couldn't look them in the eye,
It was heartbreaking.
'I wanted to say,
He was smart and he loved life,
Lived in the moment!
'Not meant for this world,
And conventional success
Just didn't appeal.
'Too mundane, too grey

He'd say, "Everyone's a slave;
*We're* not that stupid."
'His death gave me strength
To quit the drugs, but look now,
I'm no better off.
'I replaced one vice
With one just as destructive.
At least it's legal.
'I think about John
Everyday. I speak to him.
I hope he's not pissed,
'That I took his shoes
And his money and left him.
I had to survive.'

'You took his shoes? The ones he was wearing?' So many questions but this one blurts out. It seems low even by Haiku Man standards, I'm surprised.

'We were the same size!
Don't you start judging me Joe,
I regret it now.
'But they were nice shoes!
A pair of Nike air Jordans,
Those things are not cheap.
'Looked ridiculous
On my feet. Don't know if it
Was the guilt or not.
'Either way I swapped
Them for a half ounce of weed,
Glad to see them gone.
'Took all his drugs too,
And this book he carried 'round;

Basho, a poet'

He pats his coat, pulls out the book. It's cover so battered and grimy that I can't make out a title or anything. It's dog-eared and I don't want to touch it because I might catch something; unquestionably it's a haven for bacteria and infectious disease. When I don't reach for it, he carries on,

'That's besides the point.

What I'm saying is don't let

This define you Joe.

'Wanted you to know,

We all have bad stuff we've done.

We seek redemption.

'There, that's it. No more.

I already shared too much.

You are not alone!'

With that, he snatches the little book back from the bar and stuffs it into his pocket. I don't feel much better for knowing. Maybe he does. Maybe if he'd unburdened himself years ago he wouldn't be who he is now. I think it's weird he told me, I barely know him. Weird how he shared this but didn't mention that Bob and Pete are his nephews. Who is Basho? I think about how ridiculous a pair of Nike Airs would look with that coat. I'm beginning to think I have one of those faces that compels people to share their secrets. Perhaps it's my superpower.

'Just try to get through,

The next week or maybe two,

It might be OK,

'And then hopefully

We can all get on with life,

Put this behind us.'

He reaches out, pats my back. We, us. I'm not alone. I glance at my new tattoo that affiliates me to these people. Until the cops call. We sit quiet for a couple of minutes. He's done, and I don't know what to say. So, I grab my snacks, 'Yeah,' I say, 'I'm gonna take these upstairs.' I leave.

# Easy Life From Now On:
## Wi-Fi And Weed

Pete's door is open down the end of the corridor, I hear talking as I walk upstairs. Bob sticks his head out the doorway,

'Alright, Joe?' He looks exhausted. I half smile.

He walks towards me, so I say, 'The Haiku Man says I should stay out of your way. Just want to put some stuff in my room.'

Bob sighs, 'I didn't say you had to stay out the way.'

'Want me to help with anything?'

'No, nothing. I don't know, maybe later. I'm trying to talk some sense into Pete about his weed factory up here.' He gestures over his shoulder. I am curious to see it but the offer doesn't come.

'I can work tonight if you still want me to.'

'Yeah, that's great kid.'

'I texted Kitten, I think she might let me stay with her, I don't know.'

'OK, good. See you at six, yeah?'

'Yeah. Um, are my clothes still in the washing machine?'

'I put them to dry, go get them.' He turns to go back to Pete, so quickly I ask,

'Uh, Bob… any chance of the WiFi password?' He stops and turns on his heel.

'You serious? You cheeky little shit!' Then he grins, 'I suppose so. The router's in Pete's room, password's on the box, c'mon.'

Yes! I quickly drop my snacks in my room, follow Bob up the corridor giving next door a wide berth, pulling my phone out ready. But, I'm not prepared for this; Pete's room is insane!

The room is large, like Bob's. High ceilings, picture rails, those big sash windows, classic Victorian. This building must've been grand once. But Pete's decor couldn't be more different from his brothers, I've never seen anything like it. For starters, there's a full hydroponic setup on one side of the room, so many plants, blinding lights and it fucking stinks, fills my lungs. No natural light in here, the windows are covered with black out blinds. It's the sort of thing you see in movies, or newspapers. The other half looks like a spoilt delinquent teenager's bedroom; unmade bed, strewn with clothes and magazines, a laptop, the walls covered in posters of semi naked girls, all breasts and thongs. An Epiphone Les Paul hangs on the wall. Lava lamp, ashtray overflowing, a whole load of smoking paraphernalia even though Bob said *I* wasn't allowed to smoke up here. I can barely see the floor for discarded clothes and debris. Again, nothing like Bob's room. No artwork or chairs or rugs. Bob seems positively sophisticated in comparison.

My mouth agog, Pete says,

'Alright, Joe? Welcome to my humble abode!' He's standing in front of his horticultural hoard, smiling and waving an arm across the spectacle of his room.

'Hi Pete.' It's all I can say. Bob's fiddling by the TV,

'Ready Joe?' I clumsily tap on my phone for the settings, and Bob reads out the password. I connect.

Pete asks me, 'What d'you reckon on these plants, Joe? You think we're in the clear?' He's looking at me for back up. I want to be in the clear, but it's barely been twenty-four hours so it's wishful thinking to believe it's over. Bob sits on the edge of Pete's bed,

'No we're fucking not. Tell him, Joe, he'll go to prison and I ain't visiting him.' I'm not taking sides. I look at them both in turn and shrug.

'Why are you so paranoid, man? They only need a few more weeks and then I'll get rid of the lot, I promise.'

'We haven't got a few weeks. What if the cops call?'

'Well, they'll need a search warrant. We'll worry about it if it happens.'

I say nothing but something's caught my eye. A set of wooden rosary beads, hanging from a hook by the head of the bed. Unintentionally changing the subject I ask,

'Are you guys Catholic?' Bob looks at me like I'm an alien.

'Fuck off, no, what sort of random question is that?' Pete's laughing.

'Oh. Just saw those beads is all.' I point at them.

'They were our old man's. *He* was Catholic. Used to take us to church when we were kids, fucking load of bollocks. Jesus Christ Joe, all the weird shit in this room and you notice some fucking beads? You not noticed that ganja farm there?'

'Yeah, sorry.' Bob always seems to be looking at me like everything I say is ludicrous. He used a lot of fucks in a short space there, I might've pissed him off again. I carry on, trying to explain myself, looking at my feet. I'm shit at conversation.

'My family were Catholic once, a long time ago. I went to the church earlier.'

'What? What the fuck did you go *there* for? You think Jesus will save you?'

'No.' Alright, don't take the piss Bob.

'What church? St. Judes?'

'Yeah.'

'You want to avoid that place, the priest's a fucking nonce. Again, what the fuck did you go there for? You didn't tell anyone did you?' I've definitely pissed Bob off.

Also, noncey priest, bit of a cliche.

'No, of course not.'

'You fucking sure?'

'Yes! I just went in a minute because the door was open.'

'Keep the hell away from there, that church is riddled with corruption. Did you see the priest?' He says this with absolute vitriol.

'I saw him, didn't speak to him though.' Yeah, Father Thomas. I lie, because I don't want to explain myself. I feel stupid having gone there now.

'Old guy? Going bald? Glasses?'

'Yeah, I guess.' Bob looks at Pete.

'Old cunt's still there then. Fucking sick bastard. Stay away Joe, I'm not joking.'

'I wasn't planning on going again. I'm not religious or anything.'

I look at the plants, hoping to divert the conversation back to them. I've never seen cannabis plants in real life and I've never smoked it. Can't deny I'm curious. Is Pete a drug dealer? It works anyway, because Bob forgets me and says,

'Anyway, Pete, this is the score. If you keep these plants and we get busted by the cops, it's solely your responsibility. You get me? Whatever happens this is the last lot. I mean it. We ain't kids anymore. I can't take the stress. Want an easy life from here on in, we're going to toe the line.'

'Yeah, last time, I swear. You're right bro, easy life.'

'Good. Same goes Joe, you're still entirely responsible for yesterday, yeah? I'm not going down for shit I didn't do. I'm not your fucking carer. If it comes to it, you will not take us down with you, right?'

'Right, yeah.' I nod eagerly.

The cops will never believe I did all that shit on my own, unnoticed. I hope I can stay at Kitten's tonight. Pete relaxes enough to leave his plant-guarding position, climbs onto his bed, opens his bedside drawer and pulls out a tin. Reaches down the side for a tray, upon which, with three papers, he starts rolling a massive cigarette which I realise is actually a joint. I'm watching him the whole time, standing there like a spare part.

'Right, that's clear then. I'm going to lie down for an hour, I'm fucking knackered.' Bob lifts himself from the edge of the bed, I sidestep as he walks out the door.

I don't know if I should leave too, so I say to Pete, 'You play guitar?'

'Yeah a bit. You?'

'Not really, only know four chords.'

'Four chords is all you need. Shut the door Joe, have a seat.'

There's nowhere to sit, but Pete pushes a load of crap onto the floor, signals for me to sit next to him. I feel weird because I'm just not used to hanging out in people's rooms. I shut the door and self-consciously place myself on the edge of the bed. It's stiflingly warm in here, from the lights I presume, which are blinding.

I ask him, 'D'you sleep with those lights on?'

'Yeah.' He reaches under the pillow behind him, pulls out an eye mask, grins at me. Dropping it again he carries on rolling. 'So anyway, used to be in a band, we were shit, but y'know, we were young,'

'Cool.'

'Yeah, my old man bought me that guitar for my sixteenth birthday.' He nods at the Les Paul.

'What were you called? Your band?'

'The Fucks.'

'Nice.' Pete's finishing up, pushing a torn piece of cardboard flyer in one end for a makeshift filter. He lights it, inhales deeply, grabs the ashtray and plonks it in front of him. I don't know how to talk to Pete but I find some words.

'You know what you said last night, how I freaked you out because you felt like there was someone else with me?'

'Yeah.'

'You got that feeling now?'

He inhales, exhales. Takes a minute, eyes shut. 'Yeah, suppose I'm getting used to it now, it's no biggie.' The smoke stinks, it's powerful, distinctive. Musky? Sweet? Pete hands me the joint and I'm hesitant but take it because I haven't had a cigarette for a couple of hours. I tell him,

'I've never smoked a joint before.'

'Are you fucking real? Well crack on, Joe, first time for everything.'

I take a drag, way more smoke than I was expecting probably due to the lack of an actual filter. I guess I don't care about hepatitis anymore. Grandpa said, I should be seeking experiences. I nearly cough, but somehow swallow it back while Pete continues; 'Thing is with weed, it can go one of two ways. Either you'll end up paranoid and jumpy, or it'll chill you the fuck out, take away your worries.

Inhale it deeper, it's not a fag, take it into your lungs, hold it.' I do as I'm told. I don't want to feel paranoid and jumpy, especially as I've got something to legitimately to feel paranoid about. That second exhalation I feel it; a virtual massage, my shoulders relax, my back, everything. My scalp tingles, in a good way. I smile to myself lazily, look at Pete who cracks up laughing, 'There it is, good shit, huh?'

I ask, 'How come you're allowed to smoke here and I'm not?'

'Cos the rules don't apply to me, this is my fucking gaff.'

I giggle, It's not funny but my brain thinks otherwise at this point. Now I'm thinking about Pete's old band and I say,

'You know your band was called The Fucks?'

'Yeah?'

'It'd be cool if it was Fucks with an X, like The Fux. F U X' I feel like a genius.

'Yeah man, yeah! You wanna start a band?'

'I can't play. Or sing.'

'Told you, four chords is all you need.'

'Can you sing?'

'Like a fucking angel. You passing that back or what?' He's holding out his hand, fingers poised, and reluctantly I pass the joint back. I guess I like weed. I remember when Pete was singing at me before and, yeah, he does sing like an angel.

'You a drug dealer?' I ask. Probably too personal a question but I feel like we're bonding or something, it's not like he can deny it.

'Well, I sell this shit to someone, and they sell it on, you get me? This is too much shit for one guy to smoke alone, even for me.'

'Yeah. Does Bob smoke it too?'

'Not for years. He's pretty straight edge, apart from a few beers here and there.'

'I like Bob. He scares the shit out of me sometimes, but I like him. I'm grateful for everything y'know?'

'Yeah, he's a good guy, a good brother. I'd be in a gutter without him, Joe, I'm a natural born fuck-up, just like you.' I don't know why I find this funny but I do, the bit about the gutter. He says it so sincerely. A natural born fuck-up. It's funny. I start laughing, which sets Pete off too. He passes the joint back, 'Don't forget to share, yeah? Spliff politics.' Still laughing. That tips me over the edge, spliff politics. I snort the smoke out of my nose, and I feel like a stereotypical stoner from the movies, and it's not so bad. 'Stop fucking laughing and smoke it!' He's jovial, amused by my intoxication. I never saw Pete as a classic stoner, too much energy, too jittery. Perhaps that's why he smokes, to take the edge off. It works I reckon because right now he seems pretty chilled. 'Y'know one day this shit will be legal here, Joe. I guarantee it. It'll take time but we'll get there. You see how America are dealing with this stuff? It's revolutionary! You can get it on the NHS now.'

Some time later after talking about nothing and everything I leave Pete and go to my room. The sandwich I bought earlier is the best I ever ate, and shop sandwiches are shit. My phone says it's two fifteen, and I lie down for a bit because I feel a bit floaty, disjointed. I fall asleep.

I wake up around an hour later, disorientated and groggy. I feel panicky, because I remember yesterday all over again; the blood, the teeth, his eyes, the smell. I mournfully think I'll recollect these grim details every time I wake up the rest of my life. It passes eventually. My clean clothes are downstairs, and after taking five minutes to come around, I get up and quietly go downstairs, aware that Bob's sleeping. Except he's not, he's sitting in the kitchen, staring at the wall again.

'Uh, just came down for my clothes.'

'Hey, Joe.' His eyes don't leave the wall. My clothes are dry, creased as fuck, but clean. I feel like I should say something more. He looks like crap. The green dye in his mohawk is fading and the sides are growing out. I guess it's a high maintenance look.

'Thought you were going to sleep?'

'I tried. Can't.'

'Yeah.' Even though I just had a pretty good nap. I feel bad, I drop my clothes on the table, sit opposite him.

'I just want to say thanks, Bob, for everything.'

'You think we did the right thing?' No. We should've called the police. It's not what I say;

'I don't know. I'm sorry though. I don't know why you helped me.' I'm not sure it was help, but as I said, I feel bad, this is my mess.

'Me either, Joe, me either.'

Neither of us say anything for a minute, but then Bob muses, 'I felt sorry for you, Joe, when you turned up with the Haiku Man the other day, all pathetic and shy. New kid in The City, backpack full of dreams or whatever. I looked at you and thought, ah, we can work with him, give him some confidence, help him belong.' He takes his eyes from the wall, looks at me. 'Felt a bit proud of you that first night, when you confronted that wank-stain Tyler. Thought you were gonna be alright, a kid with morals and shit, just in need of some acceptance and nurturing. Pete wasn't here and you fucked my bar up, but it was admirable all the same.

'Listen to me, I sound like I give a shit. And here you were, celebrating your eighteenth birthday working the bar. You know what I did on my eighteenth?'

I'm touched. 'No, what?'

'I got wasted, Joe! I had good friends and we went on a massive fucking bender, me and my mates, pilling my face off, I double-dropped, got wrecked, dancing, shagging. It was a good night. My old man bought me a car. You spent yours here, not a friend in the world, no family, no birthday cards. Your fucking grandfather just died. I'm a cold bastard, Joe, but I felt for you. Reckoned you were brave, starting over, wanted to help you out. The tattoo? Thought you'd like it, y'know, be part of our little gang or whatever, someone you could count on.

'I can't believe this shit. I have never done something so fucking terrible in all my life, and believe me when I say I can be a right cunt.' I believe him. 'Anyway, that's it. I am not getting involved with any fucking dodgy shit ever again.'

What can I say? I already said sorry and thank you. I nod. I say, 'I like the tattoo.'

I really do.

Later in the bar, Kitten is cheerful, but when I ask about staying at hers she says,

'Not tonight, Joe. We'll go shopping tomorrow if you still want to. Then you can bring your stuff to mine. Not tonight though, yeah? My flat-mate's home, I can't be bothered to persuade her. And it'll only be temporary OK? My place is tiny. Where'd you lose your jacket?'

Pete burned it because it was covered in the blood and brain matter of the guy upstairs I killed yesterday. I don't say this out loud obviously.

'If I knew that it wouldn't be lost.'

She rolls her eyes, but smiles. Bob's quiet, Pete's lazy, the Haiku Man is drunk.

# Communicating

I wake to the haunting thoughts I'd expected. I slept alright, fucked up dreams aside. I lie for a couple of minutes before I pick up my phone, Google Jack Jones soldier. Nothing except the same as yesterday. I Google train delays. Nothing relevant. I search through news sites. I find something;

*The discovery of a body on the Eastbound train line to The City is being treated as suspicious by police.*

*The police are currently unable to confirm the identity of the male, whose body was discovered yesterday afternoon. The line was closed for several hours.*

*Officers are investigating the circumstances as to how he came to be on the tracks.*

My heart's pounding. Officers are investigating. It's suspicious. Suspicious means they know it's not a suicide. Of course they know, it was an insanely stupid idea. It's only eight thirty, too early to tell Bob, though maybe I won't tell him anyway. What good will it do?

I could murder a coffee, no pun intended, but don't feel at home enough to go make myself one in the kitchen. I get up, still in yesterday's clothes. I'm done with sleeping fully dressed, done with this shitty bare mattress, I miss warmth, a lamp, a kettle, carpets, sofas, pillows, normal stuff. I'm instantly pissed off. I'm going to Starbucks.

With my cafe latte in front of me, my crumpled clothes still scented with sleep, I connect to the WiFi. Casey has messaged me;

*Hi Joe, what you up to today? Told my mum about you, she's relieved but worried.*

I reply,

*Nothing much today, what you up to?*

I text Kitten,

*Know it's early. You still up for going shopping?*

The texts sends, I haven't been cut off yet. Sipping my coffee and waiting for responses I think of my situation. I haven't done anything remotely constructive since I got here. I just want to survive. I'm a killer. Accidental, but still. I'm a criminal, it's a strange feeling; I know I did something terrible, but I'm still the same person, I'm not what I thought a murderer was, calculated and cold, I'm not dangerous, a threat to society. I'm genuinely sorry. I feel I need to live a life for Grandpa, and for Jack Jones. I'm overwhelmed. Casey replies,

*Nothing. School's over. Lying in bed thinking about you. Feel like running away like you did* Winky face emoji.

On a whim I message back,

*Do it!* Smiley face.

*Can I join you?*

Shit no, I have nowhere. It would be good to see her.

*Crashing with a friend, but I'd love to see you!*

*But I have no cash* Sad emoji.

Thank fuck for that.

*I have cash* Sunglasses emoji.

What the fuck is wrong with me? She can't come, she can't depend on me, not now. Yet I send these messages.

*I'm tempted!* Crying laughing emoji.

I'm sure she's not actually crying with laughter. I stop responding because I'm scared she's going to turn up. It's gone nine, still nothing from Kitten. I order a bacon and gouda breakfast sandwich. What the fuck is gouda? I just want a bacon sandwich, I take the risk because I'm hungry. Despite eating nothing but junk since I got here, my jeans tell me I'm losing weight. It's an effort, buying food and eating all the time. Makes me appreciate Grandpa all the more.

Gouda is cheese I'm guessing, because my sandwich turns up with cheese in it and it tastes pretty good. I finally get a text from Kitten,

*Just woke up. Give me an hour. Where u want to meet?*

*I'm at Starbucks. Where do you want to meet?*

*Meet u there? Which one?*

*I don't know, how many are there?*

*Shitloads!*

*The one nearest the bar?*

*OK, see u soon* Smiley face.

I can't wait to see her. I buy another coffee and wait.

# Only Saw Him Twice

Kitten arrives and plonks down into the worn leather sofa.

'Can I get a coffee before we go, Joe? I'm fucking knackered.' I buy her a coffee. 'Hey, listen to this! Tyler called me yesterday, said he'd seen that guy from the bar in the news, asked if he was still staying there. Did you read it, Joe? I mean, shit, who knew?' She didn't mention it last night. I nod, yeah. 'I was talking to Bob about it last night, he was weird, huh? Did you ever speak to him?'

Yes, and I killed him. 'No. Only saw him maybe twice. Did Tyler call the police?'

'Hell no!' She thinks it's funny for some reason. What is everyone's issue with the cops around here? I feign laughter, trying to look like I get her.

We catch a bus across town, a part of The City I've never seen. It's cool, all indie and quirky and there's so much variety and colour here, the streets are like art galleries, the people like living exhibits; I'm instantly in love. Why didn't I end up here? I feel out of my depth but I've got Kitten by my side and she has enough confidence for both of us. We wander around vintage shops. I think they smell just like charity shops, except the clothes are more expensive and there's no benevolence. Kitten's fun, trying on hats and feather boas, taking selfies, she engages with strangers in a way I never knew people did in real life. She's friendly and contagious and my mood is lifted. It feels good to laugh again. She's beautiful and I wish she was my girlfriend. She posts a picture of us together in bowler hats to her instagram and I promise myself I will sign up to every social media platform she has, if only to see photos of her.

She fawns over an umbrella patterned with skulls and I buy it for her and she hugs me. She has me try on jackets;

'Too big.'

'Too old man.'

'Too country.'

'Punk as fuck! I love it!'

I hate it. It's covered in studs, I feel like Rob Talbot. Not me at all, I don't want to give the wrong impression. I find one though, as similar to my old one as possible. I try it on. I like it, it feels almost familiar. I unzip the pockets, slip my hands inside.

'Very you, Joe.' It has pockets inside too, and I slip my hand in one to discover a £20 note. 'Whoa, nice, it's a sign! Buy it!' She whispers it, discreet, gives me eyes to hide it. I do. And then I buy it. She hasn't mentioned about me staying at hers and neither have I.

'You want to get some lunch? I'm paying.' I ask.

'Well yes, you're fucking loaded, Joe!' I'm feeling mildly euphoric, she's such lovely company.

There's a ton of food places around here, all ethnic stuff, street food that smells amazing that I have no idea how to pronounce.

'What do you recommend?' I ask Kitten. I'm hoping she'll order us something so I don't have to embarrass myself.

'Hot wings!'

I can pronounce that. 'Let's get those.'

So we do, and we sit on a bench where pigeons pester us. The wings are messy and Kitten has hot sauce on her cheek and her perfect lipstick is smudged and I love her anyway. Without me asking she says while chewing,

'D'you still want to stay at mine for awhile?'

'Yeah, if that's OK?' I say it too keenly and cringe internally.

'It's only the sofa, you know that, right?'

'Yeah, that's fine. Have you seen my room at the bar?'

'Shit yeah, Joe. What a fucking pit. Bob's a good man, he's been good to me. But that place, that's no way to live. You need to look for something better.'

'I know.'

'You serious about staying here? I think you should. I know it's scary, because I was in your shoes once. I was frightened and overwhelmed, but it's the best thing I ever did. It's just liberating. I love this City, look at it. Beautiful isn't it? I promise it'll work out.'

She pats my knee, it's entirely platonic. I think about telling her what happened. I can't. I haven't decided if I will stay much longer or not, but I'll give it a few more days and being away from the bar will make things better, give me some clarity. Where else can I go anyway?

After the wings I awkwardly tell her she has sauce on her face. I'm proud of myself because normally I'd be too embarrassed for her to say anything, and then later she'd be like, why didn't you tell me? And I'd be, I dunno, sorry, I didn't notice. I suddenly realise

I had the chance to completely reinvent myself when I came here, I could've been anyone, could've made up some elaborate and interesting back-story, but instead turned up just being myself. I think I've been braver than I would've at home, At least I'm learning to talk to people.

We catch a bus back to near her place, and she tells me to go to the bar to get my stuff, come back when I'm done, she'll be waiting for me. Here goes, I try again.

# Ruminating, And The Trip

My mood is decent after hanging with Kitten. Being with her is like therapy. I feel good, then five minutes or so later I remember everything that happened, and when she mentions Tyler I get a surge of adrenaline and anxiety, that shitty feeling in my gut. My heart pounds, I sweat and shake. It's hard to focus on anything else, but I try and eventually, I force my brain to cling to something optimistic, until five minutes passes and it happens again. It's draining. I have no right to feel good about anything, I *should* suffer for what I did. I accept the fact that I'm going to feel like crap a lot of the time. I deserve it.

Back at the bar Bob greets me. He seems better than yesterday, more chirpy, less tired. He sees me in my new jacket.

'Where've you been, boy?'

'I met Kitten, we went shopping.'

'Ah nice. Didn't tell her anything did you?'

'No!'

'I know. Good lad. How're you feeling?'

'OK. You?'

'Yeah, better. Got some sleep finally.'

I wonder if I should mention what I read this morning but it'll just piss him off so I keep it to myself. Instead I say,

'Kitten says I can stay at hers. I can still work if you want me to.' He might not let me go if I tell him the truth.

'That's great, Joe. Good for you. And there's work if you want it, can't rely on Pete at the minute. Monday's are quiet though, have a night off.' He smiles, gold teeth glinting. He really does look better.

'Cool, thanks. I'm going to pack my things, take it to Kitten's.'

'Go for it son.'

Son? It's just how he speaks but I feel a twinge of warmth.

I go upstairs, and as I'm opening my door Pete sticks his head out of his room.

'Alright Joe?'

'Hey Pete,' I smile, he feels like family to me today.

'Fancy a smoke?' He grins, waves a joint at me. I do actually, yeah.

'Yeah.' I pull shut my door and walk towards him.

'New jacket? Nice!'

'Thanks.' I forgot how blinding his room was, and say, 'Shit, it's bright in here, doesn't it do your head in?'

'A bit. Worth it though. Besides, I got these.' He slips on some sunglasses, they make him look like a right cool fucker. Or blind. 'Here, I got more, for guests.' He laughs, hands me a pair too. I put them on and sit on his bed, same as yesterday. Now we both look like cool fuckers. He lights the joint, 'What you been up to, Joe?'

'Went shopping with Kitten. Got this jacket. I'm going to stay at hers for a while.'

'Oh yeah? Meant to ask, d'you fuck her the other night?'

'Yeah.' I smirk. So much for me being gentlemanly. Pete brings out my coarse side.

'Ah ha, nice one, Joe, she's hot, man, no doubt!'

'It was a one off,' I say, 'I'm only going to sleep on her sofa.'

'Yeah, we'll see.'

'What've you been doing?'

'Nothing, not long woke up.'

'You smoke that shit for breakfast?'

'Yes. Yes I do.' He passes it to me. I inhale, fuck it's good. Numbs that crappy gut feeling I was talking about. 'Tunes?' says Pete. I nod. He gets up and fiddles around with his CD player. A song kicks in.

'Who's this?'

'Minor Threat.' Never heard of them but I give them a chance, take a few drags. Wouldn't describe it as tunes to be honest. They're noisy, lacks melody. No idea what the fuck they're saying. No intro, no solo, no breakdown. First track's over in a minute. They're shit. I was hoping for some seventies stoner rock, but I suppose I admire the energy, it suits Pete. I pass the joint back, ask him,

'Would you sell me some of this?'

'Yeah. How much do you want?'

'I don't know.'

'You want some crisps?'

'Fuck yeah!' I'm suddenly starving. Pete passes me a multipack from down the side of the bed. I rummage about and settle on some cheese and onion.

He asks, 'What do you reckon is the best flavour crisp?'

'Depends,' I say, 'If it's for a sandwich, or if it's as a stand alone crisp.' I'm instantly into this, it's a complex matter. 'Also, define crisp. Are we solely talking about deep fried sliced potato crisps, because what about chipsticks? Maize based snacks? And Wotsits? Pringles? Do they count?'

'Jesus Christ Joe, that's a lot to think about! Let's go with standard potato crisps first yeah? Not in a sandwich?'

'Salt and vinegar.'

'But you chose cheese and onion?'

'There's no salt and vinegar left.'

'Ah, yeah, I ate them.' He passes the joint back to me, 'Agreed, salt and vinegar is the king of crisp flavours.' We're both nodding, I'm satisfied. But,

'In a sandwich, I prefer smoky bacon.'

'Nah Joe, prawn cocktail!' I like this inane conversation. Pete's rummaging in his bedside drawer. He pulls out a tin, opens it. It's filled with weed. 'So, how much? What do you want to spend?'

'I don't know. This is new to me, I never smoked before. Enough for a week or two? Not enough to get me locked up or anything.'

'Ha, two weeks worth would get *me* locked up. But yeah, good thinking, small quantities. How about this? Thirty quid? Should last you a while.' It looks like a decent enough amount, I don't know, when Pete rolls he mixes it in with tobacco. I don't think he's ripping me off.

'How about fifty quid? What would you give me for that?'

'That's a lot for one person man, don't let it dry out, you'll have to keep it airtight.'

'OK.'

'This much? I'm being generous, mind, I ain't no dealer, just a gardener. This is my own stash. Only because my plants are almost done that I've agreed to this yeah?'

'Yeah, thanks.' Pete finds a bag to put it in. Sets about rolling another joint.

He says, 'Alright, here's one for you. Would you rather travel to the past or the future?'

'Would I have to stay there forever?'

'No.'

'Future.'

'Why?'

'Dunno. I bet there's cool stuff in the future. The past's already written down. I could get the lottery numbers?'

'Good point, Joe. Me too. OK, what about this, would you rather be a girl with a dick, or a man with a vagina?' Pete's mind is strange. This feels like an interview.

'Tough call.' I pull out the money I have, not discreetly because I just smoked a joint and I don't give a shit. Pete doesn't notice. I give him £50. 'Would I have tits if I was a girl with a dick?'

'Hell yeah!'

'Then yeah, a girl. I'm not bothered about having a vagina.'

Pete shrugs, 'Same, sounds good. We got a lot in common, Joe. Tits are life. Right, this one's a tough one. Imagine you're in prison...' Shit, thanks Pete. I might actually be in prison by next week. 'Would you rather get fucked in the arse and then get a nice blowjob. Or would you rather fuck someone in the arse but then give them a blowjob?' Oh fuck, I hope I'm never in this predicament.

'Those are both shit.'

'Yeah, but you gotta pick one.' Seriously? I consider this a minute.

'I think I'd rather fuck someone then give a blowjob.' I'm scared at the idea of taking it in the arse. Stuff comes out, it doesn't go in.

Maybe I'm missing out, but I don't want to try. 'What about you?' I ask.

'Depends if there's lube. I love a good blow job.' I don't have a response to that. He carries on, 'OK, I got one more Joe. Would you rather swim 300 metres through human shit, or dead bodies?'

'I can't swim.' How much is 300 metres?

'You can't swim? Are you fucking retarded? Christ! If you *could* swim, which would you choose?'

'The shit. It's got to be better than dead bodies, easier.'

'Well, that's your opinion. You want a cup of tea?' Pete's up, puts the kettle on.

'Yeah, thanks. You'd pick the dead bodies?'

'I would. I'd puke if I had to swim through actual shit. Sugar?'

'Two.' As if he wouldn't puke swimming through corpses? He's so weird. Pete has a mini fridge with milk in, some beers and chocolate bars. He's giggling.

'What's so funny?' I ask.

'Nothing, you.' He hands me my tea.


Ah shit, here we go. Bad move. Bad Pete. Mad Pete. Don't drink the tea, Joe, don't drink it! Too late. This could be interesting.


He sits back down on the bed, carries on rolling a joint. He asks, 'You ever wish you were someone else Joe?'

All. The. Time.

'Yeah.'

'Who?'

'Dunno, someone else. Someone confident? A really rich person?'

'Like who? Pick a real person you'd rather be.' I don't know. I always presumed it would be easier if I was someone else. I'm embarrassed to name someone though. Can I say Kurt Cobain? Yeah, he's dead, but he left a mark, a legacy. Something of significance. I suppose I could pick Jay-Z or someone. He seems to have a pretty good life; a mansion and Beyonce. Or the Queen? But I do not want to be Jay-Z, or the Queen. Money's not really my thing.

'Dunno, maybe Kurt Cobain?'

'He killed himself though.'

'I know. But he was cool, his legacy lives on doesn't it?'

'Yeah, I'm not saying it's a bad choice.' I'm embarrassed, so I deflect, ask,

'What about you? You ever wish you were someone else?'

'Fuck yeah, all the time. Let me think, someone groundbreaking yeah?' I nod in agreement, I can't wait to hear.

'Hmm. Reckon I'd be GG Allin.' I'm disappointed because I have no idea who that is.

'Who's GG Allin?'

'Are you serious? What are you? Jehovah's Witness? A Mormon? Fucking Amish or something? Fuck Joe, Kurt knew about GG Allin.'

'No.' I'm embarrassed again. Pete's shaking his head, looking disappointed in me.

'Ah man, you're fucking missing out! Let me tell you about him,' I try to look cool.

'GG Allin; Jesus Christ Allin. He was the punkest motherfucker who ever lived! Had the weirdest childhood, his old man was some religious psycho recluse, but it made GG a fucking warrior, Joe. He was a car crash, didn't give a shit about anything, that's admirable right? Not giving a shit is the key to happiness, trust me.' I'm not sure I agree with this philosophy, but I'll hear him out. He lights the joint, takes a massive drag, 'So, he was a legend. The biggest arsehole in the world. He had no conscience, no morals, no filter. Straight fucking crazy, didn't believe in government or religion or rules, Joe, a pure anarchist. If you went to a GG Allin show, you'd get pissed on or shit on, probably take a beating, unless you were tough enough to be the one dishing it out. Like, seriously, his gigs were fucking mental; GG would be naked, covered in his own shit and blood, he'd stick his dick in your mouth and kick you in the head. He said that if he wasn't a performer, he'd be a serial killer.'

Sounds charming. I say, 'He sounds crazy.'

'He *was* crazy! He's dead too, heroin overdose. The point is, the reason I admire the fucker Joe, is that he was the embodiment of everything that society hates, a real fucking rebel. Chaos personified, lived by his own rules and everyone could just fall in line or fuck off. No one does that! Takes a lot to not give a shit that much. I think that's brave, takes guts.' He's really animated now, but I think GG Allin sounds like a psychopath. Pete shrugs, he's smoking the shit out of that joint, I hope he doesn't forget to pass it. 'Look at me, all of us, fucking conforming, pretending to be subversive, making out like we're challenging the system. Reality is, we're all complying; none of us have the balls to do what the fuck we want to do, to take what we want. We live in fear of the consequences, and even when we do break the rules, we do it discreetly or whatever, because we're trying to fucking blend in, look normal, seem like respectable upright citizens. Because it's fucking safer, it's self-preservation, Joe! And it's not just our lack of rebellion or fear of repercussions; most of us have empathy and shit, we don't want to go around being arseholes, hurting people, right? We care about our friends and family, and their feelings.

'But just imagine it, being able to act on all your desires without guilt or conscience. Now, that sounds like freedom to me, living without a care. Am I right?'

Huh, maybe Pete's actually smarter than I thought. He passes the remainder of the joint finally. And it's weird, he's like a different person suddenly. The weed must be really good for him; he's gone from jittering and erratic simpleton into, I don't know, someone with actual opinions. He's got some valid points, some observations I hadn't considered before. Some of them are ridiculous too, I mean, a lack of conscience is surely a bad thing.

Yep, ignore it Joe, Pete's really not that smart. The weed is good for him though, alleviates his hyperactivity, to the point where he's lucid and he can have a regular conversation like he's almost normal. But normality should not be mistaken for intelligence.

'I really believed in anarchy once Joe, the concept is attractive, right? It's everything that punk stands for, but now I'm tired, that shit's a young man's game. At your age I believed in a better world, had a real sense of cause, you feel that way, yeah? And fucking go for it kid, fight for it! Because a time comes where your spirit just breaks, you soften, lose heart, and then you just trust that those after you will continue to run with the baton.'

Well shit, I do not have a cause or an ideal. I'm just not political, but now I feel I should be. I do care about stuff and I'm glad there are people out there fighting for progress, I'm just not the right person for thc job. So, at least I won't get old and jaded like Pete? Also, anarchism sounds extreme. He's still on one.

'When GG died, he had an open casket. He'd wanted to kill himself on stage, said once he'd reached his peak he'd go down in front of a crowd. Kind of like Kurt, right? Better to burn out than fade away or some shit? It never happened, but can you imagine if he did that? He wasn't embalmed. Laid in his coffin, stinking of shit and piss, all swollen and bloated, wearing a jockstrap and a leather jacket, bottle of whiskey beside him, all his mates fucking taking photos, all discoloured and fat. It'd be troubling, if you didn't get him.'

It is fucking troubling. Confirmed, Pete's insane.

I don't mean to criticise the sentiment of punk rock, but GG Allin is not the poster boy for this movement. Pete could've picked a far better advocate of such ethics. Anyway, doesn't matter, Joe's moved on already. And Pete doesn't have it in him to be a massive cockwomble like GG either. He's a bit of a knob, damaged, but he's still got a heart. It's not his intention to corrupt Joe.

'Pete?'

'Yeah?'

'D'you think we're gonna get caught?'

'Nah. Shit, don't get paranoid Joe, stay positive.'

'I'm trying. You burnt all the stuff right?'

'Yes, good and proper, don't worry about it.'

'What did you do with his tags?'

'Threw them off a bridge, miles away. Honestly, let it go.'

I'm trying. I ask him, 'Don't you feel bad?'

'I didn't do anything, Joe, you did.'

'It was an accident.'

'So you say. I believe you, never had you down as a stone cold killer.' He laughs, 'Change the subject, Christ, what a downer.' He lights another joint, starts giggling again.

'Sorry.'

'No worries. You up for hanging out this afternoon?'

'I have to take my stuff to Kitten's.'

'Can't that wait?'

'Not really, I pissed her off the other day, you know, everything that happened.' Pete passes me the joint. I'm already feeling it after those first two, I wouldn't mind a nap, but I take it anyway, finish my tea.

'What was she like, Joe?'

'What do you mean?'

'Kitten! When you fucked her?' What am I supposed to say? I have nothing to compare her to, and I'm not sure what the protocol is discussing these things. I'm glad for the change in subject, but the music's pretty loud and I don't want to have to shout anything out. It was good, what I remember. Awesome. Is that enough? I think I totally fucked her, but the word makes me cringe a bit, sounds disrespectful. So I say,

'We were drunk. It was hot.'

'Details Joe, details!'

'It was just sex.'

'She suck you off?'

'No.'

'Oh. Nice tits?'

'Hell yeah.' They're the only tits I've ever seen in real life, of course they were nice.

'What are her nipples like?' I don't know. Like nipples? I suppose one was a bit bigger than the other. I shrug, pass the joint back.

'Aw come on, are they little pink nipples? Big brown beef burgers? What are we talking here?' I nearly choke laughing; beef burgers? Christ!

'Nah, small I guess, pale pink. They're cute.' I'm still chuckling. I'm not going to say anymore, I feel bad.

'Ah just as I'd imagined then.'

I think of meeting Pete that first night, how scary and unhinged he looked. I still think he's unhinged, but he's not frightening, not really. I ask him,

'How old are you?'

'Not sure, stopped counting. Forty three? I think. Christ Joe, stop bringing me down man, age don't mean shit.' Wow, he's ancient. No wonder he still has a CD player. He looks younger, would've guessed maybe thirty. He looks like a child right now, grinning with his fake Ray-Bans on.

'Do you have a girlfriend?' I ask. I know the answer already, I haven't seen him with anyone. I presume he's not gay with all these half naked girls on his wall, and him asking about Kitten's nipples. Don't know why, I just expect people in their forties to be married with kids and stuff.

'Nah, women are hard work, they expect too much. Can't be arsed.'

'Any kids?'

'Fuck no, what would I want them for? Fucking Hell. You Joe, you're just a kid still, don't fall into the trap.' He's shaking his head, as serious as he gets. 'Anyway, stop asking me questions! I've got something to tell you.'

'What?'

'I put something in your tea.'

'What do you mean?'

'I mean I put acid in your tea. Have a nice trip.' He's sniggering, looking mischievous. What? He'd better be joking.

'Acid? What? Are you serious?'

'Yeah!' He's laughing now, almost hysterically, clutching his stomach. He's not joking.

'What do you mean? Like LSD?!'

'Yeah!'

'Fuck Pete, I've never done it before… why? Why would you *do that?*'

'For a laugh.'

'It's not funny! You're taking the piss, right? What's going to happen? I feel OK, maybe stoned? 'Fuck Pete, I've got to go to Kitten's! Tell me you're joking?' I'm scared. I don't know what to expect. Is this it? Because this is fine, I can deal with it. I'm taking deep breaths but I feel like I'm hyperventilating.

'I'm not joking. Relax Joe, takes a while to kick in, you'll be fine. Here, I'll drop some too, we'll trip together.' Pete thinks this is hilarious. I'm shitting myself. What if I think I can fly or some shit? Try to jump off a building and end up dying? I'm frightened.

'I'm scared, Pete.' He's over by the kettle.

'Here, I'm doing it too, Joe, it's fine, honest. Embrace it! Enjoy, it's fun, I promise.' I watch him, small glass vial in his hand, he squeezes a couple of drops onto his palm, licks it.

'Fuck!' I get my phone out. I'm texting Kitten;

*Pete just spiked my tea with acid, I'm still coming I promise, but I've never done acid before!!!*

I ask him, 'What's going to happen?'

'You'll know when it kicks in.'

'How will I know?' I'm freaking out.

'You need to calm the hell down Joe, or it'll be shit. Relax, enjoy the ride, we'll have a laugh. You're safe, I'll look after you, quit whining!'

Kitten texts back;

*R U 4 real? Pete's a fucking twat! FFS!*

Pete's phone is vibrating, on the drawers beside his bed. He picks it up.

'It's Kitten,' he says, answers it, 'Alright Kitty?' I can't hear what she's saying but she's angry, I can hear her ire, even over the music. A high pitched rant, she's not letting Pete say anything, he looks perplexed. He's looking at me, eyebrows raised. Now he's gesturing, smiling at me, feeling imaginary tits. He says down the phone, 'Chill out, everything's fine!' I can still hear her. 'Alright, calm down, Kitty, Christ!' She hangs up, and Pete is like, 'Fucking Hell Joe, what did you tell her?' My phone rings. I'm not in the best frame of mind to answer, it's Kitten. I answer anyway.

'You OK Joe?'

'Yeah.'

'Stay where you are, keep calm!'

'I'm fine.'

'I'll see you in a while OK?'

'OK.' She hangs up. I start to laugh. 'Sorry Pete, I text her.'

'Fuck, Joe, she gave me a right mouthful.' He's laughing too.

'I'm sorry, I feel fine, it's no big deal. I need to get my shit together, go to Kitten's.' I wish I were brave and familiar enough to call her Kitty.

'You can't go now. Take it easy, Kitten knows where you are, it hasn't got you yet.' I've calmed down, nothing bad is happening. I feel normal. I just want to go. I say,

'I'm gonna go, thanks for the smoke Pete.'

'Ah man, you sure? I mean, I wouldn't if I were you, you haven't come up yet, give it a while. I don't want you freaking out, it's no fun on your own.'

'I'm alright.' Still sitting on the bed, my body's not making any effort to move.

'Look, hang out for a bit, I'll come with you to Kitten's, yeah?'

'OK.'

'Good, stop thinking. Clear your mind, just relax.'

'Can you change the music?'

'Yeah, yeah I can, something more chilled right?'

'This guy sounds so angry.'

'He is, that's why. Straight edge motherfucker needs some weed! Don't worry, I'm on it.' After a minute of sifting through his CD collection, he says, 'Don't tell anyone, Joe, but I really like The Beach Boys.' OK? It's less offensive to my ears, cheerful at least. Fucking weird though. I have a strange metallic taste in my mouth. 'Right Joe, trick is to think happy thoughts yeah? Beach Boys will help. Keep this shit quiet, mind, don't ruin my reputation, I'm trusting you.' The music reminds me of my father. I don't have any happy thoughts, just panic with an undertone of self-loathing.

A knock on the door, it's Bob, he lets himself in. He sees us both sitting on the bed with shades on, in a fog of pot smoke, listening to Good Vibrations.

'Fucking hell Pete, don't go turning Joe into a waster.'

'Haha, yeah, alright bro? What's up?'

'Nothing, just checking in.'

'It's all good.'

'Alright, don't get too messed up, I gave Joe the night off, be good to see you downstairs later though?' Bob looks concerned.

'Yeah, no worries.'

'Aren't you going to Kitten's, Joe?'

'Yeah, soon.'

'Alright. See you later then.' Neither me or Pete mention the acid. Bob backs out the door, looking like a disappointed parent.

When the door shuts, I say to Pete, 'This song reminds me of my dad.'

'Me too, Joe, me too! Your old man must be alright.'

'Nah, he was a bastard.'

'Oh right, sorry. He's dead?'

'Don't know, don't care.'

'Ah man, that sucks. My old man was alright, this CD makes me feel sentimental and shit. Don't say anything Joe, but I like Elton John too.' What can I say to that? Suppressing a snigger and unrelated, I ask,

'How old is Bob?'

'Two years older than me. You know he's got a kid right?' I didn't.

'For real?'

'Yeah, he'll be about fifteen now. Bob's ex missus, she moved up North years ago with him, got married.'

'Wow, does Bob ever see him?'

'No, not for years. And get this, his name's Joe.'

'Fuck off!'

'Serious!' Pete's laughing. This is funny as fuck for no reason, we're both weak giggling. I'm feeling jittery, restless. This song has way too many layers. It's complex as fuck. All that vocal harmonising, all those instruments. Pete says, 'You coming up?'

'I don't know.' Coming up where? Is this drug talk? Presume so, going with it.

'Go with it, don't fight it.'

The Beach Boys, did they consider how this song would sound on drugs? Because it's a lot to deal with. To be fair, it's giving actual good vibrations, but my brain's overloaded. I think of Kitten. The character of the song changes completely, that lull, that change of tone, are they trying to fuck with me? It's genius. I tell Pete,

'I'm good.'

'Ha, close your eyes, lie back.'

I'm laughing, sounds like he's going to suck my dick or something. I do it anyway, relax my head, lie back on his pillows, try to stifle my mirth. He'd better not try to suck my dick because I will kick him in the face.  As soon as I close my eyes, technicolour perfection. Fuck. Wow. I remember something. My eyes still closed I ask, 'Pete? Is that other person here?'

'What other person? Oh, right, *that* one.'

'Yeah.'

'Yeah, actually. Didn't say it was a person though.'

I've got my eyes shut still, kaleidoscopic visions. Colourful little plastic beads falling when I move, I feel good. Blissful actually. Why did I think it was a person?

'Tell me more.'

'Nothing more to say, I'm used to it now. To be honest Joe, I think whatever it is, a presence or an entity or something, it's judging the fuck out of me, you don't feel it?'

I take a couple of seconds to see if I can feel it. I feel something, but it could just be the drugs. I open my eyes, and no, just me and Pete. Everything's beginning to look a little distorted though, the light is weird, and inanimate things are looking a bit shaky, things are shifting. It's not unpleasant.

'Nope, don't feel it, but Pete, what is up with your plants?' I'm looking at them, and the leaves all have fingers, each leaflet, every point of every leaf is a finger. Shit. That is strange behaviour for a plant. They're beckoning, waving long green-painted fingernails, feminine, hundreds of them, the light surrounding them an ethereal greenish hue. Pete looks at the plants, looks at me,

'You tell me, Joe.' He's smiling, delighted.

'They've all got fingers!' It's not as disturbing as it sounds. The fingers are gentle, they're calling me, guiding the way. Pete's creased laughing,

'Ah brilliant, you're definitely there, good shit right?' I have to close my eyes again because it's some trippy shit. Literally. And when I do, my eyelids are filled with a psychedelic rainbow of colour and movement. I like the music now. It's buoyant, matches the moment. The colours match the rhythm. I say,

'I don't want to open my eyes again.'

'Ah, but you must Joe! That's the best part, the stuff you see.'

Pete's voice sounds distant, I tune him out. Lying there I feel as though my head's falling through the pillow, like I'm sinking into the bed, and I briefly open my eyes, I haven't moved or sunk, but looking at the ceiling it's as though it's drifting away from me; am I descending, or is it rising? Don't know. I shut my eyes again, feels safer.

I lose myself in thought, waves of insight wash over me. It's intense, and I have this realisation that I'm immortal. I mean, I know I'll eventually die, but my body will in turn continue to exist as atoms, as matter within the earth, the water and air; I'll be reborn as something new, some essence of myself eternal and enduring. We're just carbon. It's comforting, what with being an atheist.

I have another thought about destruction. It's our nature to destroy, to ruin, to kill, to hurt, to break. We lie and we cheat. It's sad and I could cry. Why do kids like to kick down the sandcastles they built? Knock down their building blocks? I know why; violence is a necessary tendency in order for us to survive, to obtain our basic needs of territory or whatever. But is it not also our nature to create? Destruction feeds creation. We're a contradiction, not intended to be static. Both destruction and creation exist entangled with one another, neither can be without the opposite. Yin and yang. Dark and light. Juxtaposition. The circle of life. It is not a new concept, but this is the first time I ever really understood it so completely. My mind's blown.

I remember where I am, the sounds of the room come back. Awareness of music, of Pete. I open my eyes, it takes more effort than it should. I think I've forgotten how to be human. What is time? Pete's not on the bed, but instead sits on a clothes strewn chair near his blacked out window. I'm looking at him in profile, he's like some modern painting; Punk Reclining on Chair. His head thrown back, he's still and I momentarily worry that he's dead until I see him smile. I call him,

'Pete?'

'What?' He doesn't move.

'Nothing.'

'You OK, Joe?'

'Yeah.'

'You up for going out? Taking a walk?'

'No.' Oh God no. I feel like doing some drawing though. I raise myself up on my elbows, look around. The plants don't have fingers anymore. They're still waving though, in unison, like arms at a soft rock concert.

'Ah come on Joe, I need visual stimulation, let's get out.' Plenty of visual stimulation on his walls if you know what I mean; I can barely look at these posters because I'm feeling warm and relaxed and I'll probably get a hard-on if I see any more tits and butt-cheeks. Pete's head turns towards me, and this is when my trip takes a turn for the worse.

Fuck! Pete's jaw is half missing, bloodied ripped skin hanging from his face, teeth missing, I can see his tongue moving through the hole where his cheek should be. He's talking to me but I've no idea what he's saying because I'm freaking out. I leap up from the bed, I'm on my feet backing away, there's saliva and blood dripping onto the floor and he's walking towards me, his jaw wagging up and down, incoherent babble spilling out. I make out, 'Don't tell anyone about The Beach Boys!'

# Running And Everything
## Fucks Up Again

Fuck! I'm gonna run, I'm not going through this again, I will not be held prisoner. My back hits the door, I turn around and frantically pull at the latch, let myself out, slam it behind me, and run for my life, down the hallway, down the stairs. The floor feels like sand. Through the doorway and I'm behind the bar, confronted by Bob who is not looking normal. There are customers, the bar's open and everyone's eyes are on me and I'm freaking out! I lift the hatch and I get out that front door as fast as I can, run down the street, checking back over my shoulder to make sure the dead guy's not following me, I need to find somewhere safe. Nobody follows. I slow to a jog, then a fast walk. I'm aware that I might look a bit of a state. I don't want to draw attention to myself. I'm not out of breath from running, more out of fear, and I want to rest.

Ah, bugger. I said it would get interesting, didn't I?

I end up outside the church again, and it feels like a sign. Churches offer sanctuary, right? It was peaceful there yesterday. Was it yesterday? The door's closed, but I push it anyway and it opens. It's dark inside, and I realise I still have Pete's sunglasses on, so I push them up onto my head. The air's cool, it's empty. I instantly feel better, my breathing is levelling, my heart calming. Maybe I overreacted. I walk slowly down the aisle, and at the end, the altar, is a huge effigy of Christ on the cross; it's so detailed, the loincloth, the bloodied holes where the nails hold him in place. His face pained, a thorny crown impaled upon his brow. His long hair falling about his face. I'm fascinated, I walk closer, studying every detail and I swear he's moving. He's not as emaciated as I'd expect Jesus to be. His head is bowed to one side, but it's turning, I can see it, he's real! But he is not Jesus, he is Kurt fucking Cobain!

Guess I'm tripping.

His head turns towards me,

'Hey, Joe.' he says.

'Uh, Hi, Kurt?'

'Yeah, it's me.' It's him, it's his voice. He's actually handsome as fuck too.

'But, aren't you dead?'

'Do I look dead?'

'Kind of, you're nailed to a cross.'

'Huh.' I don't know what to make of this, it feels like real life. I love this guy! Kurt Cobain is right here, alive, I'm talking to him, he knows my name! I feel a bit awkward because he's only wearing a loincloth, but I think I might be smiling. I tell him,

'I accidentally took some acid.'

'We've all been there, kid.'

'I accidentally killed someone too.'

'Don't be so hard on yourself.' Maybe he is Jesus and not Kurt, because he's very forgiving. He continues, 'Joe, I'm not here for long, so listen to me. You need to do something.'

'What?'

'Burn this motherfucking church to the ground!' I didn't expect that. Can't we just have a chat?

'Why?'

'Because it's your duty man, it's your purpose.'

'It doesn't sound like the right thing to do. It's arson.' Here I go again, sounding like a twat. I am so not cool. Kurt Cobain is telling me to do something, I should fucking do it. He asks,

'You got a light?'

'Yeah.'

'Look at all those candles, look at all that flammable fabric, light that shit up!'

'But what about you? You'll burn too. I can't get you down, you're nailed up there. Does it hurt?' He's dripping blood on the floor.

'I'm already dead, remember?'

'Oh yeah, right. This is weird. You say it's my purpose?'

'Yes, yes it is. Trust me.'

'OK. I'll light all the candles. You got any other advice?'

'Um. Yeah. Abort Christ!' Kurt's laughing, his torso quaking against the restraints holding his arms. This seems like shitty, if not impossible guidance.

'Surely burning a church is bad?' He shakes his head side to side,

'This place is depraved. It is saturated with sin and wickedness. It's very foundations were built on deceit. It's your responsibility to make a difference, bring about progress and change. You'll be doing the world a favour, Joe.' That American drawl is seductive.

'Really? OK. Anything else?' I don't know what I expected from Kurt, but it wasn't this.

'Yeah. Remember it's better to burn out than fade away.' Wow, I can't fucking believe we're having this conversation. As I look at him he's changing, back into a resin cast Christ. It's over. What the fuck did I just see?

I fish around in my pocket, find my lighter, and a bag of weed, I'd forgotten about that. It takes me a while, but I light every candle in the place, and I have to admit it looks cool. Spiritual as fuck. I sit myself down in the front pew, roll a cigarette, smoke it, because there's not a No Smoking sign in here. Those candles; little flames are dancing atop every wax platform, it's mesmerising, tiny twirling ladies of light, writhing and swaying flirtatiously, a hundred fairy-sized burlesque dancers. They're telling me it's not enough, I have to do more. Kurt was right, there's a lot of flammable material in here. Do churches have smoke alarms? Can't see any. There's a swath of heavy white fabric draped over this table at the front of the church, just below where Kurt visited. I get up, slowly edge forward. Do churches have CCTV? Can't see any. I get my lighter, hold a flame to the bottom corner of the tablecloth. It ignites, no problem, the flame creeps along the fringes, enveloping it in fire before I can even step back, seat myself, enjoy the show. The red carpet on the floor of the altar has caught alight too, where burning specks of cloth have dropped. I think I should get the fuck out of here. Why am I even doing this? Shit.

I know. This is messed up. I had to communicate with him somehow. Of course that wasn't Kurt Cobain, it was me. Revealing my true form to Joe would've frightened him, and so, I chose an avatar, something Joe would be comfortable with; I manifested as Kurt. The acid turned out to be useful. I just figured, while he was here, intoxicated beyond sound decision-making that we may as well make the most of it. I feel bad about the 'Abort Christ' thing, I was only having a laugh, and I had to chuck in some stock Cobain quotes to make it seem believable. Anyway, this church should've been burnt to the ground years ago, so many young lives already ruined. Better late than never. I should've told him that killing the soldier was OK, that it was the right thing to do. But I didn't, he wouldn't understand.

Joe has no idea that Father Thomas is, as is often the case, drunk on whisky and sleeping in the sacristy, slumped in his chair. As Joe makes his way outside, the priest is trapped, oblivious in his slumber. Smoke inhalation is a painless way to go. A blessing.


I quick step up the aisle, out the front door and I pull it shut behind me. Despite the fact I'm off my face, I'm aware that I'm in a city full of spy technology, cameras everywhere. The sun is blinding bright and I pull the glasses down to cover my eyes, keep my head down and walk, no looking back. Fuck! How much can I mess up? My phone rings. It can only be Kitten, and I answer; I'm casual, normal.

'Hey.'

'Joe? Are you alright? Where are you?'

'I'm taking a walk.'

'I came to the bar to get you, Bob said you ran off all spooked.' Shit, yeah I did.

'Is Pete OK?'

'He's fine, where are you?'

'Not far. I'll come back. You still at the bar?'

'Yes. See you soon?'

'Yeah.'

She hangs up, and I make my way back. I won't mention the church or Kurt. Perhaps I didn't actually do anything, maybe it's just the acid. I know I'm kidding myself, I literally just started a fire in a church and I'm definitely going to Hell.

I'm back outside the bar, but I'm nervous to go in because I still don't feel right and I'm scared that Pete's face is still fucked up. I know now it was Pete, not Jack Jones, but I'm thinking of what I read on the news this morning, and I worry that Kitten's phone call was a trap and the cops are in there waiting for me. I text her;

*I'm outside, don't want to come in*

Moments later the door opens, and it's not the cops, it's Kitten, hands on hips, regarding me with pity and concern.

'Jesus Christ Joe, I was worried. Are you alright?' I'm not alright.

'I'm fine.'

Bob appears, 'Alright boy? Had me worried there. Come in, relax for a bit, drink some water, eat something.' Ah shit, I can't take this attention. Kitten stands beside me, puts her arm around my shoulder, I feel pathetic. She leads me through the door, and it's the same as earlier, all eyes on me. I tell her,

'I can't cope with the people.'

'I know, keep walking, we'll go in the kitchen.'

'Where's Pete?' I ask, 'Is his face normal?'

'Yes, of course it is! Everything's fine, he's upstairs. Bob's super pissed off with him, so am I. He's a twat,' Through the bar hatch, into the kitchen, Kitten pulls out a chair at the table, 'Sit down, I'll make you something to eat.'

'I'm not hungry. I don't think my mouth works.'

266

'You need to fight it now, Joe. Eat, soak up the poison. You fancy anything?' She's looking in the fridge but there's not much in there.

'I suppose I could eat a crisp sandwich.' Been fancying one since Pete's room.

'Perfect, because there's definitely crisps here.'

Bob says, 'I gotta man the bar, take it easy, Joe.' I don't look at him because faces are messing with me. Kitten finds bread, I sit like a kid waiting for my dinner. I study the wood grain on the table, it slithers about and I just want this to end so I shut my eyes. I'm done with this weird shit, I'll never do acid again.

'Here you go.' I open one eye, Kitten puts a plate and a glass of water in front of me and I'm totally up for eating now. She's going on about how irresponsible and childish Pete is. He is a twat for spiking my tea but I still like him. I smile to myself because it feels like Bob is my dad and Kitten's my mum, and Pete's my naughty older brother, grounded, confined to his room, and they're like my little family now. I want to say to her, I don't want to live with dad anymore, I want to live with you, but I know she won't get it. I'd like to lie down in a dark quiet room. I can hear sirens, I'm sure of it. I think about the church. I really fucking did that. Wow, what is wrong with me?

Bob pops in, says, 'The church is on fire.' Shit.

# Unworthy, Yet Everyone's Still Kind

A little later Kitten says to get my bag, we'll go back to hers and I can sleep off the drugs. I feel much better, still hazy, and I go upstairs and knock on Pete's door because I feel I owe him an explanation. He opens it and thankfully his face is intact and he's still wearing the glasses and he grins at me and I grin back. He pulls me in for a man hug, and he's all like, 'Ah Joe, man, you lost the plot there! It's good to see you.'

'You too, sorry Pete, I freaked out. You looked weird, your face was bleeding.'

'It wasn't. I'm fine, see? Still fucking gorgeous!' He stands back, jutting his jaw out, swaying his head back and forth. 'Wanna smoke?'

'Nah I can't, I'm going to Kitten's before I fuck up again.'

'Ah, alright Joe, got you. Don't be a stranger though.'

I get my bag, and I'm ready to go. I can't wait to get out of here. Kitten and I are off, walking down the street and oh my God. There are cops everywhere, three fire engines and an ambulance; the church is burning, under control but still mildly aflame. It's blackened, the heat palpable, smoke billowing out of the remainder of the roof. Kitten stops, stands alongside the large crowd of spectators already gathered. The Haiku Man's here. I don't want to stop and watch, I read once that arsonists usually return to the scene of their crime, and I can feel all the police looking at me.

'Wow, can you believe this, Joe? Shit.'

'No, it's crazy!' I reply, trying to sound and look shocked. I am genuinely shocked, I thought you needed petrol or something to destroy a building so completely, I only lit some candles. Man, I really messed up this week. Why is there an ambulance? The church was empty, right? Apart from me and Kurt, and I assume he was just a hallucination. But the more I think about it, I realise the door wouldn't have been unlocked if it was empty. Did I kill someone else? Did I kill the fucking priest? Fuck! I need to go, and I nudge Kitten and quietly tell her, 'I need to go, this is freaking me out and I don't think it's worn off yet. The cops are making me feel paranoid.' She looks at me, understands.

'Yeah of course, come on, sorry Joe, let's go.' But the Haiku Man is suddenly next to us, and he says,

'The Priest was inside,

Trapped at the back of the church.

What a way to go!'

Again, oh my fucking God. Kitten asks him, 'D'you know what happened?'

'People are saying

Was probably a candle,

Just speculation.'

'Huh. Gotta go Haiku Man, catch you later.' But before we can leave he looks at me and comments,

'Are you alright, Joe?

You look so pale and frightened,

You sick or something?'

Kitten whispers on my behalf, 'Yeah, he's best left alone, Pete gave him acid today.'

The Haiku Man starts to laugh, looking at me like this explains everything.

'I love LSD!

Didn't know Pete was holding,

Gonna get me some!'

And he's off, with more energy than I realised he had.

We start walking and Kitten asks how I'm feeling. I'm sad and worried, but I tell her I feel OK, a bit floaty even though my bag is really heavy. The acid's still happening because in my mind I've interpreted the heavy load on my back as a metaphor for the burden I'll forever carry, my albatross. Analogy or not, it's true. I'll never shed this weight, this guilt. It's crippling.

We make it back to Kitten's and her flatmate is there. A hot brunette, big blue eyes, big boobs. Reminds me of Casey. And shit, Casey might DM me again. I need to ask for the WiFi password but is it too soon? Kitten's flatmate is asking who the fuck I am and why the fuck I'm here. She's hostile, not asking me, instead directing her questions at Kitten and looking at me with disdain. I stand with my backpack still on, trying not to take up too much space while attempting to look endearing.

Kitten tells her, 'This is Joe, he's my friend, he's new here. I work with him at the bar. He's just hanging here for a bit, no need to be so rude, Jess! Say hi, Joe.'

'Hi.' I say, I hold up my hand in a feeble wave. Here I go looking lame again. Her initial scorn diminishes fractionally and she responds,

'Hi.' with the same flimsy wave I gave her. I don't know if it's meant sarcastically but I suspect it. Whatever. She's preoccupied, looking for shoes. She says at Kitten, not me, 'Got to go, see you later.' She's out the door. Kitten says to me,

'Relax, Joe, drop the bag. You hungry?'

'I'm alright.' I had a crisp sandwich.

'Well I'm hungry, you wanna buy us a takeaway?'

'Yeah, OK.' I drop the bag, just next to the door and I don't know where to put myself. I'm not relaxed. Maybe still tripping a little. Kitten's dropped herself onto the sofa so I sit next to her. Still don't feel comfortable. She starts talking about the church burning down and I don't want to talk about it because it makes me feel like shit and I know I've killed the priest and I can't believe I killed two people in three days. Only a matter of time before I'm found out. I really don't want to go to jail, so I think leaving here and starting fresh elsewhere is the best thing I can do. I'll still live a life of self-condemnation, I will punish myself, aim for some redemption. Maybe change my name, cut my hair. Still, I just got here and don't feel ready. Who knew I'd end up a drifter?

I remember I have a load of weed on me and ask Kitten if she ever smokes it. She tells me yeah, roll one up, but can we order food because she is starving. I tell her I only know how to roll one paper rollies and not those fancy three skinners that Pete does, that I don't mind what we eat because she made me that sandwich. She looks at me impatiently,

'Pass it here, I'll skin up.' Rolling her eyes. So I do, and she is clearly a pro. She tells me to order some food but I explain I have never done that online and am in no fit state and can't pay over the internet because I don't have a bank account, and she rolls her eyes again and says, 'Forget it Joe, I'll make some toast!' I'm fine with that, I just want to sleep. She's shaking her head but I can see she's smiling. I wish I could tell her everything. She finishes rolling and we're not even talking, the TV is on and I am weirdly engrossed in some soap where this alcoholic is on a rampage through his town. Kitten says, 'Shall we turn this off, music instead?'

'Yeah,' I say, What's your WiFi password?'

Casey has sent me some DMs, she's seriously considering coming here. I reply telling her I'm crashing on a friend's sofa. Kitten asks me who I'm texting and I tell her a friend from back home. She can see I'm being secretive so she says,

'A girl?'

'Yeah.'

'Your girlfriend?'

'Not really.'

'Aww, show me Joe, show me a picture?' Casey's twitter picture is slutty as fuck, all pouty lips, breasts and filters. I show it to Kitten and study her face to see if she's jealous. She doesn't seem so, and why would she be? The other night was clearly a pity fuck, and that's OK I suppose because at least I got to have sex. Still, would've been nice if she feigned some kind of possessiveness or insecurity. Nope. She's like, 'Nice Joe, she's pretty, great tits too.'

We've finished the joint and I'm tired and Kitten says I look like shit and that I can sleep in her bed and she'll take the sofa, but only tonight because I had a bad day. She opens her bedroom door and waves me inside. My eyes are heavy and I feel bad for taking her bed and I tell her we can share because it's a double and she shakes her head and says no, it's fine. I take off my boots and she shuts the door leaving me alone and I lie there sniffing her pillows which smell of shampoo and makeup and I fantasise that she'll join me any minute, undressing herself, undressing me… then I remember I'm a killer and don't deserve anything, let alone sex or Kitten or pillows. Instead I lie there and dwell on my actions and I don't want to live anymore but I'm not brave enough to kill myself.

I think of painless ways to do it, because if I just die I won't have to face consequences and won't have to suffer for all eternity because the more I think about it, I'm certain the concept of Hell or Heaven is ridiculous, I've always known this and it'll be fine, sleep eternal. Overdose is best right? A shitload of pills? Just fall asleep? I hate swallowing tablets but I can't hang myself, it seems painful. I can't jump from a bridge because I'd never have the courage. Same with slitting my wrists and that seems messy and not certain to work, because what if someone found me? Where will I do it? Not here, not now. I have to plan this. I think of Kurt and the shotgun, and suicide is somehow courageous. A tear runs down my cheek onto Kitten's pillow because I am a gutless little shit. Lying here, contemplating my death, I fall asleep.

# Praying For A Sign

Today I will not kill anyone. It's my first thought when I wake in Kitten's soft bed. I inhale her pillows again because it's lovely, the scent of femininity, though somewhat tainted now by my own odour; the smell of guilt and pot and dirty hair. All suicidal thoughts have been extinguished for now but I still hate myself but I need a plan because otherwise I'm just stagnating in this town instead of the last. I sit up, still dressed except for my boots, and I want to read Grandpa's letter to remind me why I'm here, but it's in my bag, still by the front door. It's early, only quarter to seven but I get up and quietly open the bedroom door. I pad gently past Kitten to my bag, and as I crouch down to rummage in the pocket of my rucksack I hear her stir. I look at her, she's awake.

'Morning,' I say. She groans, and mumbles,

'That was the shittest sleep I've ever had.'

'Sorry.' She gets up and goes to her room and flops onto her bed without closing the door. I sit on the sofa and unfold the letter. I break it down, what he asked of me.

*Don't stay.* Check. *Don't bother with education.* Check. *Don't get in debt.* Financial, check, though there's still time. Emotional debt, I got a lifetime of that. *Get laid.* Check! Go Joe! *Meet interesting people, make friends.* Check? Kind of. *Try new things.* Check? Alcohol, drugs, arson; I don't suppose it's what he meant. *Do the things you enjoy.* I don't even know what I enjoy. *Don't seek wealth, seek experiences.* I definitely had a lot of experiences this last week. *Enrich people's lives.* Nope. *Leave a mark.* No. Unless murder counts as leaving a mark? *Help and be kind, don't hurt people.* Well, I truly fucked that one up. *Eventually find love.* Plenty of time for that. It's an end goal I'll never deserve. *Believe in yourself, be brave.* I did, for a couple of hours when I first left home. Not so much now. *Speak up.* I find it hard, but I'm honestly trying to say how I feel. *Do not compromise yourself.* What does that even mean? *Do or die.* And this? Like, do all the above or die? What does this shit mean?

I read the whole thing again. I started out with good intentions, I really tried. The more I think about it I realise there was no intended outcome, no actual mission for me to accomplish. It makes me feel lost when I had only looked at this letter for purpose, for guidance and hope. I can't find it. God I wish I could talk to him. *Grandpa, if you are still around in any way at all, I could really do with a sign. Please, help me Grandpa.* I feel like I'm praying, which is ridiculous. I fold the letter up, and slide it back into my jeans pocket. I'll go out to get coffee, let Kitten sleep. I leave my bag, just take my money and my phone. As soon as I shut the door I realise I don't have a key so I'll just have to stay out until later. Starbucks will be open, right?

# The Haiku Man's Encouragement

Technically homeless, I need to find a place to stay and I'll make this my first goal. I have money to set myself up and I guess I'll have to share accommodation because cities are expensive.

I'm sitting in the window at Starbucks when I see The Haiku Man coming down the street. I bow my head and look at my phone because I don't want to have to acknowledge him or for him to see me. I have my headphones in and try to look engrossed in my phone but I can see him peripherally, standing outside. I think he's smiling, waiting for me to notice. He bangs the window and I can't help but look up. Fuck, he's grinning at me. I give a half smile, pretend I'm surprised to see him and he makes his way to the door, comes in,

'Buy me a coffee?

With cream and sugar please Joe,

White Russian for me.'

He chuckles. I have no idea why he's on about Russians. Embarrassed to know him I get up and order him coffee, gesture towards the window seats to the barista, give him a shrug and an eye roll. I go back and sit beside him.

'You're up early Joe,

Can't sleep eh? Well, me either,

Been a weird few days.'

'I'm staying with Kitten. Looking for a place to live, can't carry on like this.'

'And then what next Joe?

Figured out why you came here?

Need to make a plan!'

It's like he read my mind. I don't know why but I take Grandpa's letter from my pocket, offer it to him. I tell him it's why I came. He unfolds it, starts to read. His coffee arrives and he stops for a moment to indiscreetly pour a large swig of vodka into it, adds three sugars, stirs, then goes back to reading. I watch his expression as he scrutinises. Amusement turns into scepticism turns back into amusement. He finishes, folds it up and hands it back to me.

'What do you think?' I ask.

'Grandpa was a fool

To think you could survive here

Alone and so young.'

That's not what I wanted to hear. I'm not that young and I tell him so.

'But you are naive,

And you have no idea

What you want from life.'

He muses a moment and says,

'You write poetry?

Could do with an apprentice,

Take over the reins.

'When I'm dead and gone,

Carry on my legacy?

I don't have long left.'

It's not really a job with prospects. I decline. He shrugs, unoffended.

'Do what you enjoy.

Remember when you told me.

You had ideas?'

I remember saying that but I don't know what they were. I think I was just excited for adventure, for new beginnings. I never had a plan. I tell him,

'Yeah. I never had a plan, ideas. I just came here on a whim. On Grandpa's whim.'

'You're good at drawing,

Grandpa was right about that.

Still, not a plan though.'

I think he's trying to be helpful.

'It's been a rough couple of weeks, I just want to hide away from the world, find a cave and cry; pathetic, but it's true. I've no place here, no purpose.'

'Hide away from what?

From the police? Or living?

That's not a plan Joe.

'It's easy to hide,

I lived on a roundabout

For over a year!'

That's weird. Kind of cool, but weird. Some roundabouts are like mini forests, untouched and ignored, the heart of them hidden from human view. Little islands of nothingness. Maybe I could live on one. The Haiku man leans in close and whispers,

'Can you live with it?
What happened the other day?
If you can then good.'
and louder now,
'You must move forward,
And focus on your future.
Your Grandpa was right,
'You can if you want,
Got your life ahead of you,
You are smart enough.
'Can be anything,
You can do something worthwhile,
Make your Grandpa proud.'

For the first time ever, I'm grateful for his company, for his lilting counsel. It's encouraging.

'Find another job,
Something more conducive to
Your interests and likes.
'You got this shit, Joe,
You like drawing and comics?
Take that direction;
'Comic stores all over,
Beg for a job, hone your skills,
You might get lucky.
'Comics are for kids
but someone has to draw them!
Why can't it be you?'

Because I have no education? Because I'm not that good? Still, worth a shot, right?

'Thanks. I mean it.' I feel inspired. Something like promise and exhilaration. I've forgotten his name, he's just The Haiku Man now. I might write a couple of haikus, leave them around in homage;

*The Haiku Man said*

*I should chase my hopes and dreams.*

*You should do it too!*

See? Easy. I haven't seen a single comic store since I got here but I'll find one and get a job. Kitten will help me. I'll still work at the bar too. I'll draw every spare minute I get.

Nice one, Haiku Man. Pointless, but nice one, lifting Joe's spirits, elevating his mood. Boy needs it now more than ever. What Joe doesn't realise is that he's officially a wanted man in connection with the fire at the church and the subsequent death of the priest. Potentially murder, at best manslaughter. CCTV from the opposing property clearly shows Joe entering and then, somewhat suspiciously with those sunglasses on, exiting the building. The police have enlarged the image of his face, and these photographs will later be released to the press. God help him if they connect Jack Jones to all this. Tonight's news will feature the priest's death as one of their headline stories. The Parks family will see it. Tyler will see it. The Haiku Man will watch it, because he'll happen to catch the news when he visits a regular haunt to purchase some tax free illegally imported tobacco. The story catches his eye because it's local, and upon seeing Joe's grainy, enlarged mugshot, he'll exclaim, flabbergasted by the kid's propensity for bother.

'Oh for fucks sake boy!

Can't you stay out of trouble?

It's beyond a joke!'

He'll rush to the bar and tell Bob, whispering across the bar,

'Have you seen the news?

It was Joe who burned the church.

Kid's a disaster!

'Was it on purpose?

Who knows, Bob? Who fucking knows?

But he's got to go.

'We can't take the risk,

Boy's a liability…

He's not your son Bob.'

The Haiku Man will shake his head, Bob will be solemn. Pete will be oblivious.

Around the same time, Joe and Kitten will be at her flat, they both have Mondays and Tuesdays off. They'll be joking and smoking, Joe will think he's making headway, when Tyler will call Kitten on her phone and tell her what he just saw on TV; knows it's that kid from the bar, the one who started the fight.  She'll be disbelieving, won't mention that Joe's next to her. She'll hang up, and ask,

'Joe? That was Tyler. Said he saw you on the news, that you're wanted in connection with that fire at the church? Did you do that?'

She'll be simultaneously looking it up on her phone, Joe's face will drain of colour, his world will come crashing down. She'll say he can't stay, she can't harbour a wanted man in her flat sorry, even if it was an accident. She can't believe it, why didn't he say anything? She'll tell him to go back to the bar for now. Things will not get any better from here on. At least not until the end. Enough spoilers, I'm skipping ahead. Back to Joe.

I say goodbye to The Haiku Man, thanking him again. I'm going to put this week behind me and start again, stay out of trouble. I'm going to draw, I got this really cool idea for a story too. I'm psyched!

I get back to Kitten's flat and bang on the door until she answers, sleepy and disoriented. She looks beautiful, heavy lidded, make-up free, fresh skin, but I don't tell her because I don't think she wants me to be attracted to her. I want to tell her my ideas and hopes, but she's clearly not in the mood. While she heads to the bathroom I rummage through my bag for a sketchbook and pencils and I plant myself on the sofa and I draw. It feels good, I catch myself smiling and decide to draw Kitten, make her this kick-ass character, a cross between Tank Girl and Catwoman, less gross than tank girl though and less villainous than Catwoman. Am I just going to end up ripping off these characters? Will Kitten think it's creepy? Doubt starts infiltrating my mind, and I have to block it out. The Haiku Man will make an incredible character too; I'll make him more visually and socially palatable, more brawny, less smelly. I'll allow the drink problem. Kitten gets out of the shower, and without giving her a chance to do anything I say,

'Will you help me find a new job?'

'Yeah. You're perfectly capable though, Joe.' I can hear her roll her eyes. She might be right. Still, be nice to have some moral support. I ask,

'You know any comic shops?'

'Uh yeah, there's a few.'

'Cool. I want to work in one. Don't laugh, but I want to draw comic books.'

'I'm not laughing, good for you.'

I don't like to say graphic novels, it sounds so grown up and elitist. But I want to draw them. I've been doing it since I was eleven, Self-taught counts for something, right? I ask,

'Will you help me find a place to live?'

'Yeah Joe.'

'Thanks. I saw The Haiku Man this morning at Starbucks.'

'Oh. That's why you're so wired huh? Too much coffee? I see you're better after yesterday?' I'm just blocking yesterday out of my mind. She sounds moody.

'Yeah I'm fine.' I say. And then I shut up because she's obviously not a morning person. She sighs,

'I'll try to help you Joe, just not today. I'm not in the mood.' Maybe it's her time of month or that she only just got up. I nod, tell her it's cool. I carry on drawing. I know she catches a glimpse and reckon she's impressed, but she goes to get dressed. Comes out of her room, says she's going out. She leaves me, and I don't know if her flatmate is home, so I'm quiet, not daring to snoop around just in case. I plug in my headphones and I sit and draw, hungry, waiting until she gets back.

# It's The End

Tuesday night. I'm sitting with Kitten and we're having fun. She's smart and funny, we're laughing and I definitely love her. She tells me her flatmate is never here and I finally feel comfortable. Earlier we went out to get alcohol and Chinese food, which was a luxury for me because although Grandpa liked Chinese takeaway it was kind of expensive and we only had it if it was a birthday or something. Kitten and I smoked a couple of joints, we're drinking wine and we're giggling like idiots. It's the best I've felt in days, weeks, maybe years. She looked through my sketchbook earlier and she was blown away. I think she likes me a bit more now, since she thinks I have some talent. I tell her I want to draw The Haiku Man as a character and she laughs and agrees, says it's genius.

Her phone rings; her ringtone is AC/DC's *Back in Black* and she's literally the coolest person I've ever met. Before she answers she rolls her eyes.

I can't hear what's being said but her face changes. 'You sure?' She's frowning, 'Like, positive? Huh, right, OK, didn't need you to ring up all gossip queen.' She hangs up. Her face grave. She takes a deep breath, looks at me, 'Joe? That was Tyler,' She pauses, thinking what to say. 'He said he saw you on the news, that you're wanted in connection with that fire at the church? Did you do that?' I feel sick. Blood rushes to my face. I gulp. I don't know how to answer. The news?! She's tapping on her phone, looking at me, looking at her screen.

'What do you mean?' I ask, and then, because I know she knows, 'It was an accident. I'd taken that acid, I didn't do it on purpose, I'm not a criminal! Tyler saw me on the news?' She's not saying much, just nodding intensely into her phone. She looks up eventually.

'Jesus Christ Joe. What the fuck? Look.' She holds up her phone, there's a picture of me, with those stupid sunglasses of Pete's, my hood's up, I couldn't look more like a criminal if I'd tried. There's barely any background, just a big grainy zoom on my face, I can't pinpoint when it was taken. How the fuck can everyone tell when I had those glasses on? 'Did you do it?' she asks again.

'I, I don't know.' I hang my head in shame. I did.

'Well, it looks bad. Fuck Joe. You can't stay here!' I look at her beseechingly, she turns her face away, 'I'm serious, I can't be harbouring a wanted man here. I'm sorry! Why didn't you say anything? Are you insane?' Maybe. I wish I could rewind. I wish I never came here. I can't tell her about Kurt, she'll think I'm crazy. I say,

'I'm sorry. I would never hurt someone on purpose, I didn't know he was in there!' She looks at me both pitifully and confused, I think she believes me. Shaking her head,

'Who the fuck sets fire to a church? Go back to the bar, Bob will take you in again.' I'm stoned and a bit drunk. I stand, unsteady. My phone is charging, I unplug it. I can see I've got DMs from Casey, she's seen the news too. Fuck. I grab my sketchbook, seek out my bag which I never get to unpack, stuff it in. I grab my jacket from the back of the sofa, I want to cry, but I won't. She says it again, 'Sorry, but you know where I'm coming from, right?'

'Yeah.' I wouldn't have me here either, and she doesn't even know about Jack Jones. What a fucking waste of space I am. The lump in my throat is obstructing my breathing. I tell her, 'Sorry.' I walk the few steps to her door. Kitten doesn't move from the sofa, her phone still in her hand.

I leave, down the stairs, I'm scared to go outside, half expecting a swarm of cops with guns waiting for me. No one. Just dark empty streets. I can't think straight, I'm frightened and I don't think going back to the bar is a good idea. But where else? Home? I can't. Everyone will know there too, Casey knows. I wander slowly and people pass me and I hide my face. I need internet. Can the cops trace my phone? Are they tracing it right now? No, they don't actually know who I am yet, or maybe they do, because someone will have phoned and told them by now. My heart quickens and I turn it off immediately. I'm screwed. I consider turning myself in at the nearest police station, I'll tell them it was an accident.

I decide I'll swing by the bar, I don't have to go in if things don't seem right, and as I near the building I see The Haiku Man amongst a crowd of smokers outside. He sees me, looks concerned or angry or both, I can't tell, but he stomps towards me. He knows. Grabbing me by the shoulders, he roars, 'I saw what you did!

Are you fucking insane, boy?
Are you a nutjob?'
'No, it was an accident—' he cuts me off, shaking his head
frantically,
'You said that last time!
Get the hell out of here kid,
Don't ever come back.'
'I don't know where to go.'
'I don't give a shit!
Anywhere but here is fine,
You need to leave now;
'You could steal a car,
Go drive yourself far away,
Get a haircut too.
I tell him, I can't steal a car, I can't drive.
'You can't fucking drive?
What kind of retard are you?
Are you a retard?'
'I'm not a retard! I'm eighteen, I never learned.'
'Then don't steal a car,
End up killing someone else—
Just get the fuck out!'
He's quite vitriolic, so I step away as he spits these words out,
the weight of my backpack pulling me backwards, I'm scared. I ask
him, 'Does Bob know? Pete?'
'Yes they fucking know!
Your face is on the TV,
No choice but leaving.'


Actually Pete doesn't know. He's left the bar, beckoned
by social media to a protest not far away. Pete loves a

protest, any reason to get angry or violent and he's in. And The Haiku Man means no wrath, he's more concerned that Joe gets away for his own sake, he likes the kid. Bob knows too, but truth be told, he's glad the priest is dead. He's never forgotten what happened back when they were kids, what Pete told him about the time he'd stayed behind to help Father Thomas clear up after communion. Once, Bob was just biding his time, plotting. But, Bob mellowed with age. He doesn't harbour hostility like he once did. The anger is still there, but with a more mature attitude on how to deal with it. He trusts in karma, from some poncey, hippy philosophy he picked up from his misspent youth with easy vegetarian girls with nose-rings and dreadlocks that he met at gigs and festivals.

If he knew where Joe was right now, chances are he'd take him in. He likes the boy. He's already called Kitten, Joe already left. He knows Joe's an innocent, and looking out for him had felt like redemption for all the shitty things he'd done before, at least until the kid fucked shit up by killing that guy. Bob would still help him.

He won't get the chance.


I could be wrong but The Haiku Man looks a little sad. My eyes are welling up again. I need to control this shit. I adjust myself, turn away, walk.

'Joe? Maybe call Bob,

Once everything has calmed down.

He'll be worrying.'

I hear him but I don't look back, and he doesn't say anything else. I'm on my own again.


You're not on your own Joe.

# Opposition

I walk and formulate a plan. I'm lonely and frightened, but I'm sucking it up as best I can. Haiku Man's right, I'm definitely going to have to get a haircut. I have to think of a new name too. I need to get out of The City first. I definitely don't have the skills to steal a car. I think I'll go buy some scissors and cut my hair, then catch a few buses until I'm a hundred miles away. I need to look confident, innocent. I need to blend in. I'm going to jail unless I become someone else.

I walk for ages, no one notices me or my sadness, no one mugs me or accosts me which I find surprising, but I'm grateful. I glance behind me, and oh God, two cops are walking up the street behind me. They're quite a way off, do they know who I am? Shit! Keep walking, head down, look normal, I daren't look back again and I can't run, that's a dead giveaway. Are they tailing me? My heart is pounding, I'm waiting for one of them to grab my shoulder, or worse, tackle me to the ground. Fuck.

By some wondrous miracle, I see a large crowd up ahead. I've no idea why they're there, maybe there's some celebrity in town? No, not that, some kind of march or protest. I reckon if I get myself into that mass of people, blend in and look like one of the group, I can lose the cops, get out the other side unscathed. Escape. I walk quickly towards them and they envelope me as one of their own.

**Oh, the delightful naivety, isn't he something? I'm just observing, waiting, I know what's coming.**

They're rowdy, the crowd. As I immerse myself within the mob, I see them, feel them all, angry and animated; they have a cause, a purpose, an end goal. I feel like I'm a jellyfish or something, some spasmodic mass, undulating towards an unknown point and I mimic them; try to look angry about whatever they're pissed off about. They're shouting, their eyes searching mine, looking to recognise the anger they feel. I reciprocate the emotion, feign feeling, I wish I knew what the problem was. Wait, maybe they all saw me on the news and, shit, this was a terrible idea! Are they angry that someone burned the church? Fuck! What was I thinking? Why are they all out here at this time of night? Aren't protests a daytime activity?

I shuffle my way through and there's a huge cordon of police on the other side, kettling the crowd. Of course there's fucking police. Man, I'm so dumb. What is wrong with me? It feels more aggressive here, and I know I'm going to have to go back the way I came. This stupid rucksack is such a hindrance. I begin to back out to get away from the scores of police I can glimpse by their hi-viz jackets, away from the contemptful and angry frontline crowd, their shouts of 'PIGS!' I read a placard, a piece of cardboard box with a length of wood gaffer taped to it. Black marker pen declares, WE ARE THE 99%, and another, EAT THE RICH. I still have no idea what's going on.

EAT YOUR PHEASANT, DRINK YOUR WINE! YOUR DAYS ARE NUMBERED BOURGEOIS SWINE!

Creative that one, I bet they nicked it off the internet. To be honest I don't really give a shit, as far as politics go I'm indifferent, I don't feel like it affects me. I don't feel I should be entitled to anything, you know?

Yes, they did nick it off the internet. The 99% are done with austerity, with cuts, the annihilation of public services, the downgrading of the free health service. When politicians are claiming expenses in far excess of one hundred million per year. When they spend more than half a million feeding and watering foreign ministers. When some of them claim three thousand for rent in The City per month. Not to mention what they claim for their sandwiches, newspapers, and paperclips. There's no money though, for the ten thousand rough sleepers, the eighty thousand homeless families; that's an excess of one hundred thousand homeless children! How do they sleep at night? No money for the NHS, but there's over two hundred billion for Trident. They voted in favour of reducing corporation tax alongside a reduction in welfare spending. Voted against rental homes being fit for habitation, against equal rights, against everything that matters. I could go on.

The Government had it coming. They've taken the piss a bit. And now someone has to fight for those hard won rights of the people, for those living in poverty despite working fifty or sixty hour weeks, using food banks, never sleeping soundly because they don't know how they're going to get through the week when they've got to pay the gas bill, the kid needs new shoes and they've got only tinned peas and mouldy bread. Sad times, tough times. And they're congregated because here, in the building that the police guard, the Prime Minister, his deputy and their wives are currently engaged in talks and a shockingly expensive dinner (paid for, of course, with taxpayer money) with the foreign minister and his wife of a questionably dangerous and war-mongering country. They're an ally in a financial sense, but not for the benefit of the ninety nine percent.

Those ninety nine percent are tired, hungry, poor, and frankly, seething. They are young. They cannot afford education, or property. Hell, they can't afford to eat... all that shit about millenials and the Gen X'ers and their avocado on toast and quinoa; you having a laugh? Who eats that shit? I'll tell you who. The privileged.

Do not underestimate the beautiful agenda of a disadvantaged youth. The anger is directed at those people who hold the power to help them and don't. The threat of Martial Law, along with all the scandal and corruption, the misconduct, the underhand and immoral behaviour of those who rule has become too much to stomach. Finally, apathy is cast aside, torn asunder from the hearts and minds of the suffering, the common man. It's been slow. Very slow. It's amazing what injustice the masses will tolerate but eventually, it becomes too much.

Time for revolution. It needs to happen, it is history and it is nature and it is fact. The cycle of humanity. We wait for it, these moments of triumph in favour of the majority. It's important and necessary. The greater number conquers. The snowflakes start an avalanche.

The crowd's getting bigger by the minute. There's been footage of it on TV and more importantly, social media; it strikes a chord with so many, and the outrage and hostility is gaining momentum at an incredible pace. Joe is now within a crowd double the size it was when he walked into it. Within another ten minutes it will be triple. This isn't a protest, it's a riot.

A wise and peaceful man once said, 'A riot is the language of the unheard'. It is. You have to ask yourself; who are the unheard, and why is no one listening to their plight? Poor Joe, will he even make it out alive? Every revolution needs a martyr.

It feels chaotic here, hot. All I want to do is leave, but I can't seem to swim my way out the soup. This fucking rucksack. I'm lost in the crowd, struggling against a tide of passion and anger and I'm too weak to escape. Right in front of me, without warning, this huge fucking thing drops from above, just misses me; it takes a moment to process.

It's a sign! Not from God, but from a roof above, an actual sign from the pizza shop has dropped into the crowd. It lands on the head of an angry student, I'm assuming, just judging from appearances here, and it knocks him unconscious to the ground; there's a moment of near silence as everyone registers what's happened. We all look upwards and there are people on the roof, did they throw it down? The crowd aren't happy, in fact they're fucking livid. I'm near the front, and next thing I know someone picks up that sign and they throw it forwards towards where the police are lined up, and I think it hits one of them because an eruption begins. There's suddenly violence. It's terrifying, immediately everyone is hell bent on hurting the opposition; it's no longer a peaceful endeavour and it's nothing to do with me, yet here I am caught up in it, too delicate to participate but stuck nonetheless amongst the frenzy. Holy shit, God help me please!

There's a theory circulating on the internet that the catalyst for a riot is undercover cops and FBI or whatever, acting as agitators, agent provocateurs; deployed to ruin the peaceful protest by lighting fires and smashing cars and windows, sparking a wave of chaos and discredit over said protest. A conspiracy theory, you might say. Well, everything is a conspiracy until it's not, eh? Anyway, in this case, it's entirely organic, the riot is sparked not by an employed agitator lobbing a sign into the crowd below, but by someone who's a bit drunk and stoned and simply along for the ride. He only leaned over and accidentally knocked a loose and rusty screw from the fixing. Totally random and perfect!

Things escalate quickly, I'm crushed from both sides. My rucksack is slipping and people are grabbing at it, I've got to get out but I can't see to the front or back of the crowd and everywhere there are elbows, contorted faces, shouting. This feels like a do or die moment, I think I get that now. I muster some courage, I stand tall, ground myself, and I'll fight my way out if I have to.

The police are not holding back, brutal; I catch glimpses of batons, I see blood spatter, and the crowd did not come unarmed either. Knife blades glint in the street lights, but the police are gaining territory and it would be easier for me to go forward than back but I'm worried they're going to hit me. What if I put my arms up? I see riot vans pulling up, cops emerging in their full gear, shields and helmets. I edge myself sideways, more like barge, shoving my elbows into ribs and backs, anything to get through and there's a side street to my left and it's my goal, I can get there, breath again. I've never fought so hard for anything in my life. I battle my way through the crowd, they're all against me, striving for the front while I summon the power to escape. I think of Grandpa and jail. The crowd thins and the pressure against me eases, I can make it.

It hasn't even been a week since I left and it's been the most eventful, horrifying, terrifying, exciting, and exhausting week of my life. An education. Despite being a wanted criminal, despite the killing, despite my new friends all abandoning me, I feel a glimmer of hope. OK, I know I'm definitely going to jail, but, I have to try yeah? I'm not a bad person. I imagine a future, far away from here, I can buy a new identity right? That's a thing? I'm going to head North. I've just got to get out. Fuck following dreams and everything, I only need to survive. I'm kidding myself.

I made it! I am on the side street, away from the manic throng of anarchy. I stop a moment, peel my rucksack from my back, breathe deeply. This street is dark and narrow, little more than an alleyway that smells of piss, and I don't know where it leads. The riot cops are gaining ground because behind me I see the protesters being bulldozed backwards, people dropping to the ground, being crushed as they lose their footing. It's started to rain, an intense summer rain, heavy drops and I pull my hood up, cover my hair. I've got to go. The police are in my eyeline again, they're battering their way forward and I can't risk being recognised, I pick up my bag, haul it onto my back and start walking away. Someone shouts from behind me, 'Oi!'

I look back, it's a cop, a regular one, and I daren't stop to chat so I can only make a run for it now, hoping I can lose him or he won't bother to give chase because clearly, there's more concerning matters to attend to right where he already is. I start running but I hear him again, hear his footsteps as he starts to run too, he shouts, 'Oi! Stop! Police!'

I'm not going to stop, no way, I'm not going to fucking jail. I don't think anymore, just run, as fast I as I can with this cumbersome bag filled with my only possessions, raindrops lashing my face and I'm nearly out the other side; I can see another alleyway parallel to this one, just across the road, I'll head that way, and then swing a left and hope for the best.

I'm almost out of this corridor, I've got good speed, I make it, I dash across to reach the other lane and there's a humongous BANG! Something halts me. A weight, an incredible weight! An impact so great that it knocks the breath right out of me. Something big, I have never felt this way… and I don't feel good, can't breathe, can't go on. My legs don't work, my arms, I'm somehow on my back on the wet ground and where's my bag? I can't lift my head to look.

Let me describe the scene for you because Joe's not making much sense now. Joe's running full pelt, so frightened of being caught that he doesn't pay attention to the fact he's sprinting straight into a road upon which The Prime Ministerial car, over three and a half tonnes of custom built armoured Jaguar XJ, is speeding away from the venue of a dinner cut short due to the baying crowd outside, and the inevitable riot that is taking hold. Behind the Jag is an unmarked Range Rover, containing protection command officers. Ordinarily, the motorcade would be larger, more organised, but this whole event was meant to be low-key and discreet, under the radar. So, there are no police motorcycle escorts to halt the traffic, no excess security. The car takes the corner, the driver's got his foot firm on the accelerator, he wants out, and the windscreen is wet, huge pelting drops of rain, visibility limited, but he knows these roads better than he knows his own wife. He's not worried, until... he collides with poor Joe, all that metal and glass, and although Joe is small, flung fifteen metres down the road, the Jag is halted. It skids somewhat in the rain as the driver has the capacity to brake after the impact.

Neither the Prime Minister or his wife had the time or sensibility to put their seatbelts on. The PM's neck is instantly broken as he slams into the reinforced bulletproof glass partition, a quick and painless death. His wife also hits the partition, sideways, breaks her arm for sure, several ribs. Splits her nose open, and her recent facelift becomes unstitched in its delicate healing phase. She's not dead. Minorly disfigured, but not dead. Unimportant, she's of no significance. The Range Rover slams into the back of them. The Deputy PM slams into the back of the Range Rover. Severe whiplash. He'll step down from his post in a couple of days; the Prime Minister is dead, he's not up to replacing him; and the party is tainted by the revelations that soon come to light; the backhanders and the offshore tax havens are mild when you consider the paedophilia links, and when the PM's laptop is seized, dear God. God help them all. Or not, actually, they don't deserve it.

I do not care for your politics. Joe certainly doesn't. None of it matters in the grand scheme of things. But this incident will lead to a chain of events that will benefit the majority, which is kind of the point. With corruption cast aside, a new dawn breaks for this nation. A new government, better than the last. Progress.

We were there. Tiananmen Square. Gandhi's salt march. The storming of the Bastille. We stood beside the Suffragettes, the Slaves, the Revolutionaries. We stand with the Palestinians. We stand with Antifa, with the kids opposing the NRA, with Greta Thunberg. Black lives matter. We'll continue to do so. Recognise the oppression, for fuck's sake. We're losing faith though, things never seem to improve with you lot. We are trying our best, we want you to succeed and flourish. Help us out, for goodness sake.

Anyway, I digress, let's get back to the moment in hand, because this is when we finally claim him, we collect Joe and he joins us in our quest.

# No True Change Happens
## Without Conflict

I realise what's happened, I got hit by a car. People are crowding around me, that policeman kneels over, 'Can you hear me?' I can, but I can't answer, my tongue just lolls about my mouth unable to articulate anything sensible. I'm struggling to keep my eyes open. There's some pain, not much, but I can't get up. I'm worried about my bag and my money. There's someone else here too, they're bright, really hurting my eyes;

'Don't worry Joe, you can't bring them with you.'

What the fuck? I am so confused right now.

'No need to be confused.'

I didn't even say that out loud, but this thing, this person (is it even a person?) can clearly read my mind. Is it a ghost? It's blinding!

'No, I'm not a ghost. We met before Joe, at the Church. Remember? Kurt?'

Kurt Cobain? Because you don't look like Kurt, I say, telepathically. I can still faintly hear the cop,

'He's lost consciousness!' I hear sirens, so many sirens.

Joe has no idea of course, but the accident, the noise, has attracted the attention of the protesters. They think he did it on purpose, that Joe threw himself at the car, sacrificed himself. This was all part of the plan. No true change happens without conflict. It's an ugly scene, watching them spit and kick at the Prime Ministerial car while he's slumped dead inside, his wife severely injured. There's wickedness on both sides. They can kick all they want, that car's armoured with titanium and kevlar. In a minute the driver will press a button that releases tear gas as a crowd dispersant. That'll really piss them off.

'No I don't look like Kurt because I'm not him. Never was. I was just, well, pretending. Sorry, try not to think too much about it. You're dying Joe, almost dead. You're in limbo. Not long left.'

Something else happens now, I make myself visible. Fuck it. It's chaos here and everyone needs to chill the fuck out. I can do that. You know who sees me first? Pete. Mad Pete is here. But I think he's seen me all along. He shouts, 'I know him!' and bounds over, some cops hold him back; he's calling to Joe, not me. The others, they register what's happening. I know they can see me because their mouths drop open, they shield their eyes and drop back. The noise calms, the crowd stops their assault. An ambulance arrives, slows to a halt, and the paramedics sit upfront their cabin awestruck. They can't hear me, I can't speak to them, only Joe. But the effect is there, they're dumbfounded.

I feel incredibly powerful now. I like it, I shut them right up. Yeah, I know what I've done, perpetuated that religion myth. Still, what's the worst that could happen? It's already a shit-storm here. People are filming me on their phones. There's a TV crew too, I hope they get my good side. This shit will go viral.

I'm dying? This is the end? Will they save me? Who are you? This is all telepathic because my body is useless now. Limp, wet and smashed.

'Yes you're dying. Don't fight it, don't worry. They can't save you, it's too late. Don't want to freak you out, kid, but to put it in terms you'll understand, I suppose you could say I'm an angel. And you will be too, very soon.' Pete has dropped to Joe's side, he's unfazed by my presence and it's sort of sweet, but Joe sees only me.

An angel? Are you fucking kidding me? What do you mean?

'Ah come on, you know what I mean. More like a guardian, whatever. Just trying to help out.'

What? Like God and shit? Sorry I'm swearing so much, I'm just shook up.

'Hmm, God's not what you think. Doesn't matter right now, you'll learn in time. The cursing is fine, Joe, fuck it!'

I think I'm being funny, but maybe it's not the moment for comedy.

Ha, well that's something…what now?

'Shall we go? You ready?' I'm sad to leave, enjoying the attention.

Yeah I guess. Where's Grandpa?

'Not one of us Joe. Don't concern yourself now.' Shit, there's so much I want to say about Grandpa.

What do I do?

'Just a moment and we'll go, don't let your body hold you.'

What do you mean I'll be one soon too? An angel?

'Yeah, something like that.'

But I'm a terrible person. I'd laugh if I could! I'm mentally chortling. This is a bit much. Wait... did *you* tell me to burn down that Church?

'Yeah.'

What? Are you an angel from Hell or something?

'There's no such thing as Hell.'

The priest died. And I killed someone else, a man.

'I know.'

Then surely I'm not, y'know, suitable? This shit is fucking mental, am I on drugs again?

'I think you smoked some weed. But those men were meant to die Joe, they were bad people. It was your purpose.'

Huh. It would've been nice to know at the time. I've been feeling like shit about it.

'Yeah, sorry. You ready?'

Yeah.

And on that note, Joe is with me. It's intangible, difficult to describe. We can manifest ourselves as physical but were not tied to it. It's science honestly, you'll get it one day. The crowd see it, they watch Joe's wings unfurl, smooth and fluid; it'd be painful if he could feel it. All that back pain Joe's been suffering was symbolic, a representation of the burden, preparation for the weight of these feathered appendages he'll have to carry for the rest of his existence. He'll need to work on his posture. That's probably the only shit you got right about us, the wings. Yeah, they're pretty cool.

His body remains crumpled on the road. There's two of him for a moment, the physical and the ethereal. It's breathtaking to see, I hope they all get good footage on their phones. The sceptics will still think it's photoshopped. Pete's grinning at us, I swear I see him do a fist pump. I like him. Joe and I leave this plain. He has so much to ask, so much to learn but I know he's going to be good at this. He's a pure soul.

Well this is a turn up for the books. I'm thinking about Bob, The Haiku Man, Pete, Kitten and Casey. I'm hoping to see Grandpa now I'm here. I'm worried about my sketchbooks. I wish I'd left them somewhere, with someone. I had so much left to do.

'Kitten will claim your possessions Joe, she'll say you were her boyfriend. That she had no idea about anything. She even gets your money.'

Still reading my thoughts then, 'Well thanks, I feel a bit better.' I guess?

'Just wait Joe, everyone saw what happened. Everyone. It's on the telly! You're famous. We're famous!'

'That's not much use now is it? Where's Grandpa?'

'No, I suppose not. Jesus Christ, Joe, put a damper on it why don't you? I thought it was cool. Gives them all something to think about. Just wait, see what happens. And hey, you like comic books right?'

'Yeah. Where's Grandpa? Do I get to see him?'

'You'll be immortalised Joe, literally, in human terms. You'll be a bestselling comic book hero, The Avenging Angel. You'll love it! The Haiku man's your sidekick. Kitten's your accomplice. They're based on your sketchbook drawings. It's pretty kick ass.'

'You serious? That's awesome! Who writes that? Who draws it?'

'I don't know Joe, I'm not into that stuff. But it's true.'

'I'm actually immortal now?'

'Yeah.'

'Cool. Where's Grandpa?'

'For fucks sake Joe, Grandpa? That's all you can think about?'

'I miss him.'

'Well this is so new for you, I don't know if you can take it.'

'What do you mean?'

'I mean, I don't think you can take it.'

'I can! I killed people, I can take anything. Wait, he's not in Hell is he?'

'Hell's not real Joe, remember? See? This is a lot to digest, all in good time.'

'But what about Grandpa? Is he OK? Is he here?'

'It's complicated.'

'What does that mean?'

'Do you believe in God?'

'No. I didn't anyway, I mean, maybe now. Grandpa thought it was bullshit. Is he real?'

'Well, yeah, but he's not what you think.'

'What do you mean?'

'He's lazy. He doesn't contribute. He gets bad press to be honest, he doesn't do anything bad, not really, But he doesn't do much good either. He just exists.'

'Oh, right. So he's real? Wow.'

'Yeah, it's not like you think, not like all that bible stuff.'

'OK, I get you, he doesn't do anything. So what's the point in everything? All this?'

'I don't know Joe.'

'Seriously? *You* don't know?'

'Nope. Imagine you were God. What would you do?'

'I don't know, good stuff, help people?'

'Ha, yeah? That takes effort.'

'I guess.'

'Well this is the thing. God just pisses about. He gave you all free will, figured he could just relax after that, enjoy himself. Total waster if I'm being honest.'

'Huh. So, where's Grandpa?'

'What was Grandpa like Joe?'

'I don't know, he took care of me. He was there when I had no one. A good guy. Clever. I just miss him.'

'OK, let me tell you something about God. Since the beginning of time, he likes to play human. It's his thing. Like a virtual reality thing. He inhabits a meat suit, and he lives it through from beginning to end. I can't think of a better analysis at this point, like virtual reality? Like computer games? You get me?'

'Not really, I never had a Playstation or Xbox or anything. Is God just fucking about?'

'Yeah, pretty much. Don't hold it against him. He didn't expect this level of difficulty, he's just completing one mission at a time. levelling up occasionally. It's a tough game!'

'God, I mean wow, yeah. I bet.'

'Right? I don't know where he is now, but I know where he was, until recently.'

'Yeah? Where?'

'Want to hazard a guess?'

'I don't know. I mean, he could be anywhere in the world, give me a clue? What's he like, God?'

'For fucks sake Joe, you can't figure this out? I mean, you probably know him better than me.'

'What?'

'What?'

'What do you mean?'

'I have to spell this out to you? Thought you might be smarter than you look.'

'Well clearly not. Man, this is all so weird. Where even are we?'

'God likes to inhabit human bodies right?'

'Yeah?'

'Well he just finished with one, fuck knows where he is now, but he'll turn up somewhere. Takes a while for us to work it out.'

'Oh. So what's he like?'

'You tell me Joe, for fucks sake, you've been living with him for years!'

'What?'

'You heard me. Are you retarded or something? How long does it take?'

'What? Grandpa? What?!'

'Yeah, finally. So you tell *me* Joe, what's he like?'

Mind. Blown. This is a joke right? Grandpa wasn't God, no fucking way. I mean, if you were God and that was your thing, would you choose to live in a council house in a deprived and backward town? Everyone's miserable, no money or prosperity, your wife dies, your kid leaves you and dies? Seems a shitty choice. No way. This is ridiculous, if God likes playing The Sims, why doesn't he choose some wealth, some happiness? An indulgent and privileged life? Seems weird.

'Grandpa's life was indulgent and privileged, come on Joe! Think globally here? Besides, God's done the moneyed existence plenty of times, it's boring. Not a general way of human existence is it? Variety is the spice of life, and what is wealth and indulgence anyway? It's subjective. Thing is, I think God likes suffering. Sees it as the ultimate mortal experience. Where do you think he'll go next? He's not always a he.'

'I don't know! Perhaps he'll pick an easier ride this time. Actually, if he has any sense he'll just get an Xbox or something.'

'Yeah, don't count on it. We were hoping you'd have some clues or something.'

Wow, I'm still processing everything, I can't think straight. Grandpa? He was a great human. Shit at cooking, smoked all the time.

'Yeah, sorry. Take your time. I know, God likes a smoke, he always does that. You'll forget all this eventually.'

Yeah? I don't want to forget it. He hated religion. Maybe not, maybe he just had opinions. It's a lot to think about. Man, he had opinions. God opinions! This is pretty epic, I wish I'd known.

'Of course he hates religion, haven't you seen how he's portrayed? Doesn't matter, you're going to have to move on from this.'

'Will I see him again?'

'Grandpa? No. God? Not as God. Like I said, you'll forget, move on.'

'Be nice to see him, have a chat. I really tried.'

'You did well. That stuff there, it was nothing to do with him, you know, we're doing all the work in his absence, trying anyway.'

'Huh. You think he'd approve?'

'Don't know. We're trying to maintain a balance, seeing as he doesn't contribute or give a shit. None of us know. Maybe he's pissed off you ended up dead, in which case, perhaps he'll turn up and put the world to rights? Didn't work when we killed off the rest of his family. We hope we're doing OK. He could help us out if he wanted to. I don't know his plan. If he's angry, probably a killer virus. '

'So we have no goal here? You don't know what you're doing? You killed my mother?!'

'Well, if you put it like that it sounds shit. We're trying to do good! I knew you'd have questions, but this is kind of a promotion for you; thought you might appreciate it more.'

Do I appreciate it? They killed my mum? My Grandmother? What sort of mafia organisation is this? If this is what angels do it's fucked up.

'I don't know, this is all still too weird. Give me a chance to get used to it.'

'Yeah of course, I know. It'll take time. Right, let's take a step back. What do you know about God? What did you learn?'

'Not a lot. School stuff. God was a dick, flooding the world. Letting Jesus die.'

'Yeah, that stuff. Sending those bears to maul a load of kids. Banishing ugly people from his churches. Lot's wife, wanting to kill Moses, all the genocide. All that shit he did to Job! It's all fiction, not a dot of it true. Lies. Do you really think he'd be that much of an arsehole? The bible's a decent novel, but it's not real life, it's fiction. Except for that bit about God wrestling Jacob, that's real. Ha, I remember it, it was funny. Most of it's bullshit though. Anyway, trust me. Look forward Joseph, we've got so much to do, all the time.'

Not surprised about the bible. No idea who Jacob is. I don't know what to think. I'm thinking of Grandpa still, and those left behind. Kitten says she's my girlfriend? That was a viable option and I'm not there to live it? For fucks sake. Wait, does this situation mean I'll never have sex again? Just that one time? That's cruel. Fuck, I don't think I have a penis anymore.

I hope Bob's not disappointed in me.

Who draws the Avenging Angel story? I wish I could tell them all, what's happened. But, avenging angel, they'll get it right? Do they know about Jack Jones? If not now, will they figure it out?

Man, I did not get closure. Also, Grandpa, the letter. I didn't achieve. Is he pissed? Is God pissed? What the actual fuck? What's going to happen to everybody?

And what do I do now? I do not have the skills for this job, I do not have the knowledge or the intelligence. I don't know what's going on. I'm ill equipped. I mean, I'll give it a go, I have to I suppose.

Yeah, let's leave Joe process, mull everything over. He's coming along for the ride, it's non-negotiable. Not even going to gratify that shit with a response, he'll get there on his own. To be fair, he seems to be dealing with everything alright. It'll take him some time to adjust to the fluidity of time and place, but I have high hopes. At least he missed out on COVID-19, that's a fucking mess.

And so, another continent, another time and place, another crisis to avert. Another story. Probably Myanmar. Maybe Papua New Guinea or Palestine. Fuck, holiday over. Hell, you guys think you got it bad? You're life is easy, you've got no idea. Fucking snowflakes. Yeah, this was a relaxing break, comparatively, please count yourselves lucky. You, with your WiFi and your tumble dryer and your socks. Socks? Who invented those? Such luxury!

Our continuing pursuit of good over evil is now at an advantage with Joe amongst our midst. Our work unceasing. Listen, I'm sorry, don't feel too guilty about your shitty ways. The line between virtue and immorality is blurry at times.

Just try to be good.

# Playlist

If you would like a playlist to accompany this book then I'm happy to oblige. The idea of a concept novel crossed my mind, has anyone ever done that? I listened to many artists during the creation of this story, I was grateful for their company and attribute much of my creativity to their inspiring and insightful lyricism. Music is everything to me, it has saved me every time I needed it to.

Had I been talented and brave enough to perform, I would've liked to be a musician. Alas, I'm a four chord wonder like Joe, and would've ended up dead in a hotel room years ago choked on my own vomit, had such a dream come into fruition, as I've no capacity for moderation and I romanticise excess and death. I would've liked to have quoted many of the songs within this book but that shit costs money.

Anyway, I would like to see every novel have a suggested soundtrack chosen at the whim of the author.

It's on Spotify. Jesus Christ Joe. Check it out.

# Miscellaneous Notes

The Yungblud bit was originally about Gerard Way, but he doesn't look like a hot lesbian anymore. That stuff about MDMA being prescribed to bored housewives is probably factually incorrect, but I liked the idea (doctors should actually do this), and it's a work of fiction, so fuck it.

Challenge the establishment. Reject the mainstream. Turn off your TV, it really helps. God isn't real. Rebellion is duty.

# Acknowledgements

Sorry mum.

Thanks Jonf and Ruby for tolerating my journey.

Thanks to Shane, Kevin, Rich, Pete, Zack, Darren for reading and advising.

Bix, you ledge, dunno what you were thinking taking a chance on this.

Nik, I'm sorry I dragged you into this. I love you.

Selby writes because it's cheap therapy, works in a library and lives in the UK. She has never published anything and has no previous accolades, literary or otherwise. Additionally, she's not a member of any relevant organisations. Selby has never won any awards. Selby is a university dropout, and thus severely under-qualified as a writer. She doesn't blog or have any worthy social media following. Despite all this, Selby spends her evenings procrastinating at her laptop and occasionally manages to churn out something that, someone, sometimes, perhaps stupidly, thinks might be worthy of publication. If asked, she would describe herself as a hopeful, yet past-their-best high functioning alcoholic, burdened by the mundanity of normal family responsibility. *Jesus Christ Joe* is her debut novel, but you can bet your life she's got more on the way. You can help validate her existence by finding them on Instagram: @switchbladeselby